Praise for Megan Abbott's
DARE ME

Shortlisted for the Crime Writers' Association Steel Dagger Award for Best Thriller, nominated for Best Novel in the 2013 Anthony Awards, named one of the Year's Best Crime Novels by Booklist, *and named one of Amazon's Best Books of the Year*

"Megan Abbott has put her spirit fingers to the task of writing the Great American Cheerleader Novel, and—stop scowling—it's spectacular. . . . It's *Heathers* meets *Fight Club* good. Abbott pulls it off with a fresh, nervy voice, and a plot brimming with the jealousy and betrayal you'd expect from a bunch of teenage girls. . . . At its core, *Dare Me* reveals something very true about the consuming, sometimes ugly, nature of female friendships. But Abbott is also on to something bigger. . . . It is this moment of adolescence that *Dare Me* captures so beautifully, the in-betweenness."
— Chelsea Cain, *New York Times Book Review*

"An increasingly addictive noir set in the world of high school cheerleading. . . . Think *Bring It On* as reimagined by Christopher Nolan."
— Joe Gross, *Austin American-Statesman*

"A compelling, compulsive read."
— Michele Ross, *Cleveland Plain Dealer*

"Chilling. . . . Ms. Abbott turns the frothy world of high school cheerleading into something truly menacing."
— Alexandra Alter, *Wall Street Journal*

"A foreboding and forbidding glimpse into the mind of the American cheerleader.... The plot's myriad twists and turns, like the precarious pyramids the cheerleaders perfect, are intriguing and unexpected."   —Donna Freydkin, *USA Today*

"Make no mistake, this is no pulpy teenage tale: It's a very grown-up look at youth culture and how bad behavior can sometimes be redeemed by a couple of good decisions."
                           —Sara Nelson, *O, The Oprah Magazine*

"Highbrow, brilliant... *Dare Me* hurtles past the glitter and angst of high school cheerleading, right to the bruising inner struggles of adolescence."   —*New York*

"Exceptional.... What *Dare Me* does with describing the body and its limits? Unforgettable."   —Roxane Gay, *The Millions*

"Megan Abbott, an Edgar-winning crime writer, drew inspiration from *Lord of the Flies* for her sexy and sinister new novel, *Dare Me,* which lays bare the cruel, confused longings of a group of high school cheerleaders, and is the perfect way to forget yourself on a turbulent transatlantic flight."
                           —Maud Newton, *New York Times Magazine*'s 6th Floor blog

"Megan Abbott has cornered the 'dark desires of teenage girls' territory too, with *Dare Me*."   —Sarah Weinman, *Salon*

"A heady tale of high school drama with grown-up stakes.... Abbott's rendering of the power plays, rites of bonding, and twisted loyalties of teenage girls is pitch-perfect. As much as *Dare Me* is a page-turning murder mystery, it is also an ode to the dark side of girlhood friendship."   —Mythili Rao, *Daily Beast*

"If cheerleaders scared you in high school, you'll finish the haunting *Dare Me* convinced you were right." —Kim Hubbard, *People*

"So disturbing and so good." —*Glamour*

"Dark high school thriller.... Having won an Edgar for her 1940s-era femme fatale novel, *Queenpin,* Abbott knows how to write a hard-boiled classic in the vein of Raymond Chandler. But what's exciting about *Dare Me* is how it makes that traditionally masculine genre feel distinctly female. It feels groundbreaking when Abbott takes noir conventions—loss of innocence, paranoia, the manipulative sexuality of newly independent women—and suggests that they're rooted in high school, deep in the hearts of all-American girls. She understands the intensity of female relationships, and she knows that some fifteen-year-olds can't be best friends until they're willing to destroy the competition." —Melissa Maerz, *Entertainment Weekly*

"Megan Abbott has been called the Queen of Noir.... Her new novel, *Dare Me,* is something of a switch for Abbott in that it's about a cheerleading squad, though—trust us—it's still quite hard-boiled.... A contemporary novel about a cheerleading squad that somehow manages to be as dark and sinister as any of Abbott's fiction." —Sherryl Connelly, *New York Daily News*

"If your image of high school cheerleaders is pretty, perky, healthy, wholesome young women, you may be shocked by the gritty, cutthroat, twisted world of cheer in Megan Abbott's sneaker-noir *Dare Me.* ... Abbott knows how to build suspense, drop clues like gum wrappers on a gym floor, and blindside the reader. The twists are the fun part.... Abbott is best in the nasty, manipulative dialogue, as Beth controls the squad with her vicious tongue, and in

Addy's confused inner monologues, where she relishes any attention from Coach French.... Some will be riveted by the complex resolution."　　　　　—Regan McMahon, *San Francisco Chronicle*

"It's an old-school B-movie setup, a girl gang seething with crushes, rivalries, and vendettas, a cold, beautiful alpha running her ring of pretties with an iron hand. Transport this viper's nest of feminine evil to a twenty-first-century high school girls' locker room, add text messages and hoodies and extreme cheerleading stunts and you've got Megan Abbott's *Dare Me,* a dark novel that will appeal to both teen readers and their mothers.... The author says she crossed *Lord of the Flies* with *Richard III*; readers are calling the result '*Fight Club* for girls.'... By the time the college recruiter shows up at the last game of the season, *Dare Me* has soaked the white sneakers in blood and turned into a murder mystery.... The potent melodrama of *Dare Me* is amped up, page after page, by the rhythm, imagery, and portent of Abbott's language.... Her take on the culture of young women is chilling and knowing, lingering on the edge between reality and sensationalism."　　　　—Marion Winik, *Newsday*

"A fascinating, almost voyeuristic, glimpse into the power struggle that goes on between teenage girls. Not just any teenage girls—cheerleaders, with their own unique hierarchy and fierce code of loyalty, which they'll protect at any cost. There's a dark and twisted love story here, told with a rich sensual undertone that lingers long after you close the last page, still breathing in your ear: *Dare me.*"
　　　　—Chevy Stevens, *New York Times* bestselling author of *Still Missing* and *Never Knowing*

"Arresting, original, and unputdownable."
　　　　—Rosamund Lupton, *New York Times* bestselling author of *Sister*

"Abbott again delivers an unsettling look at the inner life of adolescent girls in the guise of a crime story.... The question of who is emotional victim versus who is predator becomes murkier and more disturbing than any detective puzzle. Compelling, claustrophobic, and slightly creepy in a can't-put-it-down way."

—*Kirkus Reviews*

"*Dare Me* sneaks up on you from behind, pulling on long-forgotten memories of teenaged desperation, obsession, and desire. This is truly masterful storytelling." —Alafair Burke, author of *Never Tell*

"Megan Abbott's brilliant new book presents a number of possibilities—the mysterious and the erotic, as well as the inevitable and paradoxical lessons of girlhood—with such illumination that the joyful terrors of adolescence were once again present in me. Abbott's characters, confronted with unaccustomed questions and strange, new difficulties, remind us that the loss of innocence can, if we are fortunate, emerge into a lustrous wisdom."

—Susanna Moore, author of *In the Cut*

"The full range of human experience—from joy, love, and lust to greed, betrayal, and despair—can be expressed in any activity, so why not cheerleading? In this terrific novel, Abbott takes a plot that seems torn from the headlines and transforms it into Shakespearean tragedy with friendship bracelets.... Much of the novel's power comes from the way Abbott captures the fierce urgency of the teenagers' emotional lives.... This is cheerleading as blood sport, *Bring It On* meets *Fight Club*—just try putting it down."

—Keir Graff, *Booklist*

DARE ME

A Novel

MEGAN ABBOTT

BACK BAY BOOKS
Little, Brown and Company
New York Boston London

Back Bay Books / Little, Brown and Company
Hachette Book Group
1290 Avenue of the Americas, New York, NY 10104
littlebrown.com

Originally published in hardcover by Reagan Arthur Books, July 2012
First Reagan Arthur/Back Bay Books paperback edition, August 2013
First Back Bay media tie-in paperback edition, December 2019

Back Bay Books is an imprint of Little, Brown and Company, a division of Hachette Book Group, Inc. The Back Bay Books name and logo are trademarks of Hachette Book Group, Inc.

The Hachette Speakers Bureau provides a wide range of authors for speaking events. To find out more, go to hachettespeakersbureau.com or call (866) 376-6591.

Library of Congress Cataloging-in-Publication Data
Abbott, Megan E.
 Dare me : a novel / Megan Abbott.—1st ed.
  p. cm.
 ISBN 978-0-316-09777-2 (HC) / 978-0-316-25054-2 (LP) /
978-0-316-09778-9 (PB) / 978-0-316-43017-3 (media tie-in PB)
 1. Cheerleading—Fiction. 2. Psychological fiction. I. Title.
 PS3601.B37D37 2012
 813'.6—dc23   2011051323

10 9 8 7 6 5 4 3 2 1

LSC-C

Printed in the United States of America

For my parents, who taught me ambition

The curse of hell upon the sleek upstart
That got the Captain finally on his back
And took the red red vitals of his heart
And made the kites to whet their beaks clack clack.
                                    —John Crowe Ransom

DARE ME

Prologue

"Something happened, Addy. I think you better come."

The air is heavy, misted, fine. It's coming on two a.m. and I'm high up on the ridge, thumb jammed against the silver button: 27-G.

"Hurry, please."

The intercom zzzzzz-es and the door thunks, and I'm inside.

As I walk through the lobby, it's still buzzing, the glass walls vibrating.

Like the tornado drill in elementary school, Beth and me wedged tight, jeaned legs pressed against each other. The sounds of our own breathing. Before we all stopped believing a tornado, or anything, could touch us, ever.

"I can't look. When you get here, please don't make me look."

In the elevator, all the way up, my legs swaying beneath me, 1-2-3-4, the numbers glow, incandescent.

The apartment is dark, one floor lamp coning halogen up in the far corner.

"Take off your shoes," she says, her voice small, her wishbone arms swinging side to side.

We're standing in the vestibule, which seeps into a dining area, its lacquer table like a puddle of ink.

Just past it, I see the living room, braced by a leather sectional, its black clamps tightening, as if across my chest.

Her hair damp, her face white. Her head seems to go this way and that way, looking away from me, not wanting to give me her eyes.

I don't think I want her eyes.

"Something happened, Addy. It's a bad thing."

"What's over there?" I finally ask, gaze fixed on the sofa, the sense that it's living, its black leather lifting like a beetle's sheath.

"What is it?" I say, my voice lifting. "Is there something behind there?"

She won't look, which is how I know.

First, my eyes falling to the floor, I see a glint of hair twining in the weave of the rug.

Then, stepping forward, I see more.

"Addy," she whispers. "*Addy*...is it like I thought?"

1

After a game, it takes a half hour under the showerhead to get all the hairspray out. To peel off all the sequins. To dig out that last bobby pin nestled deep in your hair.

Sometimes you stand under the hot gush for so long, looking at your body, counting every bruise. Touching every tender place. Watching the swirl at your feet, the glitter spinning. Like a mermaid shedding her scales.

You're really just trying to get your heart to slow down.

You think, *This is my body, and I can make it do things. I can make it spin, flip, fly.*

After, you stand in front of the steaming mirror, the fuchsia streaks gone, the lashes unsparkled. And it's just you there, and you look like no one you've ever seen before.

You don't look like anybody at all.

At first, cheer was something to fill my days, all our days.

Ages fourteen to eighteen, a girl needs something to kill all that time, that endless itchy waiting, every hour, every day for something—anything—to begin.

"There's something dangerous about the boredom of teenage girls."

Coach said that once, one fall afternoon long ago, sharp leaves whorling at our feet.

But she said it not like someone's mom or a teacher or the principal or worst of all like a guidance counselor. She said it like she *knew*, and understood.

All those misty images of cheerleaders frolicking in locker rooms, pom-poms sprawling over bare bud breasts. All those endless fantasies and dirty boy-dreams, they're all true, in a way.

Mostly it's noisy and sweaty, it's the roughness of bruised and dented girl bodies, feet sore from floor pounding, elbows skinned red.

But it is also a beautiful, beautiful thing, all of us in that close, wet space, safer than in all the world.

The more I did it, the more it owned me. It made things matter. It put a spine into my spineless life and that spine spread, into backbone, ribs, collarbone, neck held high.

It was something. Don't say it wasn't.

And Coach gave it all to us. We never had it before her. So can you blame me for wanting to keep it? To fight for it, to the end?

She was the one who showed me all the dark wonders of life, the real life, the life I'd only seen flickering from the corner of my eye. Did I ever feel anything at all until she showed me what feeling meant? Pushing at the corners of her cramped world with curled fists, she showed me what it meant to live.

There I am, Addy Hanlon, sixteen years old, hair like a long taffy pull and skin tight as a rubber band. I am on the gym floor, my girl Beth beside me, our cherried smiles and spray-tanned legs, ponytails bobbing in sync.

Look at how my eyes shutter open and closed, like everything is just too much to take in.

I was never one of those mask-faced teenagers, gum lodged in mouth corner, eyes rolling and long sighs. I was never that girl at all. But I knew those girls. And when she came, I watched all their masks peel away.

We're all the same under our skin, aren't we? We're all wanting things we don't understand. Things we can't even name. The yearning so deep, like pinions over our hearts.

So look at me here, in the locker room before the game.

I'm brushing the corner dust, the carpet fluff from my blister-white tennis shoes. Home-bleached with rubber gloves, pinched nose, smelling dizzyingly of Clorox, and I love them. They make me feel powerful. They were the shoes I bought the day I made squad.

2

FOOTBALL SEASON

Her first day. We all look her over with great care, our heads tilted. Some of us, maybe me, even fold our arms across our chests.

The New Coach.

There are so many things to take in, to consider and set on scales, tilted always toward scorn. Her height, barely five-four, pigeon-toed like a dancer, body drum-tight, a golden collarbone popping, forehead high.

The sharp edges of her sleek bob, if you look close enough, you can see the scissor slashes (did she have it cut this morning, before school? she must've been so eager), the way she holds her chin so high, treats it like a pointer, turning this way and that, watching us. And most of all her striking prettiness, clear and singing, like a bell. It hits us hard. But we will not be shaken by it.

All of us, slouching, lolling, pockets and hands chirping and zapping—how old u think? looka the whistle, WTF—the texts flying back and forth from each hiccupping phone. Not giving her anything but eyes glazed, or heads slung down, attending to important phone matters.

How hard it must be for her.

But standing there, back straight like a drill officer, she's wielding the roughest gaze of all.

Eyes scanning the staggered line, she's judging us. She's judging each and every one. I feel her eyes shred me—my bow legs, or the flyaway hairs sticking to my neck, or the bad fit of my bra, me twisting and itching and never as still as I want to be. As she is.

"Fish could've swallowed her whole," Beth mutters. "You could've fit two of her in Fish."

Fish was our nickname for Coach Templeton, the last coach. The one plunked deep in late middle age, with the thick, solid body of a semi-active porpoise, round and smooth, and the same gold post earrings and soft-collared polo shirt and sneakers thick-soled and graceless. Hands always snugged around that worn spiral notebook of drills penciled in fine script, serving her well since the days when cheerleaders just dandled pom-poms and kicked high, high, higher. Sis-boom-something.

Her hapless mouth slack around her whistle, Fish spent most of her hours at her desk, playing spider solitaire. We'd spot, through the shuttered office window, the flutter of cards overturning. I almost felt sorry for her.

Long surrendered, Fish was. To the mounting swagger of every new class of girls, each bolder, more coil-mouth insolent than the last.

We girls, we owned her. Especially Beth. Beth Cassidy, our captain.

I, her forever-lieutenant, since age nine, peewee cheer. Her right hand, her *fidus Achates*. That's what she calls me, what I am. Everyone bows to Beth and, in so doing, to me.

And Beth does as she pleases.

There really wasn't any need for a coach at all.

But now this. This.

Fish was suddenly reeled away to gladed Florida to care for her teenage granddaughter's unexpected newborn, and here she is.

The new one.

The whistle dangles between her fingers, like a charm, an amulet, and she is going to have to be reckoned with.

There is no looking at her without knowing that.

"Hello," she says, voice soft but firm. No need to raise it. Instead, everyone leans forward. "I'm Coach French."

And you ma bitches, the screen on my phone flashes, phone hidden in my palm. Beth.

"And I can see we have a lot to do," she says, eyes radaring in on me, my phone like a siren, a bull's-eye.

I can feel it still buzzing in my hand, but I don't look at it.

There's a plastic equipment crate in front of her. She lifts one graceful foot under the crate's upper lip and flips it over, sending floor-hockey pucks humming across the shiny floor.

"In here," she says, kicking the crate toward us.

We all look at it.

"I don't think we'll all fit," Beth says.

Coach, face blank as the backboard above her, looks at Beth.

The moment is long, and Beth's fingers squeak on her phone's pearl flip.

Coach does not blink.

The phones, they drop, all of them. RiRi's, Emily's, Brinnie Cox's, the rest. Beth's last of all. Candy-colored, one by one into the crate. Click, clack, clatter, a chirping jangle of bells, birdcalls, disco pulses, silencing at last upon itself.

After, there's a look on Beth's face. Already I see how it will go for her.

"Colette French," she smirks. "Sounds like a porn star, a classy one who won't do anal."

"I heard about her," Emily says, still giddy-breathless from the last set of motion drills. All our legs are shaking. "She took the squad at Fall Wood all the way to state Semis."

"Semis. Semi. Fucking. Epic," Beth drones. "Be the dream."

Emily's shoulders sink.

None of us really cheer for glory, prizes, tourneys. None of us, maybe, know why we do it at all, except it is like a rampart against the routine and groaning afflictions of the school day. You wear that jacket, like so much armor, game days, the flipping skirts. Who could touch you? Nobody could.

My question is this:

The New Coach. Did she look at us that first week and see past the glossed hair and shiny legs, our glittered brow bones and girl bravado? See past all that to everything beneath, all our miseries, the way we all hated ourselves but much more everyone else? Could she see past all of that to something else, something quivering and real, something poised to be transformed, turned out, made? See that she could make us, stick her hands in our glitter-gritted insides and build us into magnificent teen gladiators?

3

It isn't immediate. No head-knocking conversion.

But with each day that week, the New Coach continues to hold our interest—a feat.

We let her drill us, we run tumbles. We show her all our routines and we keep our claps tight and our roundoffs smooth.

Then we show her our most heralded routine, the one we ended last basketball season with, lots of chorus line flips and toe touches and a big finish where we all pop Beth up into a straddle sit, her arms V-split above her head.

Coach seems almost to be watching, her foot perched on top of the crunking boom box.

Then she asks us what else we got.

"But everyone loved that number," peeps Brinnie Cox. "They had us do it again at graduation."

We all want Brinnie to shut up.

Coach, she's just tighter, fleeter than we'd expected, and that first week, we take notice. Planted in front of us, her body held so lightly but so surely.

We can't fluster her, and we are surprised.

We can fluster everyone, not just Fish but the endless sad parade of straw-man subs, dusty-shouldered geometry teachers and crepey-skinned guidance counselors.

Let's face it, we're the only animation in the whole drop-ceiling, glass-bricked tomb of a school. We're the only thing moving, breathing, popping.

And we know it. You can feel that knowingness on us.

Look at them, that's what we can hear them—everyone—say when, Game Day, we stride the hallways, pack-like, our ponytails rocking, our skirts like diamonds.

Who do they think they are?

But we know just who we are.

Just like Coach knows who she is. It's in the click and tap of both her aloofness and nerve. So unconcerned with our nonsense. Bored with it. A boredom we know.

Right off, she won something there, even if— or because—she didn't ask for it, care about it. Not because she's bored but because we're not interesting enough for her.

Not yet, at least.

The second day, she takes a piece of Emily's flab in her fingers. Pixie-eyed, apple-breasted Emily lifts her arms languorously above her head in an epic yawn. Oh, we know this routine, this routine which so provokes Mrs. Dieterle and makes Mr. Callahan turn red and cross his legs.

Coach's hand appears out of nowhere and reaches for the spot laid bare by Emily's tank top lifted high. She plucks the baby fat there and twists it, hard. So hard Emily's mouth gives a little pop. The gasp, like a squeeze toy.

"Fix it," Coach says, eyes lifting from the skin between her fingers to Emily's stricken eyes.

Fix it. Just like that.

Fix it? Fix it? Emily, sobbing in the locker room after, and Beth rolling her eyes, her head, her neck in annoyed circles.

"She can't say things like that, can she?" Emily wails.

Emily whose balloony breasts and hip-cascades are the joy of all the boys, their ga-ga throats stretched to follow her gait, to stretch around corridor corners just to see that cheer skirt dance.

All those posters and PSAs and health class presentations on body image and the way you can burst blood vessels in your face and rupture your esophagus if you can't stop ramming those sno balls down your throat every night, knowing they'll have to come back up again, you sad weak girl.

Because of all this, Coach surely *can't* tell a girl, a sensitive, body-conscious teenage girl, to get rid of the tender little tuck around her waist, can she?

She can.

Coach can say anything.

And there's Emily, keening over the toilet bowl after practice, begging me to kick her in the gut so she can expel the rest, all that cookie dough and cool ranch, the smell making me roil. Emily, a girl made entirely of donut sticks, cheese powder, and haribo.

I kick, I do.

She would do the same for me.

Wednesday, Brinnie Cox says she might quit.

"I can't do it," she pules to Beth and me. "Did you hear my head hit the mat on the dismount? I think Mindy did it on purpose. It's easy for a Base. Her body's like a big chunk of rubber. We're not trained for stunts."

"That's why we're *training* for stunts," I say. I know Brinnie would rather be pom-shaking, grinding, and ass-slapping during halftime, or all the time.

Brinnie's the one Beth and I have always ridden the hardest, out of irritation. "I don't like her big teeth or her chicken bone legs," Beth would say. "Get her out of here."

Once, practicing double hook jumps, Beth and I made loud comments across the gym about how Brinnie's slutty sister got caught making out with the assistant custodian until Brinnie ran off to the far showers to cry.

"All I know is," Brinnie lisps now, through those big teeth, "my head is killing me."

"If you ruptured a blood vessel," Beth replies, "you could be slowly bleeding inside your head."

"You probably already have brain damage," I add, eyeing her closely. "I'm sorry, but it's true."

"The blood may be squeezing your brain against the side of your skull," Beth says, "which eventually will kill you."

Brinnie's eyes wide and wet and brimming, I know we have achieved our goal.

On the last day of that first week, Coach calls a special meeting.

There are anxious texts and phone calls. Talk of cuts to the squad and who might it be?

But her announcement is simple.

"There isn't going to be a squad captain anymore," she says, standing before us.

Everyone looks at Beth.

I've known Beth since second grade, since we braided our bodies together in sleeping bags at girl camp, since we first blood-brothered ourselves to each other. I know Beth and can read her every raised eyebrow, every toe pivot. She holds certain things—

calculus, hall passes, her mother, stop signs—in a steely contempt that drives her hard.

Once, she dunked her mother's toothbrush in the toilet, and she calls her father "the Mole," though none of us can remember why, and there was that time she called our phys ed teacher a cunt, though no one could prove it.

But there are other things about her that not everyone knows.

She rides horses, has a secret library of erotic literature, is barely five feet tall and yet has the strongest legs I've ever seen.

I might also tell this: In eighth grade, no, summer after, at a beer party, Beth put her scornful little-girl mouth on Ben Trammel, you know where. I remember the sight. He was grinning, holding her head down, gripping her hair like he'd caught a trout with his bare hand, and everyone found out. I didn't tell. People still talk about it. I don't.

I never knew why she did it, or the other things she's done since. I never asked, that's not how we are.

We don't judge.

The main thing about Beth, though, is this: she has always been our captain, my captain, even back in peewee, in junior high, then JV, and now the Big Leagues.

Beth has always been captain, and me her badass lieutenant, since the day she and I, after three weeks of flipping roundoffs together in her backyard, first made squad together.

She was born to it, and we never thought of cheer any other way.

Sometimes I think captain is the only reason Beth even comes to school, bothers with any of us, anything at all.

"I just don't see any need for a captain. I don't see what it's gotten you," Coach says, glance passing over Beth. "But thank you for your service, Cassidy."

Hand me your badge, your gun.

Everyone pads their sneakers anxiously, and RiRi peers dramatically at Beth, arching her whole back to see her reaction.

But Beth gives no reaction.

Beth doesn't seem to care at all.

Doesn't even care enough to yawn.

"I was sure it'd be bad," whispers Emily to me, doing jump squats in the locker room later. "Like when she got mad at that math sub and keyed his car."

But, knowing Beth, I figure it will be some time before we see her true response.

"What'll cheer be like now?" wonders Emily, lunging breathlessly, paring that body down to size. Fixing it. "What does it mean?"

What it means, we soon see, is no more hours whiled away talking about the lemonade diet and who had an abortion during summer break.

Coach has no interest in that, of course. She tells us we'd best get our act together.

End of that first week, new regime, our legs are loose and soft, our bodies flopping. Our moves less than tight. She says we look sloppy and juvenile, like Disney tweensters on a parade float. She is right.

And so it's bleacher sprints for us.

Oh, to know such pain. Hammering up and down those bleacher steps to the pulse of her endless whistle. Twenty-one high steps and forty-three smaller steps. Again, again, again.

We can feel it in our shins the next day.

Our spines.

We can feel it everywhere.

Stairwell to hell, we call it, which Beth says is just bad poetry.

By Saturday practice, though, we're already—some of us—starting to look forward to that pain, which feels like something real.

And we know we will get a lot better fast, and no injuries either because we're running a tight routine.

4

The bleacher sprints are punishing, and I feel my whole body shuddering—*pound-pound-pound*—my teeth rattling, it is almost ecstatic—*pound-pound-pound, pound-pound-pound*—I feel almost like I might die from the booming pain of it—*pound*—I feel like my body might blow to pieces, and we go, go, go. I never want it to stop.

So different from before, all those days we spent our time nail painting and temp tattooing, waiting always for Cap'n Beth, who would show ten minutes before game time after smoking a joint with Todd Grinnell or gargling with peppermint schnapps behind her locker door and still dazzle us all by rocketing atop Mindy's and Cori's shoulders, stretching herself into an Arabesque.

Back then, we could hardly care, our moves so sloppy and weak. We'd just streak ourselves with glitter and straddle jump and shake our asses to Kanye. Everybody loved us. They knew we were sexy beyotches. It was enough.

Cheerutantes, that's what they called us, the teachers.

Cheerlebrities, that's what we called ourselves.

We spent our seasons prowling, a flocked flock, our ponytails the same length, our matching nfinity trainers, everything synchronous, eyelids gold-flecked, and no one could touch us.

But there was a sloth in it, I see now. A wayward itch, and sometimes even I would look at the other kids who filled the classrooms, the debaters and yearbook snappers and thick-legged girl-letes and the band girls swinging their battered violin cases, and wonder what it felt like to care so much.

Everything is different now.

Beth is tugging at her straw, the squeaking grating on me.

I should be home, drawing parabolas, and instead I'm in Beth's car, Beth needing to get out of the house, to stop hearing her mother's silky robe shushing down the hallway.

Beth and her mother, a pair of impalas, horns locked since Beth first started speaking, offered up her first cool retort.

"My daughter," Mrs. Cassidy once slurred to me, slathering her neck with crème de la mer, "has been a delinquent since the day she was born."

So I get in Beth's car, thinking a drive might do some kind of soothing magic, like with a colicky baby.

"The test's tomorrow," I say, fingering my calc book.

"She lives on Fairhurst," she says, ignoring me.

"Who?"

"French. The coach."

"How do you know?"

Beth doesn't even give me a shrug, has never, ever answered a question she didn't feel like answering.

"You wanna see it? It's pretty lame."

"I don't want to see it," I say, but I do. Of course I do.

"This isn't about the captain thing?" I say, very quiet, like not quite sure I want to say it aloud.

"What captain thing?" Beth says, not even looking at me.

The house on Fairhurst is not small. A ranch house, split level.

It's a house, what can I say? But there is something to it, okay. Knowing Coach is in there, behind the big picture window, the light tawny and soft, it seems like more.

There's a tricycle in the driveway with streamers, pink and narrow, flittering in the night air.

"A little girl," Beth says, cool-like. "She has a little girl."

"Don't think of a pyramid as a stationary object," Coach tells us. "Don't think of it as a structure at all. It's a living thing."

With Coach Fish, when we would do pyramids, we used to think of it as stacking ourselves. Building it layer by layer.

Now we are learning that the pyramid isn't about girls climbing on top of each other and staying still. It's about breathing something to life. Together. Each of us a singular organ feeding the other organs, creating something larger.

We are learning that our bodies are our own and they are the squad's and that is all.

We are learning that we are the only people in the world when we are on the floor. We will wear our smiles, tight and meaningless, but inside, all we care for is Stunt. Stunt is all.

At the bottom, our hardcore Base girls, Mindy and Cori, my feet on Mindy's shoulders, her body vibrating through mine, mine vibrating through Emily above me.

The Middle Bases in place, the Flyer rises not by climbing, not by being lifted, it's not a staircase, a series of tedious steps. No, we bounce and swing to bring everyone up, and the momentum makes you realize you are part of something. Something real.

"A pyramid is a body, it needs blood and beats and heat. ONE, TWO, THREE. What keeps it up, what keeps it alive is the bounding of your bodies, the rhythm you build together. With each count, you are becoming one, you are creating life. FOUR, FIVE, SIX."

And I feel Mindy beneath me, the sinew of her, we are moving as one person, we are bringing Beth up and she is part of us too, and her blood shooting through me, her heart pounding with mine. The same heart.

"The only moment the pyramid is still is when you make it still," Coach says. "All your bodies one body, and you DO NOT MOVE. You are marble. You are stone.

"And you won't move because you won't be able to, because you're not that hot chick bouncing down the hallway, that ponytail-swinging girl, mouth filled with nothings. You're not pretty, you're not cute young things, you're not a girl at all, not even a person. You're the most vital part of one thing, the perfect thing. Until, SEVEN, EIGHT, and . . .

"We blow it all apart."

After, our bodies spent, our limbs slick, we query her.

Sweatless and erect, she looks down at our wasted loins, water bottles rolling over our chests and foreheads.

"Coach, where'd you go to high school?" one of us asks.

"Coach, what's your husband like?"

"Coach, is that your car in the faculty lot, or your husband's?"

We try every day, most of us. The information comes slow, wriggling out. She'd gone to school over in Stony Creek, her husband works in a mirrored office tower downtown, and he bought her the car. Barely information at all. As little as she can share and still share something.

So focused, so intent, she'll only answer questions when we've done our sprints, our bridge bends, our hundreds of searing crunches, backs sliding, squeaking on the floor.

That prettiness, that bright-beaming prettiness she wears almost like a shameful thing, a flounce she keeps pulling tight, a tinkling charm she stills under her hand.

It's when she's walking away from us, it's when she's dismissed us that RiRi calls out, "Hey Coach, hey, Co-o-ach. What's that on your ankle?"

The tattoo creeps above her running anklet, a violet blur.

She doesn't even turn her head, you wouldn't even know she heard.

"Coach, what *is* it?"

"A mistake," she says. That hard little voice of hers. *A mistake.*

Ah, steel-strung coach with a reckless past, a bawdy past.

"Bet we find her in an old episode of *Girls Gone Wild: The Prehistoric Years.*" That's Beth, of course. On Emily's laptop. Beth typing Coach's name into YouTube, bottom trawling.

She doesn't find anything. Somehow I knew she wouldn't. Someone that steely-strung, there's nothing you could find.

After practice, dwindling Emily, back flat on the locker room linoleum, curls her stomach upon herself over and over, fighting to get tighter, to whittle herself down to Coach specs. I stay with her, hold her feet down, keep her pudged ankles from swiveling.

And it turns out Coach hasn't left either. She's in her office, talking on the phone. We see her through the glass, opening and closing the blinds, hand coiled around the plastic wand. Staring out the window to the parking lot. Open, shut, open, shut.

When she hangs up, she opens the office door. The shush of the door swinging open, and it's beginning.

She opens the door and sees us, and the nod of her head, permitting entry.

The office smells like smoke, like the sofa in the teachers' lounge with that hard stain in the sunken center. Everybody has a story about that stain.

There's a picture on her desk of her little girl. Coach says her name is Caitlin and she's four years old with a bleary mouth and flushed skin and eyes that glaze so dumbly I wonder how does anyone have kids.

"She's so cute," spurts Emily. "Like a doll or something."

Like a doll, or something.

Coach looks at the photo, like she's never seen it before. She squints.

"They get mad at me, at day care," she says, like she's thinking about it. "I'm always the last one to pick up. The last mom, at least."

She puts down the photo and looks at us.

"I remember those," she says, nodding at the flossy bracelets banding up and down our forearms.

She tells us she made them when she was a kid and she can't believe they're popular again. Friendship bracelets, she calls them. But we would never call them that.

"They're just bracelets," I say.

She looks at me, lighting a cigarette with a twiggy old match, like the man who sells us jugs of wine out of the back of his store on Shelter Road.

"We called this 'Snake around the Pole,'" she says, lifting the one on Emily's wrist with a crooking finger, her cigarette flaring.

"That's a Chinese Staircase," I say. I don't know why I keep correcting her.

"What's that one?" she says, poking at my wrist, the cigarette tip flush on my skin.

I stare at it, and at Coach's cool tanned finger.

"A Love-Me-Knot." Emily grins. "That's the easy one. I know who made you that."

I don't say anything.

Coach looks at me. "Guys don't make these."

"They sure don't," Emily says, and you can almost see her tongue flicking.

"I don't even know who gave it to me," I say.

But then I remember it was Casey Jaye, this girl I tumbled with at cheer camp last summer, but Beth didn't like her and camp ended anyway. Funny how people you know at camp can seem so close and then the summer's over and you never see them again at all.

Coach has her eyes on me, and there's a shadow of a dimple in the corner of her mouth.

"Show me," she says, poking out her cigarette. "Show me how to love-knot."

I say I don't have any of the thread, but Emily does, at the bottom of her hobo bag.

We show her how to do it, then watch her twist the strands, to and fro. She picks it up so fast, her fingers flying. I wonder if there's anything she can't do.

"I remember," she says. "Watch this one."

She shows us how to make one called Cat's Tongue, which is like a Broken Ladder crossed with a simple braid, and another she calls the Big Bad that I can't follow at all.

When she finishes Big Bad, she twirls it on her finger and flings it at me. I see Emily's face flicker jealously.

"Is this all you guys do for fun?" she says.

And no, it's not.

★   ★   ★

"It was like she was really interested in our lives," Emily tells everyone after, her fingers whisking across my new bracelet.

"Pathetic," Beth says. "*I'm* not even interested in our lives." Her finger slips under the bracelet and tug-tug-tugs until it snaps from my wrist.

The next day, after school, the parking lot, I see Coach walking to her sprightly little silver crawler of a car.

I'm loitering, fingers hooked around my diet soda bottle, waiting on Beth, who is my ride and occasionally sees fit to make me wait while she talks up Mr. Feck, who gives her reams of pink fluttery hall passes from his desk drawer.

I don't even realize Coach has seen me until she beckons, her head snapping toward her open door.

"Well c'mon then," she says. "Get in."

As if she knows I've been waiting for the invitation.

Driving, Coach is shaking one of those strange, muddy-looking juices she's always drinking, raw against your teeth. I don't think any of us have ever seen her eat.

"You girls have lots of bad habits," she says, eyeing my soda.

"It's diet," I say, but she just keeps shaking her head.

"We'll get you right. The days of funyuns for lunch and tanning beds—they're over, girl."

"Okay," I say, but I must not look convincing. First of all, I've never eaten a funyun in my life.

"You'll see," she says. Her neck and back so straight, her eyebrows tweezed to precise arches. The glint-gold tennis bracelet and shine-sleek hair. She is so perfect.

"So, which one of those footballers is your guy?" Coach asks, staring out the window.

"What?" I say. "None of them."

"No boyfriend?" She sits up a little. "Why not?"

"There's not a lot to interest me at Sutton Grove High," I say, like Beth might say. I'm eyeing the cigarette pack on the console between us, imagining myself plucking one and putting it in my mouth. Would she stop me?

"Tell me," she says. "Who's the guy with all the curls?" She taps her forehead. "And the crook in his nose?"

"On the team?" I ask.

"No," she says, leaning forward toward the steering wheel a little. "I see him run track in those high-tops with the skulls."

"Jordy Brennan?" I say.

There was a group: ten, twelve guys you might loiter with, might lap-shimmy, beer-breathed at parties, might letter-jacket him for a week, a month.

Jordy Brennan wasn't one of them. He was just there, barely. Scarcely a blip on the screen of my school.

"I never thought of him," I say.

"He's cute," she says. The way she breathes in, turning the wheel, you can feel her thinking all about Jordy Brennan, for just that second.

And then I think of him too.

My shirt scraping up my back, the nervy-hot hands of Jordy skittering there, and before I know it, my cheer skirt twisting 'round my waist, nudging up my belly, his hands there too, and mine coiled into little nerve-balls, and am I going to do it?

This is in my head, these thoughts, as I rustle under my Sutton green coverlet in bed that night. I've never had it happen like that before, a sharp ache down there, right there, and a put-put-put pulse, so breathless.

Jordy Brennan, who I never blinked at twice.

After, I'm about to call Beth for our nightly postmortem, but then I decide not to.

I think she'll be mad at me for not waiting for her after school. Or for something else. She is mad at me a lot, especially since last summer at cheer camp, when things started to change with us. I grew tired of all my lieutenant duties, and her no-prisoners ways, and I started stunting with other girls at camp. It goes deep with Beth and me. Our history is long and lashes us tight.

So I call Emily instead and talk with her for an hour or more about basket tosses and her shin splints and the special rainforest wax Brinnie Cox bought in Bermuda to tear off all her girl hair.

Anything but boys and Coach. My head a hot, clicking thing. I want to quiet it. I want to hush, hush it and I hold my legs together, tense as pincer grips, and clutch my stomach upon itself. I listen endlessly to Emily's squeaking voice, the way it sputters and pipes and dances lightfoot and never, ever says anything at all.

5

We're getting better all the time.

We are all locking stunts, focusing. Emily nailed her standing back handspring, which we never thought she would, with those soft-rise breasts she once had. We are stronger and we are learning how to feel each other's bodies, to know when we will not fall.

Nights, in bed, I hear the thuds on the gym floor, feel that thud through my bones, through the center of me.

Already I can feel my muscles thrusting under my skin. I even start eating because if I don't, my head goes soft. The first week, I pass out twice in calc, the second time hitting my head SMACK on the edge of a desk.

Can't have that, Coach says.

"You can't slap the treadmill before school and then expect to make it to lunch on your a.m. diet coke," Coach says, coming at me in the nurse's office. Charging in with such purpose, making even lumberjack-chested Nurse Vance, twice her size, jump back.

Her hands are riffling through my purse, thwacking the bag of sugar-free jolly ranchers at my chest.

I'm meant to throw them away, which I do, fast.

"Don't worry," Coach says. "No one gets fat on my watch."

So I start with the egg whites and almonds and the spinach, like wilting lily pads between my teeth. It's so boring, not like eating at all because you don't feel the sweet grit on your tongue all day and night, singing on the edge of your teeth.

But my body is tight–tight–tightening. Hard and smooth, like hers, my waist pared down to nothing, like hers.

The walk, her walk, feet planted out, like a ballerina. I wonder if Coach was a ballerina once, her hair pulled into a fierce dark bun, collarbones poking.

We all do the walk.

Not Beth, though, and not some of the girls, like Tacy Slaussen, who cotton more to Beth's dusky glower, the way she hitches her cheer skirt low, the way she slinks over to the freshman squad, perched in the stands to watch us. The way she reaches up and yanks the pom off one of the girl's socks and sinks it purposefully into the bottom of her plastic coke cup.

This is what Beth does, while some of us make ourselves hard and beautiful.

Jordy Brennan, fleet around the track, a soft tangle of cord skimming from his earbuds.

I watch him four days in a row, under the bleachers, my wrist wrapped around one of the underhangs, fingers clenching and unclenching.

"You got a thing for deviated septums, Addy-Faddy?" Beth asks.

"I don't know," I say, scratching my palms.

"What's the story, anyway?" she says. "He's dull as a plank of wood." She pings the bleacher post, which is actually aluminum.

"He looks like he's thinking things," I say, jumping a little on my toes, feeling like some dumb cheerleader. "Like maybe he actually thinks about things."

"Deep thoughts," Beth says, pulling her ponytail tight, "about puma treads."

I didn't tell her what Coach said, somehow didn't want her to know Coach had even given me a ride home.

Beth floats forward from the bleacher skeleton and lingers on the edge of the track.

He's pounding toward us, the huff-huff rattling in me, jolting between my hips.

"Jordy Brennan," Beth shouts, voice deep and clear. "Come here."

There's a rollicking in my chest as he slows to stop just past us, then does an about-face and slows to a cool-man stride as he makes his way over.

"Yeah," he says, up close his eyes green and blank as poker felt.

"Jordy Brennan," Beth says, throwing her cigarette on the ground. "It's your lucky day."

Fifteen minutes later, the three of us drifting along in his pocked Malibu, Beth directs Jordy to the convenience store on Royston Road, the place where the football players all buy their beer from the grim-faced man behind the counter, extra five-dollar charge just for the plastic bag.

We take the 40s, which I never like, all warm and sour by the time you get halfway in, and the three of us drive up to Sutton Ridge, where that girl jumped last spring.

Seventeen and brokenhearted, she jumped.

RiRi saw the whole thing, from Blake Barnett's car.

Right before, RiRi saw a screech owl burst from behind the water tank.

Her eyes lifted, so did Blake's, to the top of the rutted ridge. A place haunted by ruined Indians, or so we heard as kids spooking on Halloween. Apache maidens swan-diving over lost love for white men who abandoned them.

Together, RiRi and Blake watched.

Blake recognized the girl from St. Reggie's, and nearly shouted out to her, but didn't.

Arms stretched wide, her hands strangely spinning, and walking backwards fast.

RiRi watched it, the whole thing.

She said it was terrible and kinda beautiful.

I bet it was, jumping from so high, so very high, into the dark plush of that grieving ravine.

All us girls might look down into that same gorge on nights steeped in the sorrows of womanhood. I never felt so much, but looking now, I thought I might yet.

Beth walks up extra high on the ridge, swinging her 40 with surprising grace, and Jordy ducks his big boy head against me and kisses me smearily for a half hour or more.

He tells me this is a special spot for him.

At nights sometimes he runs up here, playing his music and forgetting everything.

"Maybe," he says, "that's how cheerleading is for you."

Then, he ripples his hands up and down me, gentle and with those great empty eyes of his shut tight, lashes long like a girl's. That funny way his nose bends slightly right, like a boxer's.

"Isn't she pretty, Jordy?" I hear Beth's rippling voice from somewhere, "when she looks into your eyes?"

I rest my lips on his cheekbone, near the crook of his nose, and he shudders.

The way his eyelashes tickle, and his hard heavy boy hands, grave and turbulent, I can feel all kinds of wonder and surprises charging through him.

All of this moves me, powerfully, and the day feels rare, the dusk falling purple, and I must be drunk because I think I hear Beth's voice far away, saying crazy things, asking me if I feel different, and loved.

Jordy Brennan's name buzzes on my phone that night, a spare text with "u"s and "r"s and cautious wonderings. But the thing that was there, the feeling huddling in me at the gorge, is already gone.

His wanting, so easily won—well, it bores me. I know every flex and twist of it, because there are no flexes and twists to it.

And instead I want to see Coach again, and tell her about it. I wonder what she'll say.

Beth calls after, and we have a long-winding talk, the 40-ouncers still heavy on us both.

She is asking if I remember how we used to hang on the monkey bars, hooking our legs around each other, and how strong we got and how no one could ever beat us, and we could never beat each other, but we'd agree to each release our hands at the count of three, and that she always cheated, and I always let her, standing beneath, looking up at her and grinning my gap-toothed, pre-orthodontic grin.

Such reminiscence is unlike Beth, but she is drunk and I think she may still be drinking, her mother's V.S.O.P., and she sounds affected by our time at the gorge, and possibly by other things.

"I hate how everything changes, always," she says. "But you don't."

In the parking lot the next day, Coach tilts her head and gives me a whisper of a smile.

Wanting to present this to her, I feel a funny kind of pride. Like she'd asked me to do a stunt for her, "Give me that pop cradle, Addy. Straight up, straight up—" and there I am, legs arrow-piked, and the feeling when my feet land on that hard floor, the fearsome quake through my ankles, legs, hips.

So I tell her, my hand sweeping across my mouth, like I can barely say it. *Just messed around a little. Jordy Brennan. Jordy Brennan. Just like you said.*

"Which one is that?" she says.

I feel something slither a little loose in me. Which one?

"You see him on the track," I insist. "You were talking about him. You talked to me about him and his high-tops. The crick in his nose."

She looks at me, quiet like.

"So was he a good kisser?" she asks, and I still don't know if she remembers him.

I don't say anything.

"Did he open his mouth right away?" she asks.

At first, I think I misheard her.

"Or did you make him work for it?" she continues, grinning slyly.

"It wasn't like that," I say, and is she making fun of me?

"So," she asks, her voice softer, straighter, "what was it like?"

"I don't know," I say, not meeting her eyes, my face burning. Somehow it feels like I'm talking to a boy, a guy, an older one, or from another school. "I don't think I want it to go anywhere."

She looks at me and then nods, like I've said something wise.

"You're a smart girl, Addy," she says. She pauses, then adds, "You can make a lot of mistakes, just wondering about boys."

I nod back, thinking about the word she uses, about the word "boys." Because that's what Jordy Brennan is, a boy. A boy. Not even a guy.

Coach, after all, is married to a man. Coach, after all, has known the world of men. Who even knows how many or what kinds.

She jangles her car keys into her fingers, sliding into her car.

She looks at me through the window, a winking look, but it's between us. We've shared something.

And it brings her closer to me.

6

WEEK FOUR

"Where is she?" RiRi whispers, her honey curls whipping side to side.

Beth is late for practice, and I wonder if she's going to show at all.

Something's been shifting in her and I think it's sort of like she's still captaining with nothing to captain, scratching some phantom limb.

Twice last week she didn't call for our late-night recap, our laying forth of the maneuvers of the day, who humiliated herself, whose bra is tatty, and whose fat ass is fatting up the whole squad. We've done these calls nightly since forever. But Tuesday I forgot to call and Thursday she didn't pick up. Still, I could feel her breathing somehow, could feel her watching her phone screen blinking *Addy, Addy.*

Coach rolls the media cart into the gym, fingers wrapped tight around the remote.

"Progress has been," she says, "not bad."

We watch ourselves. That bouncing yellow frill on the screen. Malibu-tanned and jerking ponytails, as ever. But we are no longer hip-shaking, pop and locking. We are bounding in perfect time, marching into a three-rowed V, jumping into our toe touches with matching precision. When we do our transition, I can't even believe it, not quite, the way we seem like one long centipede snapping and unsnapping.

We are in sync. We are tight. We are martial and precise.

"Where's Cassidy?" Coach asks, and all our heads turn from the screen.

If you're even ten seconds late—seconds she counts out with toe taps, like our third-grade gym teacher—you don't get to practice. Emily once skidded in at the five-count, blood pouring from her forehead, hurrying so fast her face had caught in her own slamming locker door.

"I think she—" I start, trying to generate an excuse.

As if on cue, I see Tacy Slaussen's hoodie pocket, red blinking from the top seam. A bass kicks up, the chorus of that song about the club, the way the heat presses tight and you know you're getting some, at da club.

She forgot her phone was on, and now she's trapped.

And I know that ring is Beth's.

Every year there are ones like Tacy, with big ole girl crushes on Beth, the kind who will skip fourth period to go on monster energy runs for her, or do dares, like running through the Sutton Grove Mall, hitching jeans low and flashing thongs at security guards. Beth likes to make these girls run.

I glare quick at her, try to get her to steady herself, but her face is panic-stitched.

A flash, and Coach is right there, her hand in Tacy's pocket.

The phone skitters across the floor, spinning madly all the way to the stretched accordion doors behind which the junior squad shouts buoyantly, *We do it like stomp-stomp-clap-clap, we do it like stomp-stomp-clap-clap.*

Tacy's jaw shakes.

Since we've never actually seen Coach have to lay it down, I don't know why we all feel it like a hammer on our chest. But we do.

Coach, though, doesn't say anything. Not for ten, twenty seconds.

She doesn't look angry exactly.

Instead, she looks bored.

It's a dismissal.

"You girls, with your phones and your sad little texts," she says, shaking her head. "Ten, twelve years ago, it was still folding notes, passing them in class. Just as fucking sad. No, this is sadder."

In an instant, it feels like all our hard work, still frozen on the TV screen, has been wiped away.

And I feel so stupid with my own stupid fucking phone, with the little skins I have for it—hot pink, butterflied, leopard skin— and how it never leaves my crimped palm, a live thing that, it seems now, beats instead of my heart.

And we all know whose fault it is.

Tacy's head is shaking back and forth, worse, much worse than the time Beth kicked her out of the car on Black Ash Ridge for spilling peach brandy all over Beth's new leather boots, licorice-shiny and magnificent and ever since creased with ruin.

"I'm sorry, Coach," Tacy blurts. "I'm sorry."

Coach just looks at her, and the look makes me think of the needle valve on that Bunsen burner, turning tight. Shutting off.

Later, Coach smoking in front of the propped-open window of her office, ponders poor Tacy and her lank, switch-straight hair and startled eyebrows.

"She's a sheep," sighs Coach.

I feel relieved I am not one of the fucking sad girls with their sad fucking phones.

"Squad needs sheep," she says. "So fine."

I nod, pressing my temple to the cold windowpane, legs still shaking from practice.

"But I don't spend my time on sheep," she says. "There's no payoff."

I nod, slower now, my forehead squeaking on the windowpane.

"But you, Hanlon. You're figuring out what you want," she says, staring at her cigarette, like it's telling her something. "Which is what you should be doing."

I keep nodding, lifting myself straight, straightening myself for her.

Still staring at her cigarette, her face slowly loosening, turning soft with youngness and fear and wonder.

I've not seen this on her, and it's like the years shuttling backwards and it's two girls inside the bathroom stall, hiding from the horrors of the world together, burning their throats, their lungs, for rude courage to face those same horrors with big smiles and white shoes.

Beth shows up at next-day practice, a note from See-Yu at the Living Heart Medical Spa assuring Coach that Beth had been suffering from severe menstrual cramps the previous day and needed an emergency acutonic session.

"Coach, no lie, they ding these big forks, like the kind you use to flip steaks on a grill," Beth says, and none of us can watch her, "and the sound just zings through you and straightens your ovaries all out."

Beth, she runs her hand over her hips, like she's showing us how quiet and subdued her ovaries now are. How she has vanquished them.

"It's hard being a girl," Beth adds, shaking her head with elaborate weariness.

Coach looks at her, hands curved lightly around her clipboard. Face blank.

She will not play.

Instead, she looks right through Beth.

"The timing is way off on the tuck jumps," she says, turning away from Beth.

That's it?

"And I know why," Coach says. "I can see sugar glazed all over you girls. You're all shiny with bad living."

Suddenly, I've forgotten all about Beth and I can only feel all the grease on me. As hard as I try, there are slips, and I feel like Coach is looking just at me, seeing the cinnamoned snack puffs I'd snuck that morning. My teeth ache with it. My stomach is swollen with it. I feel weak and desecrated.

"We're going to hit it extra hard today," Coach says. "Hit you in places no tuning forks can. Line up."

That's when we know: we're paying for Beth's sins.

The jump drill comes, and then the high kicks and then floor crunches and then running the gym track until RiRi throws up in the corner, a sloshing mix of slim-fast and sugar-free powdered donuts.

Beth, though, she sacks up. I'll give her that. At least she doesn't make it any worse for any of us. Sweat glittering on her, dappling her eyelashes, she kills it.

She will not sit down after, when we all collapse on the mats, our sweaty limbs crisscrossing. She will not sit down, will not let the steel slip from between her shoulders.

She has so much pride that, even if I'm weary of her, of her fighting ways, her gauntlet-tossing, I can't say there isn't something else that beams in me. An old ember licked to fresh fire again. Beth, the old Beth, before high school, before Ben Trammel, all the boys and self-sorrow, the divorce and the adderall and the suspensions.

That Beth at the bike racks, third grade, her braids dangling, her chin up, fists knotted around a pair of dull scissors, peeling into Brady Carr's tire. Brady Carr, who shoved me off the spinabout, tearing a long strip of skin from my ankle to my knee.

Tugging the rubber from his tire, her fingernails ripped red, she looked up at me, grinning wide, front teeth gapped and wild heroic.

How could you ever forget that?

We all want to "take it to the next level"—that's what we keep calling it. For us, the next level means doing a real basket toss, with three or four girls hurling a Flyer ten, fifteen, twenty feet in the air, and that Flyer flipping and twisting her way back down into their arms. And not even Beth has ever done a stunt like this, not this high, not without a mat. We were never that kind of squad, not a tourney squad. Not a serious squad.

Once we master a basket toss, we can do real stunts, real pyramids, because they are pyramids that end with true flying, with girls loaded up and slingshot into the air. The gasp-ahh awesomeness we've always dreamed of.

We have been YouTubing basket tosses all day, watching sprightly girl after sprightly girl get thrown by her huskier squadmates into the air and then try to ride it as far as she can. Arms extended, back arched, she is reaching for something, and only stops when she has to.

Mostly, though, we watch girls fall.

"A girl over at St. Reggie's died doing a basket toss that high last year," Emily says, her voice grave, like she's giving a press conference on TV. "She landed chest down in everyone's arms and her spleen popped like a balloon."

"Spleens don't pop," Beth says, though how she knows this is unclear.

"But I heard she had mono," someone says.

"What's that got to do with it?"

"It makes your spleen swell."

"No one here has mono."

"You don't always know."

"They banned it in my cousin's school," someone says.

"You can't ban mono," Beth says.

"You're not even allowed to do them on spring floors."

"Who could get their heels over their head like that?" spiral-curled RiRi wonders, lifting one of her legs off the floor.

"You do," Beth says. "Every Saturday night."

"So are you ready for it, Beth?" Emily grins.

"Ready for what?"

Tacy rolls her eyes. "Like it'd be anyone but you, Beth. You're Top Girl."

Beth almost smiles.

It's a relief to see it. To see how much she wants it. When Coach gives her the spot, it'll make everything better. *Maybe,* I think, high on hunger, *they will even become friends.*

Of course, we all want it. (Even me, five inches taller than Beth, a tragedy of birth.) It's the star shot, and we feel our bodies hardening, we feel our speed quickening, our blood pounding, thick and strong.

Tosses, two-and-a-half pyramids, tabletops, thigh stands, split stands, Wolf Walls—Coach says they're what separates you from just another ass-shaking pep squad.

"So we're not an ass-shaking pep squad?" Beth mutters, her voice smoke-thick, her eyes shot through with blood and boredom. "If I wanted to be an ath-lete," she says, "I'd've joined the other dykes on field hockey."

Three-oh-seven and Coach strolls into the gym, her hair wound softly into a ponytail.

"Let's get started on that toss," she says. "We need four to make the cradle underneath—two Bases, and a back and a front spot to get enough power."

She pauses. "But who's going to be our Flyer?"

Our two killer Bases, Mindy and Cori Brisky, their legs like titanium pikes, saunter over, eyeing all of us. Wondering which one of our lives will depend on the strength of their flintlock collarbones, our feet lodged there, rising high.

I think, for a second, it might be me.

And why shouldn't it be me, twisting high, propelled skyward, all eyes battened to me, my body bullet-hard and glorious?

But it has to be Beth. We all know it. Beth practically stepping forward, all five feet and ninety pounds of her, stomach tight as anyone fed solely on tar and battery acid.

She's our Flyer. Missed practices, insolence, but still she is our Flyer. Of course she is.

(Except the voice inside that says, Me, me, me. It should be me. But, if not me, Beth.)

"Slaussen," Coach says, turning to Tacy, the ewe.

I feel myself stone-sinking.

"You ready to fly?" she asks her.

There's a hush to everything, and a closeness in the air.

Not Beth.

And *Tacy?*

Tacy Slaussen, that little pink-eyed nothing, the one Beth used to call "Cottontail"?

But then I see it. Coach is putting Tacy—Tacy of the barking phone, Tacy, Beth's baby bitch—on the guillotine.

In my head, I hear the ear-popping crack, head clacking against the gym floor. Spleen splattered. So many ways to go wrong, to ruin yourself. Your legs like barrettes bent back, your body matchstick-snapped.

A pretty world of being pretty decimated in one splintering second.

That's what I secretly wanted, just moments ago?

I did. I still do. Those five inches, and no one will ever ask me.

None of us dare look at Beth, but we all watch Tacy, her flushed face. You can see her heart beating all over her skin.

When I do sneak a look at Beth, I see she's not even looking up, coiling the drawstrings on her hoodie into a candy cane twist.

"Coughlin," Coach says to Mindy, whose boulder shoulders are ringed with bruises two seasons a year. "She'll be all yours. What do you think?"

Pausing, Mindy appraises Tacy.

"I could totally base her," she replies, looking at Coach as if with a thick wagging tail.

Coach nods. "Elevator her up and let's see what she's got. *One-two.*"

Mindy and Cori grab wrists, make a square.

"*Three-four,*" Coach counts.

Tacy, her tendril limbs limply offering themselves, plants her foot in their wrist-weaved basket. One pancake palm on Tacy's back, the other just below her behind. Back spotter Paige Shepherd loads her in.

"*Five-six,*" and Mindy and Cori lift Tacy from waist to shoulder,

Tacy fumbling frantically for their shoulders, Paige hustling to back base her.

And up she goes.

"Seven-eight!"

And the girls, fingers flicking, legs rocking, toss her into the air.

Tacy's mouth open, struck.

Airborne.

Her whole body quivering like a plucked string.

Too scared to tuck, pike, toe touch, anything.

"Soften!" shouts Coach.

Tacy sinking back down, all three girls scrambling, one of Tacy's legs jamming into Mindy's collarbone.

But they catch her. They don't let her hit the floor.

Tacy, walking it off, crying like a little bitch.

For an hour, Tacy falls and falls, over and over again.

Foot to face. Shin to shoulder. Face to mat.

Mindy and Cori angrier and angrier the more knocks they take, elevatoring her up with greater and greater force.

Tacy starts sobbing a half hour in, and never stops.

Off to her office for a phone call, Coach deputizes Beth to count in her absence.

Beth, looking at her, her mouth a straight line, says nothing. But when Coach's office door shuts, she starts counting.

One-two-three-four,

*fucking ex-*tend *Slaussen!*

Who can deny it is a masterful play? Take away the princess's crown and give it to the lady-in-waiting. The handmaiden. The servant.

Never, in all my lieutenant years, have I seen anyone go toe-to-toe with Beth. Never anyone who couldn't be felled with an errant Facebook rumor, a photoshopped image (*RiRi skanking it up over spring break*), the pilfered text message sent to the entire school. This was different.

Different because no one had ever taken her on, and different because no one had ever wanted to do so on our behalf. Coach did it for us.

And her will was strong as Beth's maybe. Maybe.

Watching Tacy, shin red-streaked, a long bone bruise readying to bloom on her forearm, we all know what's happened.

We all know why, that Saturday, Tacy will be landing, at terrible and just velocity, in our meager arms—arms weary from ten hours of dieter's tea and celery shreds—we all know why.

Because Coach sees Beth for what she is and knows she has to overthrow her.

And Tacy?

A pullet-pawn.

Two days till the game, we are practicing like Tacy's life depends on it, since it does.

I'm the front spotter because Coach says I have in focus what I lack in heft.

We start with a straight ride, no twists or toe touches or kick arches. We've practiced all week and never once missed, our hands wrapped around each other's locked wrists, steeling our arms so tight, bolting them in place, a safe little girl-cradle for Tacy's quaking feet.

Then, rubber-banding our arms to spring her shaking body up into the air, all our eyes on Tacy, making that promise to her, the birdy panic on her face as she flies, flies, flies.

But, had we slipped, any of us, had one of our arms weakened, her leg curled the wrong way, her body twisted an inch or less, she'd have hit a spring floor.

And when we try to get her higher, Tacy's landings are rougher. There are incidents: elbow to the eye, index finger bent back, Tacy's grasping hand clawing my face.

But I focus on Tacy, and I don't show my fear. That's what Coach tells me. "Don't let her see it on you, or it'll swallow her."

Coach tells us you can fall from eleven feet and still land safely on a spring floor, our practice floor.

She says that knowing that, game time, Tacy will be flying high over not a spring floor but the merciless ground of the Mohawks' football field.

"Slaussen," Coach says, "you gotta want it. Don't do it if you don't want it."

And Tacy, her back straighter, her eyes clearer, her chin higher than I've ever seen on this meek and weak girl, replies, "I want it, Coach. I want it."

Tacy. Here was the head-smacking convert.

I can feel Beth's eyeroll without even looking.

"I knew that one was wasting our time," Beth says.

But I don't say anything. I am watching Tacy's avid eyes.

Friday night, when we set foot on the Mohawks' field, the frosted ground beneath us, how can we not picture Tacy's skull splitting daintily in two?

And two of the Mohawk squad bitches, the rangiest with legs like spires, circle us before and start gaming us with tales of blood sport. A mix of fish tales, trash talk, and camaraderie.

"JV year, the girl was fronting a new Flyer learning her twist," the blonde Mohawk says, gum smacking, "and when the Flyer spun around her legs came apart and knocked out

both Bases. One popped a lip and the other had to get a face
cut glued shut. Coach caught it on video and replays it at all
our after-parties."

"I was practicing my back handspring," the scrubby redhead
says, "and I kicked Heather and knocked her teeth right out of her
face. It was insane. Teeth and blood were flying everywhere. I felt
soooo bad."

There is a breathless momentum to it. I know how it goes. It's
fun when you're doing it, like hearing a ghost story.

Forty-five minutes from now, though, it will not be fun for
Tacy, standing fifteen feet in the air, two spindly girls holding her
up, ready to toss her.

Tacy is gray, into green.

Beth saunters over. She gives me a look, one I know from her
captain days. I nod.

"That's enough," I interrupt everyone. "Don't know about you
hardcore bitches, but we'd rather spend our pre-game time getting
pretty."

But the blonde Mohawk, eyes hard on Tacy, won't stop working
her. "This one kid, she had a body just like yours. And she hit the
tramp bar, hard. Her head was bleeding a *lot,* and she had to go to
the ER. Turns out the skin on her head had split and you could
see all this pink stuff underneath. She needed staples to pull it back
together. We couldn't get her to come back to cheer no matter
how hard we tried. Now she's isn't doing anything at all."

"Slaussen," Beth shouts, looming over us now. "Coach wants
you."

Rabbit-like, Tacy skitters away.

For a second, I think it's done. But it's not.

Beth surveys the Mohawk girls.

"Once," Beth starts, and I know what she's going to do, and this is why she was captain. "I was standing on this girl's shoulders and I slipped and fell flat on my back."

Everyone gasps politely.

"The crack was so loud they heard it in the parking lot," I add.

"My first thought," Beth says, shaking her head, "was how am I going to tell my mom?"

Everyone nods appreciatively.

"I was lucky," she says, her cool gaze on those Mohawks, shivering a little now in their long timbers. "I was only paralyzed for six weeks. They bolted this metal ring into my skull with pins to hold my head and neck in place. It's called a halo, if you want to know."

We two, in such sync, like the old days, like before Coach, before last summer.

Reaching across, I touch Beth's hair lightly with my fingertips. "The doctors said if she'd been an inch to the right or left," I say, "she would have died."

"But I didn't," Beth says. "And nothing would ever stop me from cheering anyway.

"They gave me the coolest purple cast. And Coach tells me I'm the best Flyer she ever had."

Under the bank of stadium lights, Tacy's face poppy pink with purpose and mania, we raise her up, her hands releasing our trembling shoulders, and she rockets herself, thrusting her legs in either direction, arms pressed against her ears and flying higher than I've ever seen.

So high that a wild shake ripples through all of us, our cradled arms vibrating with awe and wonder.

Vibrating so strongly that it runs through me, it does, and I feel my left arm slacken, ever so slightly, and a shudder bores through me, and if it weren't for RiRi next to me, feeling my tremor, flashing me her terror, a starry span of panic before my eyes, I wouldn't have driven that steel back into my blood, my muscles, my everything.

Made it tight and iron-fast for Tacy, who seemed to be in the air for minutes, hours, a radiant creature with white-blond hair spread wing-like, finally sinking safely, ecstatically, into all our arms.

It's hours later, and we're in Emily's dad's car sneaking swigs of blackberry cordial, swiped from RiRi's garage, where her brother hides it.

We're waiting in the parking lot of the Electric Crayon, its neon sign radiating sex and chaos, the cordial tickling our mouths and bellies almost unbearably.

We've never been on Haber Road before, except the time we went with RiRi's sister to Modern Women's Clinic to get ofloxacin and she told us after how she almost choked when they stuck that big swab down her throat, but it was still better than what Tim Martinson had stuck down her throat.

We all laughed even though it didn't really seem funny and none of us want to end up at Modern Women's Clinic ever, the matted-down wall-to-wall, and the buzzing fluorescent lights, and the girl behind the front desk who sang softly to herself, *"Boys trying to touch my junk-junk-junk. Gonna get me some crunk-crunk-crunk."*

An hour slides by before Tacy finally comes out of the Electric Crayon, tugging her jeans down so we can see the Sutton Grove eagle soaring there, the envy so strong it almost makes me burst.

Coach, she wouldn't come with us no matter how much we begged. But she did slip Tacy forty bucks for it. Two smooth twenties, tucked in our new Flyer's trembling hands.

We never heard of any coach doing that, ever.

Nudging my fingers under the sticking bandage on her lower back, I touch that red-raw eagle, making Tacy wince with pained pleasure.

Me, me, me, it should be me.

7

"*I've heard some* things about Ms. Colette French," Beth tells me. "I have contacts."

"Beth," I say. I know this tone, I know how things start.

"I don't have anything to report yet," she says, "but be ready."

Like bamboo slowly sliding under fingernails. She has started.

But Beth also grows easily bored. That's what I have to remember.

I am glad, then, when Beth seems to have found something—someone—else to do.

Monday morning, the recruiting table is struck in the first-floor hallway, by the language labs.

The posters blare red, the heavy ripple of the flag insignia.

Discover Your Path to Honor.

Recruiters, out for fresh, disaffected-teen blood.

"Who needs cheer?" Beth says. "I'm enlisting."

They came last year too, and always sent the broadest-shouldered, bluest-eyed Guardsmen, the ones with arms like twisted oak and booming voices that echo down the corridor.

This year, though, they have Sergeant Will, who is entirely different. Who, with his square jaw and smooth, knife-parted hair, is handsome in a way unfamiliar to us. A grown-up man, a man in real life.

Sarge Will makes us dizzy, that mix of hard and soft, the riven-granite profile blurred by the most delicate of mouths, the creasy warmth around his eyes—eyes that seem to catch far-off things blinking in the fluorescent lights. He seems to see things we can't, and to be thinking about them with great care.

He is older —he may be as old as thirty-two—and he is a man in the way that none of the others, or no one else we know or ever knew, are men.

Before practice, or during lunch, a lot of the girls like to hang around and finger the brochures. *Spread Your Wings,* they say.

Fresh off her latest breakup with Catholic Patrick, lovely RiRi spends pass time lingering at the table, leaning across it, arms pressed tight against either side of her breasts, framing them V-like and drawing one foot up her other leg, like she says men like.

"Personally, I find they like it when I lift my cheer skirt over my head," Beth says, side by side with me on the floor in front of her locker. "You might try that next time."

"Maybe you need some new tricks," RiRi yawns, eyes hot on Sarge Will. "What worked with your junior high PE teach might not roll with the big brass here."

This is how it starts, Beth rising to her feet like them's fighting words, and asking RiRi if she'd care to make it interesting.

I can tell from RiRi's face that she would not care to do so at all, but it's the prairie whistle of the Old West, high noon at ole Sutton Grove High. You can hear Beth's tin star rattling against her chest.

So much better to have Beth face off with party girl RiRi than with Coach.

It's not that Beth just rolls for anybody or even most people, but when she does, it's a star turn, it's page one. Like with Ben Trammel, or the time everyone saw her and Mike LaSalle, ebony against her ivory, in the holly hedges at St. Mary's after the game. All those forked nettles studding his letterman jacket, all up and down the felted arms, and his neck bristled red.

Everyone talked about it, but I was the one who saw her after. The bright pain in her face, like she didn't know why she'd done it, the alarm in her eyes, pin struck.

We've been angling, I have. *Coach, what's your place look like? Coach, we want to meet little Caitlin too, we do.*

Coach, show us, show us, let us in.

None of us ever think she will. We've tried for five weeks. I dream of it, driving by her house like a boy might do.

The next Saturday at the home game, Tacy kicks out that basket toss like she's been doing it all her life, and she adds a toe touch, and we do a hanging pyramid, with Emily and Tacy swinging like trapdoors off RiRi's arms, which whips up the crowd to fierce delirium.

There is such an ease to it. In the parking lot after, we're all feeling so good, like we could annihilate an invading army, or go to Regionals or State.

Beth is hoisting between her fingers a very fine bottle of spiced rum from some boy on the Norsemen team. He wants to party with us, and promises big excitement at his uncle's apartment, up on the Far Ridge.

Just the kind of wild night we'd all maneuver endlessly for, trading promises and fashioning elaborate lies, a string of phone calls home to marshal a fleet of alibis no parent could pierce.

Beth is the dark mistress of such nights and seems always to know where the secret house party is, or the bar with the bouncer who knows her brother, or the college boy hangout by the freeway where no one ever cards anybody and the floors are sticky with beer and the college boys are so glad for girls like us, who never ask them even one question ever.

But as we conspire around Beth's car, my hand stroking the borrowed bottle, mouth clove-streaked and face rum-suffused, Coach walks past us, car keys jangling loudly.

"Going home, Coach?" Emily asks, swiveling her nutraslimmed hips madly to the music thudding from the car stereo. "Why don't you come out with us instead?"

We all look wide-eyed at Emily's pirate-boldness, Tacy's head perched merrily on Emily's shoulder, like a parrot.

Coach smiles a little, her eyes, thoughtful now, wandering past us, into the dark thicket of trees banded around the parking lot.

"Why don't you all come to my house instead?" she says, just like that. "Why don't you come over?"

"The smell of desperation," Beth says, "is appalling."

Beth does not wish to go to Coach's house.

"It's not my job," she adds, as we all look at her blankly, "to make her feel like she matters."

Standing in the front hallway, we wait while Coach sends off the babysitter, an older woman named Barbara in a peach chenille sweater that hangs to her knees.

She lets us poke our heads in and see little Caitlin fast asleep. The room is blushing pink with one of those rotating lanterns that wobble pretty ballerinas all over the walls.

Caitlin, strawberry blonde, nestles under rosy gingham with a doilied edge through which she hooks one pink thumb.

Her breath is light and fast and we can hear it even huddled in the doorway, Emily and me, we're the ones who want to see. We look at her, the soft ringleted hair and the peace on her flushed face, and wonder what that peace is like and if we ever had it.

We sit out on the back deck—me and RiRi and Emily and the newly brave Tacy, the li'l cottontail whom we once ignored but whom we now gird to our chests proudly, our newly branded re-cruit, our soaring rocket.

Our cold arms buried inside our varsity jackets, at first so for-mal, we sit legs crossed tight, backs straight, speaking in light hushy tones, asking questions about the house, about Caitlin, about Coach's husband, Matt.

We sit in the chilling air, on long benches flanking two sides of the deck. And there's Coach, on a lounger, slowly sinking back, hands tucked in her jacket pockets, her hair spreading across the teak slats, her face slowly, slowly releasing itself from its school day tethers, its rigor and purpose.

The night feels important even as it's happening.

Once, Beth and I had a night like this, the night before we started high school. Kiddie-like, we'd hooked her brother's Swiss Army into our palms and pressed them tight against each other, and later Beth said she could feel my heart beating in my hand, her hand. She swore she could. We knew that meant something. Something had passed between us and would endure. We don't talk about it anymore and it was a century ago, wars won and lost since then.

And, Beth, you're not even *here* now.

On Coach's deck, we all talk in the echoey night, first shyly, awkwardly, of nothing things—the Mohawks' forward with the bowlegs, the way Principal Sheehan spins on one heel like a lady when he turns in the hallway, the doughy chocolate chip cookies in the cafeteria, the tang of the raw eggs and baking soda churning in your stomach, making you sick.

Slowly, slowly, though, we feel the dark night opening among us, between us, and RiRi talks about her dad, who moved out last month and cries on the phone whenever they talk, and Emily shows us the very first ballet step she ever learned, and Tacy says she never felt so perfect as when she was flying in the air.

Would a boy ever make her feel that way? she asks. *Would a man?*

We all look at Coach, who's smiling and nearly laughing even, leaning back on the lounger and flinging one leg over the other.

"Girly," she says, lively and light, like you rarely hear, "you have no idea the wonderful things men will make you feel."

Tacy smiles, we all do.

"And terrible things too," Coach adds, her voice tinier now. "But the terrible things are . . . are kind of wonderful too, I guess."

Tacy props her feet up on the foot of Coach's lounger. "How can something terrible ever be wonderful?" she asks, and I cringe a little. *I know how,* I want to say. *I know how, everything wonderful is terrible too.* I don't know how I know it, but I do.

"You don't know enough about wonderful yet," Coach says, her voice smaller still, her face growing more somber, more meaningful. "Or terrible."

We're so close in that moment it feels like a humming wire between us, and no one wants to say a word for fear of snapping it, silencing it.

It's very late when RiRi plucks the pint from her boiled wool pocket. Smirnoff vodka, the slummer's choice.

RiRi's move is bold, but without Beth here, somebody has to be.

"How about we all do one shot," she says, rising, stretching her arms to either side, as if to insist on the importance of the moment, "to toast the squad, and most of all Coach, who's made us..."

She pauses, then looks around, all of us watching nervously, eagerly. Watching her and watching Coach, who hasn't moved from her luxuriant slouch, whose eyes lock with RiRi's, as if deciding.

"To Coach," RiRi says, then, her voice building, "who's made us women."

Who's made us women.

This from RiRi, who's never said anything significant, ever.

Suddenly, I'm on my feet, my toes even, raising my arm high too, as if I held a champagne flute, a whole frosty magnum in my grip.

Emily and Tacy follow fast and we're all standing now, looking down at Coach, her chin lifting regally to receive us.

RiRi takes a gentle tug from that pint, then rocks her head back and forth from the kick of it. The rough, smutty smack of it. We all do. I feel it heating in me, firing up my whole body.

Then, I tender the pint to Coach, my hand trembling a little, wondering what she'll do, if we've done something here, swept her up in something with us, something we all want.

Her arm lifts serenely, without pause, her hand slipping around the pint.

Tilting it, her fingers nuzzled tight, she drinks.

Hand to hand, our warming fingers, we pass the pint until it's empty. My eyes tearing, my body blazing and strong.

Emily and Tacy go home, and RiRi is drunken-texting a new boy, who seems just like the last one and may even be the last one's brother, so Coach and I drift into the house.

*   *   *

"Hanlon—*Addy*," she says, and we pluck fruit from the big wooden bowl on her kitchen island as we walk by. "And you can call me Colette. These are Smirnoff rules."

She snags a tangle of grapes and we slide them into our mouths one after another as she gives me the big tour.

Coach's eyes are a little blurred, and it's just a gentle buzz we have, and I drop a grape on the carpet, and it smears beneath my sock, and I apologize four times.

"Fuck it," Coach—Colette—says. "You think I care about this carpet?"

And soon enough we're both kneeling on the carpet, woven wool in the deepest forest green.

"It's the face weight," she says. "That's what counts. Matt says you have to have forty ounces per square. And at least five twists per inch. He read it on the internet."

"It's beautiful," I say, and I've never really looked at carpet before. But now I can't seem to get enough of the feel of it on my knees, between my fingertips, dug deep.

"Addy," she says, pulling me up to my feet, dragging me from room to room, "you should've seen the wedding. We had a picture pool filled with rose petals. A harpist. Pin spots on every table."

She tells me they couldn't afford any of it, but Matt worked harder, until they could.

Five, six days a week, he left for work at five, came home at ten. He wanted to give her things. He let her have whatever she wanted. She didn't know what to want, but she cut out pictures from magazines. Assembled them in a book. *My Wedding*, it was called.

"I was barely twenty-one," she says. "What did I know?"

I nod and nod and nod.

"He found the house," she says, looking around, eyes blinking, like it's all new to her. Like she hasn't ever seen any of it before.

And so, age twenty-two, she had this house. And had to fill it.

He said, *Whatever you want.* So she cut out more pictures from magazines. She made a big bulletin board and called it *My House.* He saw what she wanted and he made it happen—as much of it as he could.

"He's very hardworking," she says. "He looks at numbers all day. And at home, that laptop is always open, those long columns of numbers, flashing and blinking. They never stop blinking."

Her hand skates across the pleated shade of an amber lamp.

"He does it all for me, Addy," she says. But the way she says it, it doesn't match what she's saying. The way she says, it's like it's some leaden thing.

My head isn't straight, though, the vodka still stirring in me.

But I'm not so drunk that I don't understand that the house is like any of our houses. Not as nice as Emily's, where everything is white and you can't sit on anything, but nicer than RiRi's, which has brown ceiling stains and wall-to-wall.

But the way Coach—Colette—walks through it, her voice hushed, her feet treading so softly, it starts to seem like the whole place is glowing, like the spinning lantern in little Caitlin's room, casting enchantment everywhere.

"Beautiful," I say again, my fingers slipping around a curtain pull. "Beautiful." That's the word that keeps sliding from my mouth.

"Beautiful, beautiful," she says, singsongy, as we walk past it all, as I lace my fingers through everything.

"And this is the last of it," she says, and my feet are nestling in the bedroom carpet, which is deep, rich. It's a quiet, caramely space, like a nice hotel room where everything feels soothing and featureless.

But then I think of how she chose it all, Coach—Colette— with fabric swatches, tile samples, paging endlessly through those thick magazines you see fanned on tables at the white-walled boutiques on Honeycutt Drive. From the wrought-iron chandelier, its arms looping up, nearly stroking the ceiling, to the sheer curtains dangling, twisting around the drooping spider plant. Everything touching everything else.

She made it up inside her head, and he made it real for her.

It starts to seem like so much more, swelling before my eyes. Like everything is throbbing lightly, and if you rested your forehead against it, you could feel its heart beating.

"This is my favorite room," I say.

She looks at me, then looks around, like she's already forgotten all of it. Like she hasn't noticed any of it in years, since she tacked it together on her bulletin board. *My House.*

Our eyes float to the creampuff of a bed, its linen whipped up high. The princess and the pea.

Wearily, she sinks down into it, and everything seems to puff up, tiny cream-colored pillows scattering to the corners, the carpet.

"All these pillows," she says. "Every morning I put them all back. He's already at the office by six and I'm here, putting all these little pillows, these hundreds of pillows, back on the bed."

I feel my foot sink into one of them as I stumble toward her. I've never seen so many pillows, every shade of brown, from pale honey to something the color of chicory, like the French teacher drinks every day at lunch.

She takes my hand and sets it on the duvet, soft as spun air. Her touch, a coach's touch, Feel this. Now.

"Lie down," she says. "Get under it."

⋆　　⋆　　⋆

My bare legs cocooned under the filmy duvet, I want to kick them in circles. The bed is a tremendous cream-filled pillow, no, air-filled cream, and the tickling in my belly, unbearable.

"Pretend you're me," she says. I can barely see her over the frothy mound.

And it happens just like that.

A feeling of sinking, a falling deep inside.

And I'm her.

And this is my house, and Matt French is my husband, tallying columns all day, working late into the night for me, for me.

And here I am, my tight, perfect body, my pretty, perfect face, and nothing could ever be wrong with me, or my life, *not even the sorrow that is plainly right there in the center of it. Oh, Colette, it's right there in the center of you, and some kind of despair too. Colette—*

—that silk sucking into my mouth, the weight of it now, and I can't catch my breath, my breath, my breath.

Everything's changing in me.

I guess I'd been waiting forever, my palm raised. Waiting for someone to take my girl body and turn it out, steel me from the inside, make things matter for me, like never before.

Like love can.

8

Noonish, at the Guard recruitment table, we're watching the bet unfold.

All week, Beth has kept Sarge Will in her sights, determined to take RiRi down. They both agreed: whoever can get him to do a below-the-waist touch.

Beth works those school corridors like a gunslinger, spurred boots click-clacking. They lip over her knees, tall and shiny, and you're not supposed to wear boots with your cheer skirt, you're not supposed to wear boots like that at all.

As for RiRi, her cheer skirt tugged heavenward, waistband high enough to show what her mama gave her. The two of them, they're dangerous.

Sarge, though, is above all this. All the girls are hurling themselves at him, but he never blinks, not once. He smiles, but his smile doesn't really seem like a smile but the kind of thing you do with your mouth when you know everyone is watching.

Sometimes it's like each hip swivel is a burden he strains under. So, he just smoothly shifts such attentions over to the corporal, the private, whoever the hard-jawed thug next to him is, the one we never look at, that brush of acne on his chin, that angry look on him, like the boys who get into fights after one beer, who shove their girlfriends at parties and knock their shoulder blades loose, who pop their collarbones like buttons. We never look at them. Or I don't.

The worst is Corporal Prine, the one with the barrelhouse shoulders and the broad head like an eraser stub. A few weeks ago, I spotted him standing in front of the door of my English class. He seemed to be staring right at me, his razor-burned cheeks studded red. I tried not to pay attention, but then he did something with his tongue and hand that could not be ignored.

But Sarge, he can do anything. Yet the more we try, the less interested he seems. Most days, he seems to be some other place entirely, some place in which girls like us have no place at all.

Even Beth at her tartiest can't provoke him.

I don't see it, but I hear about it—the flash of her skirt, the star-spangled panties—and I don't believe it. *I didn't flash anything,* she tells me later. Just crooked her index finger, made him lean close, and asked him if she could feel his weapon.

But Sarge didn't bat a downy eyelash.

Oh, the daily frustration on RiRi's candy-mouthed face, and worse still Beth's glower, which she wears like a black veil all day.

Between Coach and Sarge, she has much to be unhappy about.

But instead of wrath and plots, she is quiet, brooding.

There's a witchiness to it, and it worries me.

It's during those weeks that I see Coach's husband for the first time, through the half-open study door. He's reading a sheaf of paper while slowly pulling off his necktie. I can't even tell you what he looks like except there's nothing to notice at all.

The next time, and the time after, it's always like this presence. *Matt's here. Oh, that's just Matt, finally home. That's the pizza guy for Matt.* And sometimes just "he." *There he is, oh, we can't turn on the stereo, he's here. Oh, you know him, he's working. He never, ever stops.*

He is always on his cell phone and he always looks tired. Once or twice we see him in the backyard, talking into his bluetooth, pacing around. We see him sitting on a stool at the kitchen island, spreadsheets spread across the table, his laptop swiveling, screen glowing green on him.

He works very hard, and he's not interesting at all.

Or maybe he is, but Coach never seems interested. And when he's there, it feels weirdly like Dad's home. A nice enough Dad, and not a buzzkill Dad except, I guess, for Coach, who seems to sink inside a little. Once he tried to ask about how we planned our pyramids because he studied real pyramids in college engineering and wondered if it was similar. But no one knew what to say and there was a long pause until Coach, her eyes shifting away, said that we were just tired because we'd been working on sequences all night.

"Man fears time," he said, as he walked off into his study, smiling at us all and kind of saluting good night, "yet time fears the pyramids."

Once, I'm passing the door to his study and I see him there, and the computer screen flickering, reflected on the window behind him. And I see he's playing Scrabble online. And something about it makes me crashingly sad.

"Beth, just come, will you? Just once, come with us."

We have been trying for the last three weeks. But when Beth does concede, I don't like how easy it is.

"Let's see what all of you have going on over there," she says, eyes flashing. "I'd like to see for myself."

Three Saturdays in a row, we've lounged, grown-up like, at Casa French, the grill fired up, Coach flipping salmon on cedar planks. Nothing ever tasted so good, even though we all only pick at it, shred it to pink filings on our plates, our mouths focused eagerly on the tickly white wine served in fine stemware that *tinggged* when your nails clicked it.

It's harder to enjoy it with Beth there, feeling her dismissive eyes on everything. But the wine helps.

We have a routine down, Emily and me lighting all the candles, the hurricane lanterns with the hand-painted ladybugs that Matt brought all the way from South Carolina, and the tall gas torch that Coach says is just like what they have on the beach in Bali, though she's never been there, none of us have. Beth, dull-eyed and afflicted, says it's the same ones she's seen in Maui, or even San Diego, or the Rainforest Café out on Route 9.

Eventually, though, the wine whirls even through Beth and it's so fun looking around the table at everyone's blooming, candlelit faces.

Mostly, it's all of us chicken-jabbering and Coach, her silent, half-smiling self. She listens and listens, and the stories, as before, get darker and more intimate. *Oh, RiRi, maybe one day you'll find a boy who loves you for more than your double-jointed jaw. And Emily, six weeks running on splenda and cabbage broth, as caved-in as your belly looks you'll never get that round face of yours any thinner at all unless you take a hammer and chisel.*

By the time Husband Matt comes home around eleven, we are all pretty drunk, Coach maybe even a little bit, that bloom to her face and her tongue slipping around words, and when RiRi takes off her top and runs around the yard, shouting into the bushes for boys, Coach just laughs and says it's time we met some real men, and that's when we see him standing at the kitchen island, and we all think that's hysterical, except Matt French, who looks tired and flips open his laptop and asks us if we could be quiet, which we can't possibly be.

Beth, who keeps saying she isn't drunk at all, but she never admits to being drunk, starts talking to him and asking him questions about his job, and if he likes it, and what his commute is like. She squeezes her breasts together in her tank top and leans on the kitchen island, fingers grazing his computer mouse rhythmically.

He looks at her, his brow knitted high in a way that I do find sweet, and asks if her parents might wonder where she is.

Over Beth's shoulder, he's throwing these looks at Coach, who finally says she'll drive us all home and Emily and Beth can pick up their cars tomorrow.

When we're walking out, I look back at him, and his face looks troubled, like years ago, eighth grade, and my dad, who no longer bothers, watching me as I left the house with Beth, our bodies suddenly so ripe and comely and there was nothing he could do.

The next day, hung over on the L-shaped sofa in Beth's living room, I wake up to Beth's hair dangling over me. Leaning over the back of the cushion, she tells me she didn't have any fun at all. And she's talking big, which always feels ominous.

"Sitting there on the deck, like it's her throne," she says, cotton-mouthed and craggy. "I didn't like it there. I don't like the way she conducts herself." There's a hitch in her voice and I wonder if she's still drunk, or I am.

"So high on her seat," Beth says. "All of you mooning like schoolgirls."

But we are schoolgirls, I think to myself.

"You have always been soft to these things, Addy," she says. "Last summer you were."

And I don't want her to talk about last summer again, and all our bickerings at cheer camp when everyone thought we were busting up. Because this has nothing to do with that girly nonsense.

"I tell you, Adelaide, I know her kind."

Climbing over the back of the sofa, Beth swings her bare legs, nestling into me, and I'm listening but not listening because I don't like that hitch in her voice.

"She better enjoy it while she can," she rumbles, burrowing her head into the pillow I've tucked under my arm, burrowing her head into me, like always. "Because in a few years she'll probably pop out another kid and her hips'll spread like rising dough and before she knows it, she'll be coaching field hockey instead."

Twisting her fingers in my hair, she tunnels into me and the pillow behind me, hiding herself.

"Who will want her then?" she asks.

Then answers.

"None of us."

9

There is a golden period, a week, two, when Beth seems to have
settled herself, when all our days are brimful with cheer, when
everything seems, for a moment, like it will be golden-grooved
forever.

Homecoming Week is starry and sublime.

For much of the school year, the rest of the student body views
us as something like lacquered lollipops, tiara-ed princesses, spirit
whores, chiclet-toothed bronze bitches. Aloof goddesses unwilling
to mingle with the masses.

But we never care because we know what we are.

And at Homecoming, we are given full rein.

At the pep rally, they see our swagger, our balls, our badassery.
They get to see what we can do, how our bodies are not paper
dolls and how our tans are armor.

How we defy everything, including the remorseless sugar maple
floor planks nailed a half century ago, ten feet below, our bodies
tilting, curving, arcing, whipping through the air, fearless.

Homecoming Week, even those who dislike us the most—the
painted Goths, the skater rats, the third-sex drama freaks—gaze
with embarrassed wonder as we spring into our hanging pyramid
on the open quad at lunch, our bodies like great iron spokes on a
massive wonder wheel.

And at the game, as we catapult Tacy to the heavens—the

woozy screech from the stands as they seem to believe that we have flung her to her death—it inspires shock and awe.

I'm the one, strutted high on Mindy's and Cori's shoulders, who kicks off the pep rally, waving a long pole looped with streamers, Tacy running alongside with Custodial Services' pilfered leaf blower, blowing against the streamers, which unfurl like so many roman candles.

The bonfire is the highest we've ever had, our torches whirling, all the circles of light, a foam-toothed Rattlers' mascot going up in flames, swinging high above the cindery tips and all of us screaming to voicelessness, our faces hot and exploding.

Dropping our torches, we run across the dark field, Coach's voice calling out, *Toe Touch, Lock Arms, Spread Eagle...*

And there she is, ringside, watching us, eyes darting and everything about her glowing.

I remember, age twelve, watching this. From up high in the bleachers, watching the high school squad in front of the wild inferno, flames vaulting, their silhouettes doing mad jumps, leaps, death defiance. One girl picking up her fallen baton rolling across sparking grass and knowing now, knowing having held that baton, that it is searing but she smiles and dances and leaps higher than anyone else.

And twelve-year-old Beth beside me, saying:

"Look at that, look at that," her voice when it was still filled with wonder.

But, after Homecoming, returning from our glory paths, something has shifted.

In Coach's eyes there is something burning moodily. We all notice, and speculate. We try to chalk it up to post-Homecoming comedown, but we do nothing with it.

But two days that week, Coach cancels practice. We think it

must be an adult thing in which we have no interest. Mortgage payments, a broken dishwasher, a flood in the basement.

Still, everyone wonders: What could go wrong in Coach's lovely life, with her nice home and her smooth hair and all those adoring girls wreathed at her feet?

But of course, I know better. I know things, even though I'm not sure what, exactly.

The way she never meets Matt French's eyes. Watching him help her unload the dishwasher one evening, late, and she would not turn her head.

And the thing I saw, felt, under that creamy duvet of hers, that silk sucking into my mouth, the feeling of something weighing on me, on her, and I couldn't catch my breath.

Friday, Coach doesn't cancel. She just doesn't show up for practice at all.

"Maybe it's feminine medical problems," RiRi says. "That happens to my Aunt Kaylie a lot. Sometimes she has to take off all her clothes. She sits on the sun porch in her bra, rubbing ice cubes all across herself."

"That's for old ladies," Beth says. "Maybe she's just sick of your face. Can you blame her?"

Emily, dizzy from Coach's x-treme juice fast, sucking on ginger peel all day, has to lean against the padded gym wall.

"She was going to bring me the potassium broth recipe," she whispers, her face feverish.

She starts to tell everyone about the broth, counting off the ingredients on her gum-sticky fingers: *raw garlic, beet tops, turnip tops, parsley, red pepper seeds, it alkalizes and then you . . .*

I nod and nod while Emily chirps and peeps, her little twigged legs trembling against the wall.

"Someone give her a fucking Kit Kat," Beth growls.

I throw an energy bar at Emily because I can't stand it anymore either.

We all watch as she eats it slowly, picking at it with shaking fingers, and then, turning greenish white, throws it all back up again in the wrapper.

Beth leans back on the long bench, extending one Aruba-tanned leg and examining it.

"Personally, I am sick of every one of you," she continues, eyes on perpetual roll. "Sick of everything and everybody."

Beth touches these things inside us sometimes. Inside me. It is one of her gifts, deeply misunderstood by others. It sounds like she's being mean, but she's not. Sick, sick, sick. It's something you feel constantly, the thing you fight off all the time. The knot of hot boredom lodged behind your eyes, so thick and grievous you want to bang your head into the wall, knock it loose.

I wonder if that's the thing Coach feels, at home, standing next to Matt French, loading the dishwasher, scrubbing her daughter's face.

"Hanlon," Beth says, jumping to her feet. "Let's trawl."

I look at her. "But if Coach shows..."

But I can tell where that will get me, Beth with her clenched jaw, about to unsnap. It reminds me of something I learned once in biology: a crocodile's teeth are constantly replaced. Their whole life, they never stop growing new teeth.

I get up, I follow.

There's something—always, even as late as junior year, us weary veterans now—about walking the echoing corridors after school. The whole cavernous place, a place we know so well that all our dreams take place here, feels different.

It's more than the new stillness, more than the heavy bleach swabbed over every skidded, gum-streaked inch.

By day, we walk as if in a force field, surrounded only by one another—our great colored swirl of cheerness. It is not aloofness, superiority. It's a protection. Who in this ravaged battlefield doesn't want to gather close her comrades?

But after three o'clock, the school day's gush of misery rushing into the streets, TV rooms, fluorescent-lit fast-food counters all over town. And the school-after-school becomes a foreign place, exotic.

There are kids here, and teachers in odd lurking pockets, you never know when or where, a huddle of physics grinds on the third-floor landing timing the velocity of falling super balls, the barking Forensics Clubbers snarking about capital punishment in the language lab, shaggy stoners slouching, their eyes bliss-glazed, outside the shop room—now called industrial design lab—the flash of nervous Mrs. Fowler flitting out of the ceramics studio, a foot-tall candleholder thick with shellac in her shaking hands.

We stalk the halls, looking, hunting, scavenging.

I want to find something for Beth. No captain glory, no stable to call her own, not even a glance from Sarge Will to distract her, she needs *something*. Something to knock the gloomy ire from her: an abandoned joint, a senior boy and freshman girl doing furtive nastiness in some far-flung corner, his arm jammed up her shirt, up over her baby-fat girl belly, her eyes wide with panic and excitement, already, in her head, practicing the telling of the moment even as the moment slips from her.

By the time we reach the fourth floor, there's a desperation to it. Beth flashes her eyes at me, and it's really a taunt. *Get me something, get me anything.*

But it's always complicated with Beth and me, where her desire

ends and mine begins. Because when we first hear the sound, I realize it's me who wants it more. Wants something to happen.

And then it does.

A yard or two from the door to the teachers' lounge, we hear
something.

The rough rhythmic sound of a chair skidding, lurchingly, across
the floor behind the teachers' lounge door. It seems, suddenly, to
be just for me.

Scrape, scrape, scrape.

Beth's eyes nearly pop with pleasure.

We're standing outside the door, listening.

I'm shaking my head back and forth and whispering soundlessly
don't, don't, don't as Beth, bouncing on her toes, leaning against the
teachers' lounge door, dancing her fingers along it and mouthing
things to me. *I'm opening it, I am, yes, yes, I sure am, Addy.*

I put my hand on the door too, which vibrates with all that
clamor inside, that squeaking and thudding. My ear against the
humming door, I can hear the breathless pant. It sounds so pained,
I think. It sounds like the worst hurt in the world ever.

Like after RiRi lost it to Dean Grady at that party on Wind-
mere and bled for hours in the bathroom and we kept pulling toilet
paper from the roll in long, sloping drifts, like she was gonna die.
Like she was gonna—

Just like that, Beth pushes her hip against the teachers' lounge
door, and it swings open, and we see it all.

Every bit of it.

There, seated on one of the old swivel chairs, is Sarge Will, National Guardsman Will, and Coach spanning his lap, her legs bare
and looped around him like a pale ribbon, feet dangling high, and
his dress blue blazer asunder, wrapped around her snowy naked-
ness, his hands pressed against her breasts, his face red and helpless.

Her thighs are shuddering whitely and his hand curves around the back of her head, buried in her dark hair, sweat-stuck and triumphant.

Her face, though, that's what you can't take your eyes off of.

The dreamy look, her pinkening cheeks, all elation and mischief and wonder, like I never saw in her, like she's never been with us, so strict and exacting and distant, like a cool machine.

It's the most beautiful thing I've ever seen.

I feel myself jostled backwards into Beth the instant Coach's eyes meet mine, alarm and dread there. I feel myself hurling both Beth and me out the door, Beth's laughter clanging through the corridor, my hand dragging the door shut, closing my eyes to it. Wondering if I even saw what I saw.

But looking at Beth's gleeful, mocking face, I know I have. I've seen it.

Later, I think about it. It wasn't like in the movies, soft-lit bodies writhing creamily under satin sheets.

It lasted only a second, so how could it pierce me with such thorny beauty—but it does.

Coach's face that long, hectic second before she saw me.

Like someone climbing her way out of the darkest tunnel, her mouth wide and gasping for air.

And his eyes shut so tight, face locking itself into place, as if to let go would destroy everything, would bury her again, and he only wants to save her, to breathe that hot life into her.

And she, gasping for air.

By the time Coach finds us in the locker room, Beth and me jackrabbity with titillation, everything that had opened, gloriously, is shut again.

She is once more that iron ingot, hard and feverless, walking with purpose but without hurry, with no wilt or lilt in her step, no hair out of place from that shiny crest of hers.

In her office, she pulls the blinds down on the door then shakes out a handful of cigarettes on the desk.

This has never happened before, this offering.

Beth and I each take one, and I know what it means for me, to me.

And I know what it means to Beth, high on her new power perch, nuzzling her new wisdom close to her freckled chest.

But this, the extent of this, I can't think about yet.

Coach lights mine and when she does I look in her eyes and that's when I see she hasn't put on all the calm she wants. Those flat gray eyes are jumping.

Beth, leaning back in Coach's seat, kicks her legs up and props her feet against the front of the desk. Scuffing its laminated edge.

She is very pleased.

As Coach walks past me to the window, I catch the scent, just barely. Sharp and fleshy and stinging my nose and *making me think of Drew Calhoun's bedsheets that time, the smell on them, even though we didn't, but he did.*

"I need you to understand what Will—what the Sergeant and I have is a real thing," she lets her gaze flit over us quickly. "A true thing."

Out of the corner of my eye, I see Beth piano-keying her fingers along her chin.

"I never thought it would happen," Coach says, and I think she means cheating on her husband. But then she says, "I never thought I'd feel like this."

I look at her, her hands pulling at the wand of the window

blinds, lacing around it and tugging like a little girl with her whole hand wrapped around her father's index finger.

Feel like what, I want to ask, but don't.

"Do you guys understand?" she asks, tilting her head, a strand of that perfect hair slipping across her face, grazing her mouth.

I do not look at Beth.

"I waited my whole life for it," Coach says, and I feel a buzzing in my chest. "I never thought it would happen. And then it did."

She looks at us.

"Wait until it happens to you," she says, breathing hard and her body twisting with it. With these magic words.

"Wait until it's you."

Don't tell anyone.

That night, fingers plucking the buttons on my duvet cover, thumbs on my phone, Beth's texts blipping under my fingers. **Agreed. This is just us. We keep quiet 4 now.**

I shut off my phone.

Wriggling there, thinking it all through, I start to see, for the first time, how it might be for Coach, young and pretty and strong. Why should she be stuck all day rousting chickens like us, or at least like some of us, on the shellacked floors of the Sutton Grove High School gym, our hapless ponytails flying, smarting off, being lazy, spitting gum on the floor, whining about periods and boys? She spends all her days like this and then home to her kid, pucker-mouthed and red-faced, a day of sugar and agitation in preschool, and her husband at work until the nightly news sometimes.

I start to think of it differently, as a home filled not with ease and liberty but with irritation and woe. Who wouldn't need the ministrations of the likes of Sergeant Will, and what he might give her? I wonder what he gives her and why we aren't enough.

10

"I knew," **Beth** says, before practice the next day, lifting her leg into a heel stretch. "I knew there was something wrong with her. What a fake, what a liar."

"Beth," I say. But the warning flare in her eyes says I better tread lightly.

"Beth," I say, "can you show me how you get your foot behind your head like that? Can you help?"

We are in Coach's backyard after practice, just the two of us. She has invited me. Just me.

We haven't spoken about Sarge Will, not yet.

Coach is trying to help me with my standing back tuck, which is weak at best. It's really just a tight backflip from a standing position and is one of those stunts all real cheerleaders can do in their sleep. RiRi says college cheerleaders do them at parties—"Tuck check!"—to test each other's drunkenness.

One of her hands on my waist, Coach uses the other to pull my knees up, flipping me hard as soon as I'm off the ground, her arms like a propeller.

She is in that focus mode where she doesn't even look me in the eye but treats my body like a new machine with parts not yet broken in. Which is what it is.

"If you can't back tuck," she says, "you can't land most tumbling stunts." What she doesn't say: since I don't fly or do Bottom Base, I need to be able to tumble.

I need to nail it.

"The pull is just as important as the set," she is saying, her breath fogging in near dusk. I can feel it on my face as she knocks her hip against mine. "You can have the best set in the world but if you don't pull your legs around after it, you're still going to land short."

Over and over, I start strong, arms up brace-tight, only to land on my hands, my knees, the tips of my toes.

It's a head thing. I feel certain I will fall. And then I do, my foot twisting beneath me.

"You think too much," Beth used to tell me.

She's right. Because if you think about it, you realize you can't possibly jump into the air and rotate yourself 360 degrees. No one can do that.

Beth, of course, does a flawless standing back tuck, and it's something to see.

It is incredibly high and perfect.

But Beth grabs from behind the thighs, not the shins like Coach likes.

"I don't want that sloppy stuff from you," Coach says. "Don't waste my time with that."

Again and again, my shins grass-streaked and the sky heavy with dusk.

"Chest up," she shouts, every time I land, to keep me from falling forward.

Finally, I'm getting cleaner and she stops flipping me. And I start falling. She lets me fall every time.

"It's a blind landing, Hanlon," she says. "You're trying to find the ground. You gotta know it's not there."

I try to pretend I'm her. Try to feel tight like she does, so tight nothing can touch her. I think of squeezing my whole body into a tight ball.

"Ride that jump longer," her voice out there somewhere, vibrating in my ear, her hands there but not.

And then releasing.

"Open your body," she keeps saying, and it's shuddering through my whole head. "Open it."

And I feel myself doing just that, an explosion from the center of me to my toes, my fingertips.

It is just after dark, the timered deck lamps leaping to life, when I start landing it.

The feeling is breathtaking, and I know I can do anything.

I feel like I could rotate myself forever and land every time, arms upraised, chest high, body both shattered then restored. Immaculate.

The night outside her front picture window is blue-shivery, but we are curled on her sofa, our legs folded under ourselves, our bodies loose and victorious.

"Addy, I know how it probably looks," Coach is saying to me, leaning close, cigarettes and tall plastic cups of matcha green tea as my back tuck reward. "But you have to understand how things are. With Will and me."

She runs her finger around and around the rim of her cup. Her eyes are ringed darkly and it's like I always hoped it would be. I'm the one she's telling. She chooses me.

"And Matt, Addy..." She sighs and arches her back, looking vaguely to the ceiling. "Maybe you think when you're as old as I am, you couldn't want things anymore. When I was your age, twenty-seven might as well be a hundred."

"You don't seem old at all," I say.

We sit for a while, and she talks. She tells me how it started with Will.

Seeing her in the parking lot after the college fair, he told her she looked sad and wondered if she would like to sit with him in his car, parked on Ness Street, and listen to music. "Sometimes it makes me feel better," he said, and maybe it would make her feel better too.

She hadn't known she looked sad.

So they sat and they listened to some black singer she'd never heard of, a woman with a croony, needy voice. *Don't go to strangers, darling, come to me.*

And the music did something, and suddenly they were talking about big things, personal things.

She told him the way she felt after Caitlin was born, like the secret of life had been told to her at last and the secret was this: in the end all the things you think matter are just disappointment and noise.

And then he told her about his wife.

"Do you remember the story on the news?" she whispers to me, leaning close. "A few years ago. That meth head from upriver drove through the front window at Keen's pharmacy? And the customer inside who died?"

I didn't remember exactly, these stories like static on faraway currents, but something about a photo they ran on the news and in the papers that alarmed everyone. A plate glass window sheeted red. A figure slumped behind it.

"That was Will's wife," Coach says, so solemn. "She was five months pregnant."

Sitting together that night, under the pin oak on Ness Street, he told her all about it. About the things it had done to him, the way he saw the world. His year in Afghanistan nothing like the dark hole her loss drilled in him.

They talked for an hour, two, and by the time his hand dropped, almost as if by mistake, into her lap, it was like it was meant to be there.

The feeling took her by surprise, a buckling in her stomach, and he saw it, and then everything started and, eyes shuttering back, she thought, *This is happening, right now. And it had to happen. How did I not know this?*

You have something that I need, he told her. But he had it backwards.

The backseat, the seatbelt buckles cutting into her, her foot sliding on the windowpane.

After, her own hands tingling and helpless, he buttoned her shirt back up, slid her barrette back in her hair. The tenderness, like when Matt French buttoned Caitlin's pinafore, when he tied her little shoes.

When I get home, Beth is waiting in the middle of my front lawn, which she hasn't done since she was nine, and it has the same quality of ominousness it did then. *Why did you go to Jill Randall's birthday party when we said we hated her?*

Or like last summer, legs dangling from my upper bunk at cheer camp, asking when I decided I wasn't bunking with her after all.

"Where were you?" she asks. "We have items to discuss."

"At Coach's," I say, unable to stop the giddy hiccough in my voice. My body still feels stretchy and my heart proud and strong.

"She is so transparent," she says, eyeing me head to toe. "Now she wants to be your best friend, huh? Sharing secrets on her outlet mall sofa? She thinks she can work us like two-dollar whores. I hope you are not a whore, Addy. Are you a whore?"

Dare Me

I don't say anything.

"Are you a whore?" she says, walking toward me, "and is Coach your sweet-lipped Mack Daddy whispering promises in your ear?"

"I was practicing," I say. "She's the coach."

Beth folds her arms and stares me down.

I don't say a word.

"Haven't you learned anything, Addy?" she says. I'm not sure what she means, but I know I have to settle her.

We are both quiet, my hands getting cold and Beth in her puffy jacket unzippered.

I see something in her eyes I know from back when, from some girl-recesses of time spent hiding in playground tunnels together, nursing schoolyard wounds.

Nobody might understand about Beth because her seeming power overwhelms. But I can see behind things.

And so I find myself reaching my pinkie out to twine hers, and she shakes it off and gripes some more, about Coach's treachery and false friend ways, but I do see her rest the smallest bit inside, her shoulders unhunching from a toadlike curl.

We end up back at her house, down in the basement. No one ever goes down there except Beth's brother when he used to robotrip with his friends.

We lie on the sofa and the moonlight tumbles through the high window and I start it this time, our favorite thing. Or what used to be our favorite thing, but we haven't done it in so long.

Taking the vitamin E oil from my backpack, I do a soft massage on Beth's right knee, where she tore ligaments landing on the marble floor of the school hallway, which is the kind of thing Beth sometimes does.

I do these light-as-a-feather tap-taps with my fingertips, which she likes.

After, hands pearled with her sweet almond salve, she does her hard magic on me.

We started this at age ten at PeeDee Tumbling Camp and it was our thing and it was the way, always, to soothe us. Sometimes it was like a visitation, a trance.

She once said, breathless after, that it was a coolness that stilled her like nothing ever did.

We stopped when we hit fourteen or so, I guess, which is when everything changes or you realize it has. I wonder why we stopped? But time gets away from us, doesn't it? That's a thing I know.

In the basement now, there is a powerful nostalgia. This is a Beth I haven't seen for a while, the Beth of subterranean nights, our self-whipped adolescent fears and JV yearnings: *I will never what if we never will we ever.*

I'd forgotten we were like that, before we were everything.

Her hands move quietly to my calves, of which I am newly proud, the muscle there, tight as a closed bud.

Her thumb slides up the diamond shaped middle of the calf, and notches there, working slowly, achingly, pressing down to the hardest place then sliding her thumb up, the two muscle heads forking. It's like her thumb is a hot wand, that's how I always used to think of it.

I can feel Beth unloose it the way the last back tuck unloosed it. It feels warm and wet under my skin, and everything is lovely.

"You were burning this tonight," she says, so dark I can see nothing but the whites of her eyes, the silver eyeliner.

"I was," I murmur. "Back tucks."

And there's this sense that somehow she knows.

"How did it feel?" she whispers. "To nail it."

"Like this," I say, curling under the hard pressure from her hand. "But better."

11

"It's to thank you," I say. "It's like a thank-you."

We're in Coach's driveway.

"For the back tuck," I say.

She holds it up to the car light, examining it.

"It's my hamsa bracelet," I say. "You said you liked it."

When she saw me wearing it, she'd said, "What, you some kind of wicca, Hanlon?"

I'd shown her its hand-shaped charm—mirror-plated, with two symmetrical thumbs, an ancient amulet for magical protection from the evil eye.

"Sounds like something I could use," she'd said. And maybe she was kidding, but I wanted her to have it.

And now she's holding it, its crimson cord laced across her three middle fingers, like she doesn't know what to say.

Reaching out, I spin the hand charm with my index finger so she can see the big eye planted in the middle of its mirrored palm.

She holds up her wrist so I can put it on.

"It wraps around twice," I say, showing her.

"Twice the protection," she says, smiling. "That's what I need."

"You're Addy, right? Colette's favorite," he says, when I get in the backseat. Upfront, Coach is putting lipstick on in the mirror, a deep garnet shade I've never seen on her before. It makes her mouth look wet, open. It's distracting and I try not to look.

Addy, she'd said, looking at the hamsa bracelet tight on her wrist. *I have an idea.*

That's how it comes to be that it's late at night now and I'm in Sarge Will's SUV, so big it's like being in the center of a velvet-lined box, everything dark and buffered, soft sides and hard corners and the sense of nothing out there touching you.

I look at him, thinking how strange it all is. Sarge Will, but not in his uniform, and his shirt still finely pressed but some stubble on his jaw, and his eyes, most of all his eyes, not coolly watchful, as in school, as when he scours the teeming, sweaty masses of students for recruits, pinpointing all the lost souls that fill our halls, all the ones who live close to the freeway and the ones I never notice at all.

No, his eyes aren't like that at all now. There's a looseness, and an openness, and some other things I can't name. All the remoteness gone and he's this man, and he smells a little like laundry detergent and cigarettes, and he has a nick on one knuckle of his left hand, and when he turns the steering wheel I see faint sweat scalloping under his arm.

Will is drinking from a pint he's holding nestled between his legs as he drives. When he hands it to me, the bottle is so warm.

Come with us tonight, she'd said. *I want you to understand how it is.*

And now I do.

We drive to Sutton Ridge, the fall air shivery and the smell of burning leaves drifting from somewhere.

"I thought there was no place left," Will says, "where people still burned leaves."

Because they do burn leaves here, the older folks do, and I remember now that I love it and always have. The way fall feels at night because of it, because of the crackling sound and walking around the sidewalks, like when you're a kid, and kicking those soft piles, and seeing smoke from backyards and Mr. Kilstrap standing over the metal drum with the holes in the top, the sparking embers at his feet.

Where'd that world go, that world when you're a kid, and now I can't remember noticing anything, not the smell of the leaves or the sharp curl of a dried maple on your ankles, walking? I live in cars now, and my own bedroom, the windows sealed shut, my mouth to my phone, hand slick around its neon jelly case, face closed to the world, heart closed to everything.

It seems Will knows this older world and it binds us together and I realize we are meant to be close because, like she does, he opens deep pockets in the center of me I never knew were there.

"Let's go to Lanvers Peak," says Coach, voice light and high, a girl's voice. She's looking back at me now, that mouth of hers red and glorious. The excitement, and Will grabbing her thigh so hard that I can feel it, I can feel his hand shaking my own thigh to gritty life.

Lanvers Peak is not a place for cars, but it is a place for Will's Jeep, because nothing will stop him.

Driving up, Will is talking about the gorges and how they were gouged by glaciers hundreds of times over two thousand years like God's own carving hand on the dark earth, or so his grandfather used to say.

We're higher than I've ever been and we're drinking bourbon, which is the most grown-up thing I've ever had and I pretend I like it until I do.

*　　*　　*

Up high, where the sky looks violet against the peak, Coach and I kick off our shoes, no matter how cold it is, the silvered grass crunching under our feet.

"Show me," Will is saying, and he is laughing. "Show me."

He doesn't believe we can do the shoulder sit, just we two and dizzy on bourbon.

"You say it's so dangerous, but compare it to offensive tackle, which left me with these," he says, lifting his pretty lip to show me his front teeth, snowy white. "Caps, like my gramps. That's what real sports do to you."

Baiting us, he makes me want to turn my body into the lightest, most miraculous thing, makes me want to show him what I can do so that I will feel perfect and loved.

So Coach and me, we show him, without a spotter and in spitting distance of the depthless purple gorge so beautiful I want to cry into it.

I feel my phone buzzing and I don't even look at it, dropping it to the ground.

Coach and me, we're laughing now, Coach's hair tumbling against me as we scramble to the most solid patch of an unsolid turf.

Lunging forward, she calls to me and I set my bare foot high atop her bended thigh, lifting myself, swinging my other leg over her shoulder, as she rises to her feet. Wrapping my thighs around her, twining my feet behind her, and we are one.

We are one.

I never did a stunt with Coach before.

At first, we are a sorry case, weaving and laughing, and Will drill-sergeants us until we get focus, my thighs locking tight around her and Coach grinding her feet into the frosty grass.

Then I unlock my feet and thrust my legs forward, Coach reaching under and between my thighs to grab my clammy hands in hers. Dipping down, she gives me a pop, pulling me over her head, my legs swinging from behind her, then together again, my feet landing hard on the ground.

The sear up my leg is nothing at all. Nothing.

We are stupendous and Will is cheering and yelling and hip-hollering and it echoes through the ravine in bewitching ways.

Up above her shoulders, fixed tight upon her, it is something. My eyes wander down to the icy bottom of the gorge and we are higher than we ever thought we'd be.

My house is farther, and Coach gets dropped off first, which is a mind-bending prospect.

Will pulls over a half block from her house. Watching them kiss, watching the way he opens her mouth with his, her sneaky looks back at me, the pleasure on her, I feel myself go loose and wondrous inside. I want to be a part of their kiss, and maybe even they want it too.

It's only a five-minute drive to my house, but it feels like it lasts forever, all the misted lightness of Lanvers Peak gone.

"Tonight was the first time I ever saw you without that other girl," Will says. "The one with the freckles."

This seems the craziest way to describe Beth ever, but it makes everything go tight in my head and I remember, coming off the peak, flipping open my phone and seeing *missed call, missed call, missed call.* A text: **you'd best pay attn to me.**

He looks at me and smiles.

Suddenly, I want to hold the whole night close to my chest and I decide it is mine alone.

"Seeing her tonight, I understand now," he says. "She needs this."

For a second I think he means himself. And, thinking of her that night, so carefree, all the antic restlessness blown out of her, I think he is surely right.

But then he gestures toward my Sutton Eagles duffel bag, and I see he means being coach.

"She needs you girls," he adds.

I nod, meaningfully as I can.

"I know what that's like," he says. "The way you can be saved without ever knowing you were in trouble."

These are the words he says, but they sound like something I'm overhearing, a conversation I'd never be a part of.

"I guess it's funny, me talking to you like this," he says.

I guess it is. Sometimes Coach doesn't seem that much older than me, but Will, with his tragic dead wife and tours of duty, sure does.

"I know we don't really know each other," he admits. "But we know each other in a strange way."

I nod again, though really we don't know each other at all. It makes me think Will is one of those people who just tell everybody everything right away, and usually I don't like those people, those girls at summer camp sharing tales of cutting and kissing their babysitters. But this feels different. Maybe because he's right. Because we share a secret. And because I saw them together that day in the teachers' lounge, which felt like seeing everything.

"She has it hard," he says. "Her husband, he's not the guy you might think he is. She has it very hard."

Maybe it's the bourbon, or the bourbon wearing off, but this doesn't sound exactly right either, not really.

"He gave her that house," I point out.

"It's a cold house," he says, looking out the window. "He gave her a cold house."

"It's her house," I say. "I mean, even if it's cold, it's hers."

He doesn't say anything, and I feel him slipping from me.

"And Caitlin," I say, but this sounds even less convincing. "There's Caitlin."

"Right," he says, shaking his head. "Caitlin."

We both sit for a moment, and I feel suddenly like we both might know something we can't name. About how, in some obscure way, Caitlin was another thing that wasn't a gift so much as the thing that stands in place of the gift. *My wedding, my house, my daughter, my cold, cold heart.*

12

"Freaking rock star," RiRi marvels, finger spotting me.

I am doing perfect back tucks, one after another.

I know suddenly I was born to do them. I am a propeller.

"*This* is what a coach can do." RiRi grins. "Beth would never have let you get this good."

As soon as she says it, she seems almost to take it back, laughing, like it's a joke. Maybe it is.

"Knees to nose, Hanlon," Coach barks, a sneaky smile dancing there as she walks back into her office.

"Pffht-pffht," comes the sound from the bleachers, where Beth has slunk. "Watch that neck, Addy-Faddy, or it's the ventilator for you. *Pffht-pffht.*"

"Très J," whistles Emily. But I know Beth isn't jealous of my tuck. She can back handspring, back tuck me into the ground, her body like a twirling streamer.

In the locker room after, Emily kicks her leg up, grabbing her toes as she stands on the center bench. Pea-shoot thin now, fifteen pounds lighter since the month before, she's set to fly with Tacy at the Stallions game. All the hydroxy-hot and activ-8 and boom blasters and South African hoodia-with-green-coffee-extract and most of all her private exertions have made her airy and audacious.

Eyeing her, Tacy is sullen, uneager to share Flyer glory.

Lying on the far end of the bench, Beth stares abstractedly up at the drop ceiling.

"Cox-sucka," she calls out to Brinnie Cox, who is curling her hair into long sausages and singing to the locker mirror. "How's your head?"

"What do you mean?" Brinnie asks, her arm frozen. "My head is fine."

"That's a relief," Beth says. "I wondered if maybe you were still feeling the blood pushing against your brain. From that header you took a few weeks back."

"No," she says, quietly.

"Beth," I say, a faint try at warning.

"As long as you're not a purger, you should be okay out there tonight. It's the regurgitators who drop like dead weight."

At the other end of the long bench, our girl Emily releases her leg and looks at the reclining Beth, who is staring straight up at the fluorescent lights.

"Chumming all the time," Beth says, "they bust all those blood vessels in their eyes. Then one day, out on the mat, they hit their head and . . . *ping*."

Beth snaps her fingers beside her temple.

"Once," she continues, "I heard a 'mia girl fell during a dismount and an eye popped out."

Propping herself up on her elbows, she looks down the long bench straight at Emily.

"But let's not talk of ugly matters," she says. "Our girl Em's going to rock it out tonight. Going out a youngster and coming back a star."

"She'd really miss the Stallions game?"

Ten minutes before kickoff, Beth is nowhere to be found.

She's never no-showed a game. Everyone wonders if something happened, like that time she followed her dad and his paralegal to that Hyatt downtown and keyed the words MAN WHORE into the hood of his car.

Without her, we have to reconfigure the whole double-hitch pyramid. We count on Beth to be the Middle Flyer, holding onto Tacy's and Emily's inside legs as they swing out their other legs and stretch them sky high. She's the only one light enough to be that high and strong enough to support both girls. It's like juggling jig-saw pieces that don't fit and I can see Coach's face tighten.

"Should we skip the stunt?" I ask Coach.

"No," Coach says, eyes on the field, breeze kicking up. "Cox can stand for her."

I look at flimsy Brinnie with her chicken bone legs. Now I see what Beth's game was, putting the scare in Brinnie.

RiRi looks at me, squintingly. But I shrug.

"Coach knows what to do," I say.

Brinnie's right arm starts shaking during the double hitch.

I can see it from the back spot and I'm shouting at her, but fear hurtles across her eyes and there is no stopping it.

On the half-twist Deadman fall, that pin-thin arm of hers gives entirely and Emily, now just an eyelash of a girl, her head dizzy with visions of blood burst, slips and crashes, knee-first, into the foam floor.

Oh, to see her fall is to see how everything can fall.

Her body popping like bubble wrap.

In the back of my brain, I know that the clap we all hear from Emily's knee, like a New Year's champagne cork, is about that back tuck of mine.

Is about Coach and me.

★   ★   ★

I had epic cramps, Beth texts me that night.

You had it last week, I say. We all had our periods at the same time, the witchiness of girls.

Infection, she texts. Cranjuice all nite, and mom's narvox.

Come clean, I text. She has never missed a game, ever. Not even when her mother slipped on the living room carpet and dented her forehead on the coffee table, forty-seven stitches and three years' worth of vicodin.

Clean as a whistle, Merry Sunshine, she texts back. Cleaner than yr coach.

U know what I mean, I text. Em might have a torn lig.

There is a long moment and I can almost feel something black open inside Beth's head.

I have a torn life. Fuck all of you.

"Two-game suspension," RiRi tells us. "No Beth for two games. Em's down. And with Miz Jimmy-Arm Brinnie Cox spotting us, it means our heads'll be popping all over the mat."

"Tough break," Tacy Slaussen says, trying not to grin. She has her eye on the prize. With Emily and Beth out, she's the only bitty girl left to fly.

"Beth blames it all on Coach," RiRi says.

"Coach?" I say, my eyebrow twitching.

"She said Em fell because she's been living on puffed air and hydroxy for six weeks to hit weight for Coach."

I look at her. "Is that what you think?" I say, surprised at the hardness in my voice, the old lieutenant steel. It doesn't go away.

RiRi's eyes go wide. "No," she says. "No."

★   ★   ★

I find Beth lying on the bleachers out back, sunglasses on.

"I look at all of you, how you are with her. Your paper-heart parade," she says.

"You never like anyone," I say. "Or anything."

"She never should've staked Brinnie Cox, she's too short and too stupid," she says. "And you know how I feel about her teeth."

"You should've showed up," I say, trying to peer behind the black lenses, to see how deep this goes.

"Coach can't top-girl anyone else," Beth says. "She'll beg for me back."

"I don't think so," I say. "She's a rule-keeper."

"Is that so?" Beth wriggles up and stares at me, eyes like silver-rimmed globes, an insect, or alien. "That hasn't been my experience of her."

I look at her.

"She may have the clipboard and the whistle," Beth says, "but I have something too."

"We're not saying anything," I say, my voice going faster. "We said we wouldn't."

"Are we a 'we' again?" she says, sinking back down onto the bench. "And I didn't promise anything."

"If you were going to say something," I say, "you would've."

"You know that's not how to play. That's not how to win."

"You don't understand," I say. "The two of them. It's not like you think."

"Yeah," she says, looking at me, nail-hard. "You know better? You've seen into her knotted soul?"

"There's things you don't know," I say. "About him, about them."

"Things I don't know, huh?" she says, something less than a taunt, more urgent. "Illuminate. Like what? Like what, Addy?"

But I don't tell. I don't want to give her anything. I see something now. She's building a war chest.

The next night, Coach has everyone over for a party for Emily, whose fall has put her on the DL for six weeks, maybe more.

No one can even imagine six weeks. It's a lifetime.

It's too cold to be outside, but after the wine swells in all of us, we're even taking off our jackets, lounging lovely across the deck, watching the sky grow dark. Emily gets prime seat, high-kicking her boot brace for all to see, her eyes stoned on percocet. The happiest girl in the world, for tonight.

I decide to banish Beth's hex from my head. *She fell because she's been living on puffed air and hydroxy....*

Coach maps out our Saturday stunts on napkins spread across the glass-top patio table. We huddle around eagerly, following Coach's sharpie as it plots our fates.

"We have three weeks until the final game against the Celts," Coach says. "We shine there, we have a qualifying tape to submit, we go to Regionals next year."

We are all beaming.

No one asks about Beth until Tacy, Beth's former flunky, our little stone-drunk Benedict Arnold, bleats, "And who needs Cassidy? We don't need the haters. We're going to Regionals with or without the haters."

We're all a little nervous, but Coach smiles lightly, looping her bracelet around her wrist. I smile to see it's my hamsa bracelet, its eye flashing in the porch light.

"Cassidy'll be back," she says. "Or not. But she won't be our Flyer again."

She looks down at her squiggled hieroglyphics.

"She's not the straw that stirs the drink," she says.

Eyeing the Flyer spot on the diagram, I watch her pen skim right and left, a big black X right in the center.

It's not until very late that we're jarred by Matt French's car door slamming from the driveway and, the same instant, Coach's deck chair shakes to life.

Dad's home, that's what it's like, and everyone jumps. We all scurry to the kitchen, start stacking plates and shaking wine glasses empty over our mouths, and I'm helping RiRi hide the empties behind the evergreen shrubs. The bottles clanging loudly. Matt French must know. He must hear everything.

We're swooping around the kitchen island, loading the dishwasher and chomping on our organic ginger gum, and Coach is talking to him in the other room, asking him, her speech so slow and careful, about his day.

Through the swinging café doors, he looks very tired and he's talking but I can't quite make out the words.

He reaches out to touch her arm just at the moment she turns to hand him the mail.

I think how exhausted he must be, how maybe if he were my husband, even though he's not handsome at all, maybe I'd want to sit him down and rub his shoulders, and maybe get one of those lemony men's lotions, and rub his shoulders and his hands. And maybe that'd be nice, even if he's not good-looking and his forehead is way too high and he has little wiry hairs in his ears and I never think about him like that, really.

But he's tired after his long day and he comes home and there we are, bansheeing all over his house, all cranked high and slipping-free braids and ponytails, and Coach talks to him and it's like how she talks to the other teachers at school, holding their mottled coffee mugs and making the smallest talk ever.

His shoulders tucking in wearily, I see him flinching at all the clamorous girl energy radiating from the kitchen.

"Colette," I think he says, "I was calling all day. I called all day."

I'm not sure, but I think I hear him say something about Caitlin, about the day care center phoning him, asking where she was.

Coach's hand is over her mouth and she is staring at her feet in a way I recognize from myself, the nights when my dad still waited up, demanded to know things.

Suddenly, there's a loud crash from the back deck, like glasses falling.

"Coach!" someone hollers from outside. "We're sorry. We're really sorry."

13

"Everybody give the chicken a warm welcome," Coach says, giving a gentle shove to the latest recruit, a JV cheerleader getting her shot at the show. A hammer-headed girl with a body like a tuning fork. No one will mind her landing headfirst on the spring floor. She'll just *ting.*

"She's on me," Mindy surmises, curling her neck side to side. "I turn her out."

Mindy knows she can lift the shavetail rafters-high, a girl like that, not more than ninety pounds soaking wet, and she even looks wet, a dew on her that's probably flop sweat.

"Not before she pays her dues," RiRi says, arms folded. "We all fly her first."

New girls get tossed hard first time out. Initiate-style. And we like to rock them side to side.

"Mat kill," mutters Tacy, newly hard, suddenly a senior states-man of the squad.

No one asks about Beth. She's barely been in school these past three days, and Coach seems very calm in her victory.

It's after midnight when my phone hisses, rattling my bedside tabletop.

Can u pick me up? Cnr Hutch & 15.

Beth. The first text in five days. The longest stretch since she went to horse camp in the mountains after seventh grade, returning with a ringlet of hickeys from a counselor and fresh revelations about the world.

Creeping through the house, I unhitch the car keys from the kitchen door hook. Anyone could hear the car shaking to life in the garage, but if they do, they ignore it. My father nuzzled close to my stepmother, she muzzled by her nightly dose of sleep aids.

Beth is standing on the corner, and her face when the headlights hit is a surprise. It's Beth bare-faced, which is scarier than her hooded eyes, her teengirl snarl.

Her face splayed open, like it almost never is, and mascara-spattered eyes blinking relentlessly, staring straight into the center of me.

With the headlights in her face, she can't really see me, but it feels like she can. She knows I'm there.

It's a thing to see, her face so bare. I almost want to turn away. I don't want to feel for her.

By the time she's in the car, her face is shuttered tight once more. She doesn't give me much of anything, not even a hello, and sets about punching text messages.

"Where were you?" I ask.

"Guard duty," she mutters, thumbs flying on her little keyboard.

"What?" I say.

Thump-thump-thump that thumb of hers, thumping.

"What?" I say again. "What did you say?"

"Sarge Stud...," she says, and I hold my breath, "...ain't the only stars and stripes in town."

She sets her phone down and glances at me, sly smile playing there.

"Which one?" I ask. All those rawboned soldiers who stood at that table with Will, rawboned and callow, steel-wool scrubbed.

"Bullet head," Beth says. "Prine. Corporal Gregory Prine. Gregorius, let's call him. You know the one."

I picture him, tongue waggling at me, fingers forked there, that acne-studded brow and sense of frat menace.

"Well," I say, feeling sick. "Bad Girls' Club for you, eh?"

"Hells-yeah," she says, a rattle laugh.

But I look at her hands, which are shaking. She clasps her phone to try to stop them. When I see it, something in me turns.

"Beth." I feel all the blood rushing from my face. I can't quite name it, but it's a sense of abandon. "Why?"

"Why not?" she replies, and her voice husky, her hair falling across her face. "Why not, Addy? Why not?"

I think she might cry. In her way, she is.

14

Little Caitlin, her doughy face with that cherry-stem mouth, baby-soft hair sticking to her bulbed forehead.

Sitting on Coach's sofa, I watch her amble around her strewn toys, the pink plastic and the yellow fluff of girlhood, everything glitter-silted. She steps with such care through the detritus of purple-maned ponies, gauzy-winged tutus, and all the big-eyed dolls—dolls nearly as empty-eyed as Caitlin, who reminds me of one of those stiff-limbed walking ones the richest girls always had, and we'd knock them over with the backs of our hands, or walk them into swimming pools or down basement stairs. Like stacking them up in pyramids just to watch them fall.

"I know, I know. Please, will you, will you . . . listen to me, baby. Listen close."

In the dark dining room, Coach is on the phone, fingers hooked around the bottom of the low-hanging chandelier, turning it, twisting it in circles until I hear a sickly creak.

For hours she's been hand-wringing, jabbing her thumb into the center of her palm, molding it there, her teeth nearly grinding, her eyes straying constantly to her cell phone. Ten times in ten minutes, a phantom vibration. Picking it up, nearly shaking it. Begging it to come to life. We can't finish a conversation, sure can't practice dive rolls in the yard. Any of the things she promised me.

Finally, her surrender, slipping into the other room and her voice high and rushed. *Will? Will? But you . . . but Will . . .*

Now, Caitlin's play-doh feet stomp over mine, her gummy hands on my knees as she pushes by me, and I want out. It's all so sticky and unfun and I feel the air clog in my throat. For the first time since Coach let me into her home, I wish I'd gone instead with RiRi to her new boyfriend's place, where they were drinking ginger-and-Jack in the backyard and smashing croquet balls up and down the long slope of the lawn.

But then Coach, phone raised high in hand like a trophy, tears into the living room, her face suddenly shooting nervy energy.

She is transformed.

"Addy, can you do me a favor?" she says, fingering the hamsa bracelet, its amulet flaring at me. "Just this once?"

She kneels down before me, her arms resting on my knees. It's like a proposal.

Her face so soft and eager, I feel like she must feel when she looks at me.

"Yes," I say, smiling. "Sure, yes. Yes." *Always.*

"It won't be long," Coach says. "Just a little while."

She tells me Will's having a hard time. Today, she says, is the third anniversary of his wife's death.

My legs tingling, it's like Lanvers Peak again, and I have a sense of my grand importance. Jump, jump, jump—how high, Coach? Just tell me, how high?

When he arrives, Will doesn't quite look like himself, his face sheet-creased and he smells like beer and sweat, a dampness on him that seems to go to the bone. A six-pack is wedged under his arm.

He sort of burrows against Coach for a minute and I pretend to look out the window.

While Coach hustles Caitlin off to the backyard, we sit on the sofa together, the cold beer bottles pressing against my legs.

There is a long, silent minute, my eyes following the milky rise and fall of his Adam's apple, me so hypnotized, and thinking somehow of Coach's fingers there.

"Addy," he finally says, and I'm relieved someone is saying something. "I'm sorry I interrupted you two. You were probably doing things. I'm sorry."

"It's okay," I say.

When I was seven, my dad's best friend died from a heart attack on the golf course and my dad locked himself in the garage for an hour and my stepmom wouldn't let me knock on the door. Later, I think I crawled on his lap and I remember how he let me sit there for an hour and never once asked me to move so he could change the TV channel.

I don't guess I should sit on Will's lap but wish I could do something.

"Can I tell you something, Addy?" he says, and he's not looking at me but at the furred white lamb on the coffee table, its head bent. "This awful thing happened to me on the way here."

"What?" I say, rising up in my seat.

"I was coming out of the Beer Depot on Royston Road and there's this bus stop out front. This old woman was coming off the bus, carrying her shopping bags. She had this hat with a big red flower, like a poppy, the ones you wear on Veterans' Day. That's what you're supposed to wear on Veterans' Day.

"When she saw me, she stopped in her tracks, right on the bottom step. She just stopped. It was like she knew me.

"And this thing happened. I just couldn't move. I was just

standing there, beer in my hand, and we just locked eyes. And something happened."

His stare is glassy, and he has one finger tracing the tops of the beer bottles sitting between his legs.

"Did she know you from somewhere?" I ask, not sure I'm following.

"Yes. Except she didn't. I never saw her before in my life. But, Addy, she knew me. She kept staring at me from under that poppy hat. And these black eyes, like lumps of coal. She would not let me go." He shakes his head back and forth. "She would not let me go."

I'm listening, but I don't know what I'm hearing. I wonder how many beers Will has had, or if this is what mourning can look like, diffuse and mysterious.

"Addy, I think . . ." He has his eyes fixed again on the toy lamb on the coffee table, its head tilted, like a broken neck. "She *knew* things about me. It all became clear. She *knew.* The things I did as a kid, the Slip 'N Slide accident with my cousin and the sparkler bombs in the church parking lot and the time my dad showed up drunk at my job at the Hamburger Train and I shoved him and he fell on the wet floor and hit his head. And the first time in the Guard, and how now, after those bad drinking years, I only remember the MEDCAP missions, those little Allahaddin girls who slipped me love poems. I never remember any of the rest of it at all."

He pauses, his beer bottle tilting in his hand.

"She knew things I never told anyone," he says. "Like about my wife. Six years we were together, I never bought her a Valentine's Day card."

The empty bottle slips from his fingers, rolls across the sofa cushion.

"She knew all those things. And then I did."

I don't know what to say. I want to understand, to touch a bit of this shiny despair.

"What did you do?" I finally ask.

He laughs, the hard sound of it making me jump. "I ran," he says. "Like a kid. Like seeing the bogey man. A witch."

We are both quiet for a moment. I'm thinking of the old woman. I can see the poppy-blooming hat, and her face, her eyes inked black and all-knowing. I wonder if anything like that will ever happen to me.

Will leans down and picks up his bottle, setting it on the coffee table, its clammy bottom ringing the wood.

"Remember that night we all drove up the peak?" he says suddenly.

"Yes," I say.

"I wish it could always be like that," he says, twisting off a new beer cap.

I look at him.

Then he says, "Look at you," reaching out and flicking my blond braid. "You're so easy to talk to, Addy."

I try to smile.

"Let me ask you," he says, pressing the bottle against his damp forehead. "Do people see you, so pretty and your hair like a doll, and do they know about those things you hold inside of you?"

How did he know I held such things? *And what things?*

"Can I trust you, Addy?" he asks.

I say he can. Does anyone ever answer that question with a no?

And I wait for him to say more. But he just looks at me, his eyes blood-webbed and so sorrowful.

None of it makes much sense and I think Will must be very drunk or something. Something.

For a second it all overwhelms me, and all I want is to listen to music, or do a bleacher sprint, or feel the featherweight of Tacy's elfin foot in my flat palm, her counting on me to hold her up, and it being so easy.

"I'm sorry I ruined your afternoon," he says.

I'm in the backyard, leaning on the enormous dutch door playhouse Caitlin occupies, jumbo chalk jammed in her chubby hands. Still half breathless from my talk with Sarge Will, I smoke three of Coach's American Spirits and think about what's going on inside.

Nearly an hour goes by, those two inside, and Caitlin falls asleep in the playhouse, her mouth sucked over the corner of the foam table inside.

Her hair scalloped into a ponytail, Coach runs barefoot across the lawn. I think she's going to hug me, but she's not a hugger, and kind of arm-hooks me, Coach-like, wringing my shoulder.

"Thank you, Addy," she says, breathlessly. "Thanks, okay?"

And she smiles, with all her teeth, her face taffy pink.

It's like I've just done the greatest thing I could ever do for her, like a single-based split catch, like a pike open basket at the State Championship, like a balm over her heart.

For a moment, my fingers touch her hard back, which shudders like a bird's.

Touching it is like touching them, their beauty.

15

Party tonite, flashes Beth's text.

Rebs, I type back. Away game.

After, she says. Comfort Inn Haber.

Nu uh.

Uh huh.

That prickle behind my ear. The Comfort Inn. Older brothers and sisters are always talking about how it used to be called the Maid Marian, with a second-floor walkway slung so low it looked like the hookers—real live hookers like in the movies, only with worse skin—would slide right off into the courtyard. You'd only drive by when you had to go downtown, like a class trip to the museum and the teachers so embarrassed that you'd be passing Maid Marian, with all those maids all in a row

When it became the Comfort Inn, they tore out the walkway and you couldn't see the hookers anymore, but the whole place still quivered with a sense of dirty deeds.

And Beth, and her dirty deeds. I want to say no, but I want to say yes. I want to say yes to keep my eyes on Beth and want to say yes because it's a party at the Comfort Inn on Haber Road.

So I say yes.

★   ★   ★

"Whose party?" RiRi asks, reaching under her shirt, plucking first her right breast higher, then her left, so they crest out the top. "Your dealer's?"

"My dealer could buy Haber Road tip to tail," Beth says. Beth doesn't have a dealer, but there is a guy over on Hillcrest who graduated Sutton Grove ten years ago and he sells her adderall, which she sometimes shares and which feels like oxygen blasting through my brain, blowing everything away and leaving only immense joy that shakes tic tac–like in my chest and then sinks away so fast it takes everything from me and my sad life.

"So whose party?" I ask.

She grins.

I didn't believe her at first, but there it is. There's five or six of them, all from the Guard.

All Will's men.

They're wearing regular clothes, but their haircuts and close shaves give them away, and the way they stand, feet planted apart, chests puffed out. One of them even has his at-ease hands behind his back, which makes it hard to hold his beer.

I recognize the PFC with the red brush cut who walks Sarge Will to his car every day and the other one, with the ham–hock hands and the bowlegs.

There's a little bar set up on the long plywood dresser and they're huddled around it, and no one's on the drooping beds with the nubby spreads, and the lights are pitched low and soft and there's almost a peacefulness about it.

It's just a place to have a party, that's all. A little party, two adjoining rooms, the clock radio jangling softly and one PFC reaching above his hand, absentmindedly twirling the overhanging lamp, sending glades of light across the room like a mirror ball, like Caitlin's magic lantern.

Then, bullet-headed Corporal Prine steps out of the bathroom, his thumb dug in the neck of his beer bottle.

RiRi, looking at me, shaking her head, mouthing, *Hell-no.*

The other ones are all decked out in ironed polo shirts and pressed everything, but Prine is wearing a T-shirt emblazoned with skulls and bones and a big knife wedged in one of the skulls. The words LOVE KILLS are scrolled across it.

Nodding that big thick eraser-tip head of his, Prine beckons toward us.

Shrugging off her letter jacket, Beth, resplendent in a gold halter top, walks toward him, smiling slantily in that Beth way that feels like new trouble.

But RiRi is hip-shaking and she dips her hand in mine, and RiRi's ease with boys is such solace and soon we are dancing, pop-pop-popping our hips and RiRi doing the robot arm.

There's rum and diet cokes mixed special for us and all the alco-pops we can drink, and the PFCs are gentlemanly and suggest we play a game called beer blow. I never do figure out what the point is except it involves a lot of us bending over the table and blow-ing playing cards off an empty bottle, and then drinking, and then drinking again.

I don't care about anything, not the stain on the bedspread or the ceiling, or the way the bathroom sink drags away from the wall when you hold onto it, when you try to stay upright, not the crusted carpet under my feet, my shoes flung off as I climb up on the bed with RiRi, when we dance together, our hips knocking, and the Guardsmen all watch and cheer. I don't care about any-thing at all.

I don't care because it's like this: the rum, and the hard lemonade, and the shot of tequila zoom and zag through me, and the spell cast so deeply.

The whole high school world of gum-stuck, locker-slamming, shoe-skidding tedium slips away and it's all just warm and gushing perfection.

"Tell Coach to come," RiRi is burbling. "Tell her we're with the Guard." She's fumbling with my phone, trying to send a text.

Because it's all okay because these are Will's men and nothing bad could ever happen, one of them is pressing our heads together, wanting us to kiss.

"Always ready," he says. "Always there."

"We could never be girlfriends like this before," RiRi says, hugging me close. "Until this year. You were always Beth's girl. She never wanted to share you. Girl has such a hard-on for you. I was even scared of you. I was always scared of both of you."

She's looking at me, eyes wide, like she's surprised herself.

This hot, sloshing feeling low in me, I've known it before, at house parties, at bonfires on the ridge with clanking kegs and plastic cups, and every boy becomes the prettiest I ever saw. But this is better somehow—the Comfort Inn on Haber Road!—better still these men, grown men, Guardsmen—Will's men. Bearing somehow the sheen of Will.

Who am I not to curl myself under their hard, angled arms? Like Coach with Will. That could be me.

It's late when we can't find Beth.

At first I'm sure she's with Prine, but then PFC Tibbs, the sweet, gingered one with the whistle in his voice, shows me Prine passed out on the bed in the adjoining room, and there's no Beth.

Prine's jeans are around his ankles and his boxer shorts half yanked off, leaving a view of fleshy abandon. Even though he's alone, it feels sinister. Maybe it's the smell, which is ripe and unwholesome.

The PFC takes me for a walk down every hallway and into every stairwell, talking about his sister and how he worries about her at State, hears tales of fraternity lap dances and early morning walks of shame.

We look for Beth for an hour or more, and I hold on to some kind of calm only because, walking under the long bands of humming fluorescents, I'm concentrating very hard and won't miss any deodorized nook of the motel.

But each burning hallway is like the previous one, all of them yellow-bright and empty.

I'm nearly night-air-sobered by the time we find her asleep in my car, face slack and childlike, except she has no shoes and, far as I can tell, her skirt riding up, no underwear.

When she jolts awake, she says dark and woolly things about Prine.

How he took her to the adjoining room and tore off her underpants and pulled his pants down and all kinds of things are slipping from her drunken mouth.

He put his hands there, pushed down on my shoulders, my jaw, it hurts.

You're always supposed to believe these things. That's what they tell you in Health Class, the woman from Planned Parenthood, the nose-pierced college student from Girls, Inc. Females never lie about these important things. You must never doubt them. You must always believe them.

But Beth isn't like the girls they're talking about. Beth isn't like a girl at all. The squall in her, you can't ever peer through all that, can you?

It's impossible to puzzle through someone like Beth who always knows more about you than you know about yourself. She always beats you to the punch.

"I better call someone," says the PFC, standing back from us, far from my ministrations, farther still from Beth's sprawl, a seat belt twisted around her bare ankle, her feet gravel-pocked.

I try to untangle her, and Beth's left leg drops to one side and we both see the flaring red mark on the inside, the shape of a thumbprint. And a matching one on her other thigh.

"I better call the Sarge," he says, his voice strangled.

Suddenly, Beth jerks, her elbow jagging out at me, her eyes sharp and focused on the poor private.

"Call Sarge," she says. "Go ahead and call him. It's on him. I've called him five times. I've called him for hours. It's on him."

Why would Beth call Will?

I look back at the PFC. I'm shaking my head. I'm giving him a look like *oh-crazy-drunk-girl.*

Beth is a liar. This is a lie, the only thing between Beth and Will is her failed campaign. This is just Beth blowing buckshot everywhere.

"I've got it," I say. "I've got her. You can go."

Standing back, the PFC lifts his hands up.

The relief on his face is astounding.

"You cannot bring her here, Addy," Coach is saying, my phone clutched to my ear. "Take her home. Take her to your house."

I'm looking at Beth, corkscrewed into the crook of my front seat, her eyes nearly closed but with a discomforting glistening there.

"I can't," I whisper, my varsity jacket sleeve snagging in the steering wheel, *sober up, sober up.* "She's saying things. About that Prine guy."

My eyes catch Beth's purse on the car floor, half unzipped.

That's how I see her neon-lime panties inside.

Folded neatly, like a handkerchief.

You cannot judge how women will behave after an assault, the pamphlets always say. But.

"Prine?" Coach's voice turns spiky. "Corporal Prine? What are you talking about?"

I tell her about the party, the words tripping fast, my head spongy and confused. *Just let us come over, Coach, just let us.*

I don't tell her that I'm already driving to Fairhurst, to her house.

"Coach, she wanted us to call Sarge," I say, fast as a bullet. "She says she called him a bunch of times."

A pause, then her voice like a needle in my ear:

"Get the bitch over here now."

Like this, the car floating, the streetlamps like spotlights coning in on us. And Coach's voice pounding. *Why would you go to that party, Addy? Is she saying Prine hurt her? He's no high school QB. They call him the Mauler. Addy, I thought you were smarter than this.*

Climbing up Coach's front porch, I'm holding Beth up, her bare feet scraping on the cement.

She said not to knock, so I just send a text. Seconds later, Coach appears at the door, an oversized T-shirt with AURIT FINANCIAL SERVICES written on it, and a logo that looks like a winding road leading up to the sky.

The stony glare as she looks at Beth brings me straight to sober, sends my spine to full erectness. I even want to comb my hair.

"For god's sake, Hanlon," she says. *Hanlon* now. "I expected more from you."

I can't pretend it doesn't sting.

*   *   *

We are all hard whispers and shoving arms, hustling Beth to the den.

Just as Coach shakes the vellux blanket over Beth, hair streaked across her face, we hear Matt French coming down the stairs.

It all feels very bad.

He looks tired, his face rubbed to redness, brow knotted.

"Colette," he says, his eyes taking it all in. "What's going on here?"

But Coach doesn't flinch.

"Now you see what I put up with all week," she says, almost like she's annoyed with him, which is a great technique. "And now Saturday night too. These girls are nothing but boxed wine and havoc."

They both turn and look at me. I don't know what to say, but I have never drunk boxed wine.

"Colette," he says, "can you come talk to me for a second?"

They walk into the next room for a minute and I can hear his voice rise a little, can make out a few words—*responsibilities* and *what if* and *young girls*.

"What do you want me to do? These girls' parents just don't care," she says, which feels funny to hear.

A few seconds go by and then they both reappear.

"Matt, go back to bed," she says, trying for an aggrieved smile, one hand on his back. "You're exhausted. I'll take care of it."

Matt French looks over at Beth, buried on the sofa, and then away.

For a second, his gaze rests on me. His sleep-smeared face, the worry on it, and his bloodshot eyes on me.

"Good night, Addy," he says, and I honestly never knew he knew my name.

I watch him duck his head under the archway then ascend the carpeted steps.

Good night, Matt French.

Pulling me into the bathroom, Coach sits me down on the tub ledge, the questions coming so fast and the pink lights flaming.

"I don't know what happened," I say, but Beth's words keep caroming back: *hand on the back of my head and shoved it down there and kept saying, "Do me, cheerleader. Do me."*

Coach makes me repeat everything five, ten times, or so it seems. I'm getting head spins. At some point I start to slide against the shower curtain, but she yanks me up again and makes me drink four cups of water back-to-back.

"What do *you* think happened?"

"I don't know," I say. "You saw her legs, the red marks?"

But then, my hand to my own leg, I think of the dusky violet bruise I have in the very same spot from Mindy's gouging thumb, lifting me to a thigh stand.

And there's the matter of those lime panties, folded tidily in Beth's purse.

But Coach isn't listening, isn't even looking at me.

She has Beth's phone in her hand. I never even saw her take it.

She's scrolling through call history. Outgoing calls and texts to "Sarge Will," six, seven, eight of them.

Suddenly, she flinches.

A text, **Come on by, Sarge Stud, we're all waiting.** There's a picture attached that looks to be Beth's zebra-print bra, breasts pressed tightly together.

Clattering the phone against the wall, she catapults it down the toilet.

As if it mattered.

Who knew, really, what digital obscenities swam around in that phone of Beth's, what electronic blight she'd hoarded in its deepest pockets.

My drunken head and all I can think is, *Oh, Coach, she's got you in her sights. Fair or not, she's got you. Please get smarter, fast.*

Later that night, I creep from the rolled-arm living room sofa to the den. I see Beth, blanket twisted between her legs, her whole body twisting on itself like a snake.

"Beth," I whisper, tucking the throw blanket tighter around her. "Is it true? Is it true Prine did things to you? Made you do things?"

Her eyes don't open, but I know she knows I'm there. I feel like I've tunneled my way into her dream, and that she'll answer me there.

"I made him make me," she murmurs. "And he did. Can you believe he did?"

Made him make me. Oh, Beth, what does that even mean? I picture her taunting him. Doing her witchy Beth things.

"Made him make you do what?" I try.

"I didn't care," she says. "It was worth it."

"Beth," I say. "Worth what?"

"She needs to see what she's doing to us," Beth says. "I will make her see."

This is the way Beth can talk. Her Big Talk, her campfire spook story talk, her steel-toed captain talk. It's meant to put a shake on me, and it always works.

"She didn't even know we were at the party," I say.

"She thinks she can go about her sluttish ways and do whatever she wants. We're just girls and we were there, and anything could have happened to us."

"We wanted to go," I say, my voice hardening, "so we went."

"Because of her," she says, her hand lifting, coiling around her throat. Her hand, it's shaking. "We went because of her."

"Not me," I say, my voice a bark. "That's not why I went. What did it have to do with her?"

She looks at me through half-shut eyes, a glistening there beneath her lashes. Beth always knowing me. *Everything,* she is saying. *And you know it.*

"Those Guard boys, they see what they can get away with," she whispers. "They see what's okay, what's allowed."

Flashing on me, my own thoughts, hours before, hip-rotating with RiRi on the sinking mattress . . . *it's okay because these are Will's men and nothing bad could ever happen.*

"Beth," I start, trying to turn the dial to the center. "Did he . . . did he—" I can't say the word.

"What does it matter," she says.

I breathe deeply. A breath so deep it nearly pierces me.

"Addy, he might as well have," she says, her eyes blinking open, and so very drunk and lost I want to cry. "That's what counts."

More than once that night I sense movement in the house, shadows dancing past me. In my drunken sleep, curled tight on the couch, it's as if I'm in Caitlin's room, the pink-lit lantern casting ballerina silhouettes on the walls all night long.

Near dawn there is another shadow, and I feel the faintest weight on the glossy maple floors.

Rising, I creep through the living room door to the hallway, my stomach rising, the hangover scaling me with every move.

I see Coach in the den, leaning over the back of the sofa, whispering in Beth's ear.

Her face so hard.

Her hands clasping the sofa edge too tight.

I think I hear. I know I hear.

You're lying. You're a liar. All you do is lie.

Then Beth, she's talking, but I can't hear any of it, or can't be sure I have. In my nightmared head, it's this:

He held my head, he bent my legs back, he did it to me, Coach. Monkey see, monkey do. Like us with you. Didn't I jump higher, fly higher, Coach? Didn't I?

16

All Sunday long, still feeling drunk, my whole body wrung dry from it, I can't get Beth to return my texts. All I can do from my bedroom cave is wonder if she told her parents some version of her sordid story, or worse, the police.

And hovering in and out of hangover sleep, my dreams, so wretched, Prine's bullet head between Beth's tangled legs, doing tangly things with teeth, like a wild animal, the Mauler.

Or picturing Beth, teasing and goading him, slithering in her hiked skirt, saying who knew what, trying to get him to be rough with her, rough enough to mark her. I wonder how far he really got, or how far she would have let it go. Or why she did it to herself, to all of us.

Coach needs to see what she's doing to us. What does that mean, Beth?

It means nothing to me.

Sunday night, Coach calls.

"I don't know what happened," I say. "I can't get any more out of her."

"It doesn't matter anyway," Coach says, her voice flat, almost motorized. "All that matters is what she says happens. And who she says it to."

This sends a chill through me. How could it not matter? But in some deeper way, I know what she means. There's a fog upon us and there seems no piercing through.

"They've been in there an hour," Emily announces, teetering on her crutches. On the DL but she won't ever miss a practice. "At first it was *really* loud."

We're standing recklessly close to Coach's office, she and Beth knotted in there, the blinds pulled shut, and I'm worried they can hear us.

No one else seems to know about Beth and Prine. All they heard was she sidled off with someone, which Beth always does anyway.

"Do you think Beth wants back on the squad?" Tacy whispers, visions of glory slipping from her neon fingertips. "Do you think Coach'd let her back? What if Coach lets her be squad captain again?"

Little, battle-hardened Tacy, calculating three moves ahead. Time was, she was just Beth's gimp, then Beth's Benedict Arnold. Now she's Coach's gimp.

If Beth is captain again, Tacy will have to slink back into spotter slots, or worse. No more Awesomes or Libertys or Dirty Birds or back tuck basket tosses.

No more flying.

"Coach doesn't believe in captains," Emily reminds us. "Even if she changed her mind, why in the world would she let *Beth* be captain? Beth doesn't even show up anymore."

But they don't know what I know. Beth's new chit. Pay for play. I wonder, will that be Coach's strategy? It would be mine.

But it doesn't seem Coach's way. Her way: Meet swagger with swagger.

★   ★   ★

Swinging out of the office ten minutes later, Beth and Coach unaccountably snickering together, low, nasty laughs. We all watch, keenly.

I'm the only one who sees through them.

"She's a chicken," Coach says to me later. "She talks a good game, but she's just a baby chick."

About this, I know she could not be more wrong.

"You all think she's such a gamer," Coach says, shaking her head. "She's just marshmallow fluff. Like any of those JV tenderfoots. Just with bigger lungs and a better ass."

The two of them. Like liar's dice at summer camp. But Beth always won because she was good at math and understood odds, and because, when looking under the cup, she'd turn over the dice with her thumb.

"But that Prine guy. You said they call him the Mauler..."

Coach shrugs. "She told me she doesn't remember him ever hurting her. He passed out. And she guesses she didn't know what she was saying, really, she was so drunk."

I look at Coach, and I wonder who's lying, or if they both are.

"So she's not going to do anything?"

"There's nothing to do," Coach says. "I asked her if she wanted me to take her to my doctor. She said absolutely not. What she does remember is that Prine's a bantam rooster with nothing but squawk."

"So, bitch," Beth asks later that afternoon, chewing straws at the coffee place, "are you ever gonna give me my phone back?"

I picture Coach spiraling it down the toilet.

123

"Your phone?"

"Herr F told me you must've taken it Saturday night. Probably to stop me from drunk-dialing. You're a scrub, you know that, Hanlon? You're auxiliary."

"I don't have your phone, Beth," I say.

"I guess she must be wrong," Beth says, foam curled in the corner of her mouth. Her tongue unfurling, swiping. "Funny she would think it was you."

"Beth," I say, "you said you'd texted Will that night. You said you'd called or texted him a bunch of times."

She doesn't say anything, but her mouth twitches just slightly. Then she pulls it taut and I wonder if I ever saw it at all.

"Did I say that?" she says, her bright tan shoulders slipping into a shrug. "I don't remember that at all."

17

The next day, Beth is back on the squad.

And she is captain again. Honorifically.

She gets to skip chem on Wednesday for captain-coach mentor time, and study hall means she can go to Coach's office by herself and smoke. I see her when I walk by and she waves at me, head tilted, smoke swirling in malevolent plumes around her face.

Thank you, Coach, I think. *Thank you.*

"Is she really Cap?" Tacy whispers, everybody whispers, but Tacy is shaking in her bright white air cheers.

Because it appears she is.

And Beth, is that contentment I see there on your tan face?

Fuck me, I think, which even sounds like Beth. *Is this all she wanted?*

It's not, of course.

"It's okay," says Coach. "I don't have time for her, Addy. And you don't either. Let's see that back handspring."

And I am trying, but my legs won't come together and my body feels funny and stiff.

"Push off," she barks, temple sweat-dappled and her hair limp and slipping from its elastic.

"Lock out"—and with each shout her voice stronger, and my body tighter, harder—"stay tight, stay center, and, fuck it, Addy, smile. Smile. Smile."

The next morning, I spy Matt French pulling into the parking lot in his gray Toyota, with Coach in it.

When she gets out of the car she doesn't even glance behind her. It looks like he's saying something to her, but maybe not.

But he's watching her, waiting, I guess, to make sure she gets inside the building.

More and more, when I see his face I think maybe he is kind of handsome in his own tired way.

That's the hardest part, she said once. *There's nothing bad I can say about him, nothing I can say at all.*

Which somehow seems the cruelest thing to say, ever.

Which is maybe why I feel this, looking at him now. Matt French. I can't account for it, but his weariness amid all the bluster and strut of us sparkle-slitted girls—it speaks to me. Like seeing him the other night, the way he looked at me.

He's not the guy you might think he is. That's what Will told me.

But I'm not sure what he thinks I might think.

Matt French watches Coach as she walks down the center aisle of the parking lot, watches her walk through the glass doors. He watches for a long time, one arm stretched across the passenger seat, head slightly dipped.

Watching her in the way that reminds me of the way a dad might watch his daughter on the jungle gym.

She never looks back once.

"Her car's on blocks over at Schuyler's garage," Beth tells me later. "Davy saw it. There's a big punch in the front fender."

I don't know who Davy is, or how he knows what Coach's car looks like. Beth has always known people—friends of her brother, sons of her mother's exes, the nephew of the woman from Peru who used to clean her house—that no one else knows or even sees. Her reserves of information, objects, empty houses, designer handbags, driver's licenses, and prescription pads seem limitless.

I ask Coach about it later, what happened to her car anyway.

She shows me a long cut skating up her arm.

"From the seam in the steering wheel," she says, cigarette hanging from her mouth, her voice throaty and tired, almost like Beth's. "I hit a post in the lot over at the Buckingham Park playground."

I tell her I'm sorry.

"I was pulling in and had to swerve really fast. A little girl ran in front of the car," she says, her eyes losing focus. "She looked just like Caitlin."

"But you were both okay?" I ask, which seems like something you should ask.

"That's the funny part," she says, shaking her head. "Caitlin wasn't with me. I'd forgotten her. Left her at home, in her room, playing Chutes and Ladders. Or tipping over bleach, eating poison from the cabinet under the sink, starting fires in the backyard. Who knew?"

She laughs a little, shaking her head. Shaking her head a long time, flipping her Bic in her hand.

Then she stops.

"I must be the worst mother in the world," she says, eyes glassy and confused.

I look at her, all the blurry fear on her.

And I say, "Mos def."

Which always makes her laugh, and makes her laugh now, and it's unguarded, beautiful.

"She was trying to avoid hitting some kid at the playground," I say. "She hit a post."

"I don't believe it," Beth says.

"Why would she lie?"

"Plenty of reasons," she says. "I've been right before, other times. You believe people, just like cheer camp, with that St. Regina Flyer. That compulsive liar, Casey Jaye. And you licked it all up."

Beth, always sifting ancient history, scattering ashes at me. Always going back to last summer. It was our only fight and it wasn't a fight really. Just stupid girl stuff.

I never thought you'd be friends again after that, RiRi said afterward. But we were. No one understands. They never have.

"Beth, can't you leave all this alone?" I say now, surprised at the strain in my voice. "You got what you wanted. You're captain again and you can do whatever you want. So stop."

"It's not my choice," she says. "Something gets started, you have to see it through."

"See what through? What, Beth? What, Captain-My-Captain?"

She pauses, clicking her teeth, an old habit from the days we both slid retainers around in our hanging-jaw girl mouths.

"You don't understand it, do you? All that's happened. It's all her."

She leans back, spreading her long ponytail across her face, her mouth.

Then she says something and I think it's, "She has your heart."

"What?" I say, feeling something ping in my stomach, my hand fisting over it.

"She has her *part*," she says, brushing her ponytail from her face, "in all this."

But I can't believe I misheard her. Did I?

"It's not just me," she says again, teeth latching and unlatching. "She has her part."

I misheard.

18

Coach spends most of practice in her office, on the phone, her face hidden behind her hand.

When she comes out, the phone rings again, and she is gone.

In her place, Beth brandishes the scepter, or pretends to. We have a sloppy practice and Mindy wearies me, complaining about the red grooves and pocks studding her shoulder, the imprint of Tacy's kaepa toss shoe. Chicken-boned Brinnie Cox only wants to talk about her lemon detox tea.

My head bobbing helplessly, I look up into the stands and spot Emily, a white pipe cleaner propped lonely there.

I keep forgetting about Emily. Ground-bound, it's like she dropped into the black hole of the rest of the school.

God, it must be terrible not to be on cheer. How would you know what to do?

Her head darting left and right, she's watching us from the cave of her letter jacket, her ponderous orthopedic moon boot nearly tipping her to one side.

Emily, who I've known for three years, borrowed tampons from, held her hair back over every toilet bowl in school.

"Skinny be-yotch," Beth calls out to her, as if reading my mind. "How we rate to your bony ass?"

Emily shudders to life. "Tight," she calls out, eagerly.

"Tight as JV pussy?" Beth shouts.

"Tighter!" Emily laughs, and I remember this Beth, Captain Beth when Beth was feeling most captainy, most interested in wielding her formidable powers, me at her side.

Thank you, Beth, for reminding me. Thank you.

Teddy saw Coach @ Statlers last week, Beth's text reads. **Drinking, talking on cell all nite, crying @ jukebox.**

So? I text back, nearing one a.m.

I want to turn off the phone. I want to be done with Beth for the night, done with her chatter about Coach, and her car, or even the things she used to talk about: Tacy's runty legs and the antidepressants she eyed in Mindy's book bag, and the sex toy she found under her mother's pillow and how it looks like a pink boomerang made by Mattel, and maybe that's what happened to her Barbie surfboard, mysteriously lost a decade ago.

Like some polluted Little Red Riding Hood, Beth always creeping through everyone's lives.

So? I text again.

There's a long pause, and I can picture Beth pecking away her reply.

Sometimes, though, I think that how long she takes, these epic multipart texts, is all on purpose, making the dread mount each time: *What is Beth up to? What is she doing now?*

ZZzt, the phone screen flashes at me at last:

Said she ran outside + hit post in parking lot, peeled off

So...? I text back.

So why lie to us, to u? she texts. **Plus, crying abt what?**

I roll over in bed, let the phone slip to the carpet, its screen winking at me.

In the half dream that comes, the screen is a mouth, teeth gnashing.

19

I'm deep into toes-curled sleep when I hear it.

My cell, squawking from the floor.

I feel it hum under my grappling fingers.

Please not Beth.

Incoming call: Coach, the screen reads, and my favorite snapshot, from the night after the Cougars' defeat, Coach sitting on the hood of my car, sated and exultant.

"Addy," the whisper comes. "Addy, I slipped on the floor. I saw him and I slipped on something and I didn't know what it was."

"Coach? What's going on?" Words sticky in my sleeping mouth.

"I kept looking at my sneaker and wondered what was on it. What the dark stain was."

I think I'm dreaming.

"Coach," I say, rolling over, trying to blink myself awake. "Where are you? What's going on?"

"Something happened, Addy. That's what I think. But my head..."

Her voice so peculiar, thin and wasted.

"Coach—Colette. *Colette, where are you?*"

A pause, a creaking sound from her throat. "You better come, Addy. You better come here."

I'm sure I'll be heard, but if I am, no one does anything about it, not even when the garage door shimmies open, when the car leaps to life. Sometimes I don't even try to be quiet. Sometimes I turn on all the lights, leave a trail blazing from my bedroom through the garage until my dawn return, and no one has ever said a word.

But tonight, I don't.

I try not to look at my phone, which is spasming with texts that must have come in while I slept—all from vampiric Beth, who sometimes seems never to sleep at all and tonight seems especially wired with speculations and grim fancy.

I can't stop to read them now.

Nearly to Wick Park, I see The Towers, a colossal apartment complex, the only one in Sutton Grove, though it doesn't even feel like Sutton Grove but like the tenuous landing strip for a steel box dropped from high above.

I've been there once before, to pick up Coach and take her back to her car, which she'd left at school.

One of the new developments perched high on Sutton Ridge, it floats perilously over the edge, and still half empty because no one wants to live by the roaring interstate.

It's so great, Addy, Coach said. *Like a deserted castle. You can scream and shout and no one could—*

I remember when I'd pulled up Will had waved from the lobby's glass doors, his face and neck flushed, like hers. His hair wet and seal-slick. And Coach, still slipping on her left shoe as she ran to my car.

The sharp smell on her when she opened my car door, so thick it seemed to hover in the air around her.

Her face bright, her right leg still shaking.

I couldn't take my eyes off it.

But that was weeks ago, in the middle of the day, and nothing looks familiar at all now. It takes me three circuits of the complex to find the right building, and then find Will's name on the big lighted board out front.

All the while I'm thinking of Coach's voice on the phone.

"Is he there now," I'd asked, a sick feeling in my stomach. "Is Will with you?"

"Yes," she said. "He's here."

"Is he okay?"

"I can't look," she said. "Don't make me look."

She doesn't say anything on the intercom, just buzzes me in.

The drone in my ear, it's like the tornado drill in elementary school, the hand-cranked siren that rang mercilessly, all of us hunched over on ourselves, facing the basement walls, heads tucked into our chests. Beth and me wedged tight, jeaned legs pressed against each other. The sounds of our own breathing. Before we all stopped believing a tornado, or anything, could touch us, ever.

In the elevator, the numbers glow and the funniest feeling starts up inside me. It's like before a game. Chest vaulting, bounding on my toes, everything ricocheting in my head (*lift arm higher, no fear, count it out, pull it tight, and make it sing*), my body so tight and ready I feel like a coiled spring: *Let me free, let me free, I will show you my ferocity, my rapture.*

"Addy," Coach says, opening the door, startled, like she's almost forgotten she called me, as if I've shown up at her own home, unaccountably, in the middle of the night.

The apartment is dark, one floor lamp coning halogen up in the far corner. A hooded fish tank effervesces on a table by the wall, the clouded water seeming almost to smoke, a fluorescent cauldron with no fish I can see.

She looks tiny, her iron-rod back sinking into itself. Barefooted, a nylon windbreaker zipped up so high it covers her neck and the tip of her chin. Her hair dankly tucked behind her ears.

"Coach," I start.

"Take off your shoes," she says, her mouth pinched. I think it's because of the parquet floors, though they don't look that nice, and I slip off my flip-flops and rest them by the door.

We're standing in the vestibule, which gives way to a small dining area with a thick black-lacquered table. Just past it is the living room, braced by the hard angles of a leather sectional.

Turning back to her, I see something's in her hands, her tennis shoes bundled there, soaking wet.

"I washed them in the sink," she says, answering my unasked question. Suddenly, she hoists them into my hands.

"Hold them, okay? Because I need to think. I need to get my head in order."

I nod, but my eyes keep darting to the back of the large sectional sofa sprawling across the room like a spreading stain.

Maybe it's the gloomy dark, the phosphoresce from the glubbing aquarium.

But mostly it's the way Coach's eyes seem to vibrate when she looks at me, pupils like nail heads.

"What's over there?" I say, angling my head toward the sofa. "Coach, what's over there?"

She looks at me for a second, running a hand through her hair, which looks so dark.

Then she lets her eyes drift over to the sofa, and I let mine too.

I'm holding the shoes tight and inching toward the sofa.

I can hear her breathing behind me, in rasping gulps. Watching.

The parquet floors squeak and the sofa looms before me, crooking around the center of the room.

Walking slowly, the surging bleach from the sneakers nearly making me choke, I feel something skitter under my bare foot and spin across the floor. Something small, like a button or a spool of thread.

As I creep closer, ten-then-five-feet away from the living room area, the sofa back seems larger, taller than the football goalpost, than the Eagles emblem on the field, wings spread.

My right foot dangles over the circular rug in the center of the room. To step on it feels like stepping into black water.

Zzzt! My phone like Mexican jumping beans in my pocket. *Zzzt!*

I'm sure Coach heard the vibration, but if she did, she doesn't show it, so fixed is she on the sofa, what lies behind it.

Turning my body, I finger for, and press, the Off button so hard I nearly knock the phone from my pocket.

Deep breath.

Deep breath.

Me, now only a few steps from the back of the snaking sofa, peeking around the sofa's sharp corner, around its scaly leather arm. I see something on the floor.

"I let myself in with the key he gave me," Coach is saying, answering more unasked questions. "I rang the doorbell first, but he didn't answer. I walked in and there he was. Ohhh, there he was."

First, I see the glint of dark blond hair twining in the weave of the rug.

Then, stepping forward, I see more.

Coach's sneakers slip from my hands, shoe string tickling my leg as they drop to the carpet with a soft clunk.

There he is.

There he is.

There's Sarge. There's Will.

"Addy," Coach whispers, far behind me. "I don't think you want to...I don't think you need to...*Addy*...is it like I thought?"

His chest bare, wearing only a towel, his arms stretched out, he's like one of those laminated saint pictures the Catholic girls always brought from catechism. Saint Sebastian, his head always thrown back, body both luminous and tortured.

"Addy," says Coach, almost a whimper. Like little Caitlin, just waking up and scared.

I just keep looking. At Will. On the floor.

In those saint pictures, their bodies are always torn, split, lacerated. But their faces so lovely, so tranquil.

But Will's face does not look righteous and exalted.

My eyes fix on the thing that was Will's mouth, but is now a red flower, its tendrils sprawling to all corners and, like a poppy, an inky whorl at the center.

In those saint pictures, their eyes, lovingly lashed, are always looking up.

And, for all the ruin of Will's handsome face, his eyes, they are gazing up too.

But it seems to me not to the Kingdom of God but to the tottering ceiling fan.

Looking up so he doesn't have to see the ruin of his face.

Behind his head, the rug is dark and wet.

*   *   *

I can't stop looking at him, at the bright streak of his face.

It's like I'm seeing Will and I'm seeing something else too. The old woman from the bus, the one with the black eyes Will was sure could bore through to the center of him. That story never felt real to me, it felt like when someone tells you a dream and they can't make you feel what they feel. It didn't feel real to me except as something I wanted to understand but couldn't. But now suddenly I can. The woman's hat tilting up, eyes like shale.

"Stop crying," Coach is saying, begging. "Addy, stop crying."

"I didn't touch him." Coach says, and I cannot catch my breath, but she will not wait. "When I ran over, I slipped on those."

She points to three small white things dotted across the floor. The something I'd felt wobbling under my foot, that I'd sent spinning across the parquet. A button or spool of thread.

"What are..." But then suddenly I know.

Turning again to Will's poppy-struck face on the floor, the bottom half of it blown away, I know what they are.

I hear a moan come up from within me, my fingers clapping my own teeth, as if to remind myself they're still there.

"Coach, *why am I here?*" someone says in a voice I recognize, obscurely, as my own. The words just tumble out, constricted and lost. "Why did you make me come?"

But she doesn't answer me. I don't even think she's heard me.

ZZzzzzt! My phone, my phone. Like a paddle over my heart.

Beth. I'm sure I've pressed that button long enough to turn it off until the end of time, but I must've pressed it so long I turned it on again.

The way it keeps ringing, it's like Beth is there in the room too.

And I'm afraid to even touch the phone because it seems some-how Beth will know if I turn it off, like she knows everything. Like she's here right now, claws out.

"Do you see it," Coach says, still ten feet from me, she won't come any closer.

"I see *him*," I say, as calm as I can, my finger scratching at my phone, trying to hold the Off button just long enough to make it stop. As soon as I do it shudders *ZZzzzt!* again. "Of course I see him."

"No," she says, her voice going quieter still but more insistent. "On the floor."

I don't want to look again, but I do. At his hands, palms faced up, his legs, which have a queer violet cast.

That's when I spot the gun peeking out from under his left leg.

I turn to face Coach, who's standing in front of the dining room table, winding a dewy strand of hair behind her ear. She looks younger than me, I think.

"He did this to himself?" I whisper, not even wanting to say it out loud.

"Yes," she says. "I found him."

"Was there a note or something?"

"No," she says.

"You didn't call nine-one-one," I say. Maybe it's a question and maybe it isn't.

"No," she says. Before I can ask why, she adds, "I guess no one heard. He doesn't have any neighbors yet."

We both look at the walls to our left and to our right. The room feels impossibly small.

"I don't know when it happened," Coach says. "I don't know anything."

Thoughts come to me, of Will and his self-puzzled depths.

I feel a loss suddenly.

I can't hold on to it long enough to figure out why, but suddenly, shamefully, I feel sorry for myself.

In that moment, though, she's made a turn.

"Addy," she says, voice faster now. "Where's your car?"

"I don't know," I say. I can feel a bolting energy from her, her body inching toward the door.

It's like she just showed me a triple toe touch back, three fast scissor kicks, landing, then springing back for the final back tuck. Her hands never touching the ground. Not once.

But something is niggling at me. Holding me back.

"Wait, Coach," I say. "Where's your car?"

"At the mechanic. Remember?" She is curt, like I'm her slowest student.

"So how did you get here?" I ask, walking over to her.

"Oh," she says. "I took a cab. I snuck out of the house. Matt was asleep. He took two pills. I had to see Will. So I called a cab." A pause between each sentence like reading flash cards. "But I couldn't call a cab to take me back, could I?"

"No, Coach," I say. "I guess you couldn't."

"And I can't show up at home in a cab now," she says, her voice speeding up again.

Zzzzt!

My phone.

Zzzzt!

But this time she is right next to me, and she is back to being Coach, her arm whipping out, her fingers hooking over my pocketed hand.

"What is that? Who's calling?"

"No one's calling," I say, her hot fingers clamping at me, like when she pushes your body to make that jump, support that weight, the weight of five girls, effortlessly.

In an instant, it's like I'm not in Will's apartment but at practice, and in trouble.

"A text," I say. "I get texts all the time."

"In the middle of the night?" She jerks my wrist from my pocket and the phone rattles to the floor.

Mercifully, the battery flies out.

"Pick it up," she says. "Goddammit, Addy."

I start to bend down.

"Don't touch anything," she snaps, and I see one of my hands is almost resting on the shiny black lacquer of the table.

Rising, I look down at the tabletop and see my smudgy face re-flected in it, black depthless eyes.

There's nothing there, really.

"Addy, we have to go, we have to go," Coach says, her voice grinding into me. "Get me out of here."

Moments later, we dart across the parking lot, my sapphire Acura like a beacon.

We're driving, the night vacant and starless, and the whole world is softly asleep, with furnaces purring and windows shut tight and the safety of people tucked inside with the warming knowledge of a tomorrow and a tomorrow after that of just such humming sameness.

The car windows down, the crystally cool on me, I imagine myself in that world, the one I know. I imagine myself curled in just such comforts, comforts so tight they could choke you. So tight they choke me always.

Oh, was there no happiness to be had the world over? There or here?

Here in this bleach-fogged car, she beside me, still holding her sneakers between her legs. Her fingers keep running around the tongue, her eyes thoughtfully, almost dreamily on the road.

I can't fathom what she's thinking.

Finally, as we're turning down her street, Coach asks me to pull over two doors from her house.

"Roll the windows up," she says. I do.

"Addy, it's going to be fine," she says. "Just forget about all this."

I nod, my chin shaking from the cold, from the wretched loneliness of that drive, fifteen, twenty minutes in the car. She never said a word, seemed lost in some kind of moody reverie.

"You just need to go home and pretend it never happened," she says. "Okay?"

When she gets out of the car, the waft of bleach from her shoes smacks me.

Unable to turn the ignition, I sit there.

Were I thinking straight, were I feeling the world made any sense at all, I might be driving to the police station, calling 911. Were I that kind of person.

Instead, I look at my cell. I need to text Beth back.

Fell asleep, be-yotch, I type. **Some of us sleep.**

Still sitting, I wait a minute for her reply. But my phone just lies there.

No Beth.

It should make me feel better—Beth has finally dervished herself into exhausted slumber, her reign of terror over, for now—but it does not.

Instead, I have a sickly feeling I know will sit with me all night, that will join the larger sickness, the sense of nightmare and menace that feels like it will be mine forever.

I roll down all the windows and breathe.

Then I start the car and inch past Coach's house, just to see if there are any lights on.

Suddenly, I see something moving, fast, like an arrow, down her driveway and to my car.

Almost before I can take a breath, Coach's palms are slapping my windshield, my heart spurring to terrible life.

"I was just leaving, I was," I nearly yelp, shutting off the ignition as she leans in through the passenger window. "No one saw—"

"You're my friend," she blurts, an ache in her voice. "The only friend I ever had."

Before I can say anything, she's whippeting back across her lawn, slipping soundlessly into the dark house.

I sit a long time, my hands resting in my lap, my face warm.

I don't want to start the car, move, do anything.

I never gave anything to anyone before. Not like this.

I never was anything to anyone before.

Not like this.

I never was, before.

Now I am.

Finally in my rumpled bed, my eyes jitterbug through all of Beth's texts.

2:03 a.m., 2:07 a.m., 2:10 a.m.

@ Statlers, Coach drinking ginger and jacks + on phone for hour kept saying why are you doing this to me why

Bartend said she used to come when she was young and drink w. badasses from the speedway and once broke both wrists falling in that same pking lot

...kind of trash she is. She shld b glad Matt sunk so low to grab scruff of her neck cuz...

Then, by 2:18:

WHERE THE FUCK R U? You better txt back or I'm coming over. U KNOW I WILL. DON'T MESS WITH—

...and on until 2:27, the last one.

here I am, Pinetop Ct, looking at yr open garage door, but where's yr car? Hmmm...

She must be lying, I tell myself. But I know she's not. I know she was out there in front of my house at 2:27, hunched over the steering wheel of her mother's Miata. I know it.

I wonder how long she waited and what she thought.

I wonder what I'll say and how I'll ever make her believe it.

In this knot of fear, I forget everything but Beth's canny slit eyes.

Those eyes on me, even now.

In the blackest of moments that night, when sleep finally sinks me, a dream of Beth and me, little kids, Beth raking the hard bars of that ancient merry-go-round they used to have in Buckingham Park, spinning us, spinning. And we lie flat on it, on its warty surface, our heads pressed close.

"It's what you wanted," she says, breathless. "You said faster."

20

It's early, an hour before first period, but I had given up on sleeping, all those half-awake nightmares of my feet sunk in blood-wet carpet and aquariums pumping violet-red bubbles.

You saw a dead man last night. That's what I'm saying in my head. *You saw a suicide right before your eyes.*

You saw Will, dead.

So I'm slumped in front of my locker, curling the pages of my *The Odyssey of Man* textbook, fat green highlighter poked into my mouth.

Beth glides through the front doors of school.

I expect it to be immediate, her face a tanned snarl as she demands to know where I was last night, why I stopped texting her back.

But instead, hand out, she lifts me to my feet, her face vivid and mysterious, and arm-in-arms me to the cafeteria.

We get a fat-slicked chocolate chip muffin, which we heat up in the rotating toaster machine. Standing next to it, the heat radiating off its coils, I imagine myself suffering eternal damnation for sins not yet clear.

But then the muffin pops out, tumbling into my hands. Together, we eat it in long, sticky bites that we do not swallow. No one else is there, so we can do it, and Beth fills tall cups with warm water to make it easier, then spit it out after, into our napkins.

When we finish, I feel much better.

Until Beth starts telling me about her dream.

"It wasn't just any dream," she says, licking her fingers, under each slick fuchsia nail. "It was like before. Like with Sandy."

As long as I've known her, Beth has had periodic dreams of dark portent, like the night before her aunt Lou fell from her second-floor landing and broke her neck. In the dream, her aunt came to breakfast and announced she had a new talent. Then, taking one forearm to her neck, she showed them how she could turn her head 360 degrees.

Or, when we were ten and Beth came to school one day and said she dreamt she found Sandy Hayles from soccer camp behind the equipment shed, a sheet pulled tight across her face. That Saturday, our soccer coach told us Sandy had a blood disease and wasn't coming back to camp, ever.

"What was the dream?" I ask, fighting off the nerves spiking up my neck, tickling my temples.

"We were doing toe touch jumps high on one of the overlooks, like that one time, remember?" she says. "But then we heard a noise, like something falling a long, long way. I walked over to the edge of the gorge to look down, but I couldn't see anything at all. I could feel it, though, because it was vibrating, like your throat when you scream."

And I'm thinking, yes, like when all of us scream at the game, with our throats vibrating and our feet pounding, and the bleachers shaking, everything. I can hear it all in my head now.

"Then I looked back up at you. It was so dark up there and

you were so white, but your eyes were black, like one of those ash rocks in geology class."

Shoulders clustered, a preying black bird, she leans closer.

Suddenly it feels like I'm the one who's dreaming, who's still stuck in that nightmare of sinking carpets and bloody footprints and an aquarium pump glub-glubbing, opening and closing like the valves of a heart.

"But, Addy, the bottom part of your face was gone," she whispers, her fingers wandering to her chin, her lips. "And your mouth was just this white smear."

My breath catches.

"I started to slip," she continues. "You grabbed my wrist and were trying to pull me up, but it hurt and I looked down and something was cutting into me, something on your hand."

"And you lifted your other hand, and there was a mouth there, right in the center of your palm—and you were talking through it, and you were saying something very important."

I look down at my palm.

"What was I saying?" I ask, staring at the whiteness of my open hand.

"I don't know." Beth sighs, leaning back, shaking her head. "But then you did it."

"Did what?"

"You let go," she says. "Just like before you learned how to spot."

Grab for the body, not the limb.

"You had my wrist, and then you didn't anymore. You let go. Like always."

My head hot, my stomach bucking, I press my napkin to my face. I can't remember the last time I ate anything and I almost wish I'd really eaten that muffin. Almost.

"That's not a special dream," I say. "Nothing even happened."

"Everything happened," she says again, plucking lip gloss from her jeans pocket. "You know how it works. All will be revealed."

I try to roll my eyes, and that's when my stomach turns hard, and I have to reach for the napkin. The gagging is embarrassing, but nothing really comes up other than chocolate residue, a muddy slick dripping down my wrist.

"Lovergirl," Beth says. "We gotta get you your gunstones back. You're going feather soft. Now that I'm captain again, I'll get you tight. I'll get you good and tight."

"Yeah," I say, watching Beth swizzling that gloss wand like a magician. "How come I'm always the one doing bad things in your dreams?" I say.

She hands me the wand.

"Guilty conscience."

After world civ, I see Beth again. She's waiting for me outside the door.

"Splitsville," she says. "I knew it. I knew something was gonna blow. Coach and Will, *c'est fini.*"

"Huh?"

"He's not at the recruiting table today," she says. "It's just that redhead PFC."

So fast, I think. *So fast.*

"That doesn't mean anything," I say, turning. But she grabs me by the belt loop. Part of me is glad her morning spookiness is gone, and she's just regular badass Beth, but another part of me doesn't like all the jump and spark on her.

"I've done recon," she whispers, so close I can see the dent in her tongue where her stud used to be before she decided tongue rings were JV. "Bitty PFC says they don't know where the Sarge is. And he's not answering his phone."

I don't say anything, just spin-dial my locker combination.

"So get this: PFC says sometimes Sarge just AWOLs. And they don't bother him about it, don't report it. 'It's his way,' that's what the scrub tells me. They let it go because he's had some trouble in his life. Something about his wife and a plate glass window," Beth says, not quite rolling her eyes.

"So why's that mean he broke up with Coach?" I ask, pretending to look for something in my locker.

"I'm telling you, Papa's got a brand new hag," she says, whistling a little. "Who d'ya think? I speculate Mrs. Fowler, Ceramics, always rolling those clay pots with her legs spread so the boys can see."

"I don't think so," I say.

"Well, if it was RiRi she'd've posted pictures of it on Facebook by now. I don't think he goes for young trim anyway. And we know it isn't *you*."

"Who cares, really," I try, my head blurred.

She pauses a beat, taking the measure of me, and smiles. "Addy-Faddy, I wonder if that's what you were doing last night."

"What?" I whisper.

"Comforting our jilted Coach, of course," she says.

"No," I say, tapping my locker door shut.

"I have better things to do," I add, trying to match her crocodile smile, and maybe beat it.

I don't see Coach all day, until practice.

I text her four times, but she never replies.

Six hours of wondering about her, about how she's moving through her day. If she feels the same swampy misery inside of me.

Seeing the shiny brown leaf of Coach's hair from behind, her yoga-taut posture, I'm almost afraid to look at her face. For our eyes to lock and for everything to come pitching forward until I can smell the smell, hear the gurgling aquarium.

What can it be like for her?

But when she turns around—shouldn't I have known?

Her eyes breezing past me, as if we hadn't shared anything at all, much less this.

Oh, the flinty grace, it's stunning. I think it must be pharmaceutical, and I look for the slight drag to her foot, the tug in her speech. But I can't be sure.

All I know is she's got her stunt roster, her purple gel pen with the click-click-click as she ticks us off, roundoffs, walkovers, handstands, handsprings, front limbers.

Tumbling drills, two hours' worth. Best distraction ever.

We do back tuck after back tuck, bounding from standing pike into flips, handsprings. Our bodies bucking, and when I spot RiRi and watch the row of girls, I get a kind of calmness that hums in my chest. The promise of order.

My body, for instance, it can dip and leap and spring and I am as if untouched, no fear flapping behind my eyes can touch my body, which is invincible and all mine.

It's when I'm spotting RiRi on the last turn that I spy Beth, lingering tardily by the locker room door in practice shorts.

It unnerves me, but I brush it off, and instead my eyes catch the flash of hot-pink daisies that sprinkle before me every time RiRi's skirt flips up.

How is it other girls' panties are always so much more interesting than your own, I think.

"Okay, let's see those Scorps," Coach says.

Everyone groans, quietly. RiRi says she's not nearly "stretchy" enough today, but she can't do one, a decent one anyway, because you have to be small, small enough to fly. I am, or almost. I was. And I still can do it. The body remembers.

It was Beth who first taught me the Scorpion, her hands on my back leg, lifting it slowly behind me, easing it higher and higher until finally my left foot met my raised-up hand. Until my body became one long line.

She taught all of us, back when she was a real captain. She had us use a dog leash we'd tie to our ankle then try pulling it up. At the Centaurs game, when I first got that foot just shy of my forehead and made myself go straight, I knew a pain so stunning I saw stars.

After, Beth bought me a pink camo leash with my name on it in glitter.

Doing it now, I feel my body constrict, then loosen, warm, perfect.

Closing my eyes, I almost see the stars.

Opening them, I see Coach giving me a real smile, and Beth there, watching and nodding. And I forget about everything. I just do.

"It'll be okay, Addy," she says. "No one will ever know."

It's after, just after dusk, Coach driving, the two of us working things out.

"Jimmy—PFC Tibbs—told me. This afternoon, he drove out to the apartment and got the super to let him inside. He wanted me to hear it from him."

I don't say anything for a second, can feel her looking over at me. Then I ask, "What did he say exactly?"

She faces the road again. "He told me something happened

to Sarge. Then he couldn't talk anymore, for a long time. I kept waiting. It was like I almost forgot I already knew." She pauses a second. "Which was good, I guess. Because I think I really seemed surprised when he told me."

I find myself nodding because I don't know what else to do.

"He had this stuff he'd printed off the internet. *Wounded Warrior: Suicide in the Military.* He said it looks like Sarge suicided. That's how he put it. I never heard it put like that."

Suicided.

It reminds me how we'd all tried cutting. I never could break real skin. Beth scraped a big heart on her stomach and then wore her bikini top to the Panthers game. But then she decided it was a hobby for the supremely boring and it no longer seemed so gangsta to any of us after that.

Coach stops at a light and reaches for a cigarette.

"Life was always hard for him," she says, rolling the unlit cigarette up and down the steering wheel spokes.

She tilts her head a little, squinting like she's figuring out a puzzle. "I don't think he ever really got over losing his wife."

I guess maybe it's true.

"He came from a hard family," she says. "Came up hard, like I did."

I didn't know he came up hard, or that Coach did. I'm not even sure what that means. Suddenly I feel like I never knew the person who died, or the person right next to me.

"She helped him," she says, "and then she was gone."

She's not crying, doesn't even look sad precisely. But I feel like she is waiting for something from me.

"But he had you," I say. "Maybe you reminded him of her. How good she was. Maybe he found that in you."

The look on her face is grim, knowing.

"That's not what he found in me," she says, softly.

I don't say anything. It feels like some kind of furtive confession.

"I guess I knew it'd turn out this way," she says, and her voice speeds up a little, and she faces straight ahead, her foot churning the brake pedal, inching us forward with tiny bursts.

"Not just like this, but near it," she says.

She nods, as if agreeing with herself, then nods again. It's as if she's saying, *That's it, that's it, isn't it? And there was nothing we could do.*

She looks at the road, we both do, and I think about it all. About how Coach is always so efficient, so precise, her moves sharp and tight, so it makes sense she could turn this all so quickly, doesn't it?

It makes sense she could, less than twenty-four hours after finding Will's body, come to understand that it was really as it was meant to be, there'd been no stopping it, and everyone was lucky they'd had some pleasures while they could.

When I get home, no one is there, they never are, so I pluck my secret bottle of silver raz from the corner of my closet and take long gulps, then collapse on my bed.

But all I hear is Coach's voice, soft and nearly affectless: *Life was always hard for him, Addy. There was nothing we could do.*

Forcing myself to sit at my computer, eyes blurred, I make myself look.

I search for news reports on Sarge but can't find any.

I even find the police scanner website, but I can't understand it, and I keep getting distracted— *42 are we leaving the football game? didn't know you were there you told us to go here 841 Willard her back is broken that's what she said*—and my eyes all loose and stinging.

*　　*　　*

It's nearly midnight when Beth calls. I pull the covers over me and press my lips to the phone.

"Hold on, little grit," she says. "Hold on and grip hard."

"I'm holding," I say, whorling myself into the wall, my head pressing into its solidness.

"Sarge Stud killed himself."

I feel my breath go tight. I don't say anything.

"I don't know the details yet, but I'm working on it. I dispatched my remaining minions. You used to be so much more help with that, Addy. Now I have to tend to everything. But the meat of the matter is he's dead. I heard he took his head off with a shotgun."

"I don't believe it," I say, which feels like the truest thing I've said in twenty-four hours.

"Well, Addy, truth is an ugly mother, especially for you. But it's the truth. The PFC told me. That boy thinks he's my Knight in Shining. On account of the other night."

It takes me a long minute even to remember the once-world-shattering quality of that night of Beth and Corporal Prine, barely ten days past. That feels like Holly Hobbie time now.

"I told you something was going to happen," she says.

"No," I say. "You said you were going to *make* something happen."

"Well," she replies, "turns out I didn't have to."

"Why would Will do that?" I ask.

"Why wouldn't he?" she answers, her voice animated, gossipy—like we have finally hit upon the thing itself, something she's been waiting for.

"Maybe, Addy-Faddy, just maybe he saw the pointlessness of all matters of the heart and said I won't just sink in, I won't let her grab me by the ankles. Fuck me, I'll look her in the eye. I'll jump."

There is a pause, and I hear Beth's fast breaths, her tongue clicking in her mouth.

I have the sudden feeling that she might say something that will alarm and hurt me. Something I don't want to hear. About the way we are linked, my cheer shoe lodged in her steely palm. About last summer, when I said I was tired of being her lieutenant, tired of being her friend, and it seemed like the two of us were over forever, but we never could be.

"Beth," I say, my arms over my head. "I can't talk to you anymore."

"Addy," she says, somberly, intimately. "You have to."

Something has passed between us, a secret knowledge about us, and what she needs from me. But I blink and I miss it.

21

Meet me @ 7 at coffee place.

Coach's five a.m. text scissoring into my sleep.

I feel hung over, have felt hung over for two days straight, the early morning light laying dew and mystery on me as I walk the five blocks, wary of starting my car at 6:55 in the morning. Sometimes I see my dad then, lurking in the hallways, robe flapping, surprised to see me, like I'm his errant boarder.

Coach is leaning against the milk and sugar station, but when she sees me, her body seems to lift upward, her eyes jittering into focus.

She goes to the counter to get me a matcha green tea and when I reach for a pink packet, she smacks it from my hand, that familiar gesture of hers, and I almost smile but can't seem to.

We take our drinks to her car and sit there, windows rolled tight.

She tells me the police called last night and said they had some questions for her, just routine, but they thought she might wish to handle it discreetly and come to the station house.

At first, all her words just flap at me. I listen and nod and slide my drinking straw behind my teeth, grate it along the roof of my mouth until it hurts.

"Luckily, Matt's out of town," she's saying. "Did I tell you that?"

I shake my head.

"He flew to Atlanta yesterday for work," she says, eyes lifting to the rearview mirror.

I hadn't even been thinking of Matt French. Or how she was going about her life with him amid all this, hiding such a monumental secret. But maybe it wasn't that different. Maybe it wasn't different at all.

"So I got Barbara to stay with Caitlin and I went to the police station. And it wasn't like I thought at all. The detective told me that...he told me what we knew. And he said that they were conducting a routine investigation and they had found my phone number in his call log."

She pauses, her chest heaving a little. That's when I realize her voice is faster than yesterday, with a new wariness to it.

"He asked me if I thought Will was depressed. And if I knew whether he kept any firearms in his home. And about how we knew each other."

"Did you tell?" I ask, sinking my chin into the plastic lid of my drink. "What did you tell?"

"I was as honest as I could be," she says. "It's the police. And I have nothing to hide, not really."

I lift my head and look her in the eye. I wonder if I've heard her right.

"I mean, I *do*. Have some things I'd rather...," she says, shaking her head, like she's just remembered. "I told him we were friends. And that Will probably did have firearms, which is all I really know."

"If he saw the call log," I say, trying to get her to look me in the eye, "wouldn't he know you're more than friends?"

"Will and I didn't really talk on the phone that much," she says, briskly. "Besides, all that has nothing to do with what happened."

I don't know what to say to this.

A voice spins from me, small and wild. "Will the police call me? Will they be calling all of us?"

It suddenly seems like it could happen, and I think: this is how your life can end.

"Listen, Addy," she says, turning to me. "I know this is all really a lot for you to take. I know it all seems scary. But the police are just doing their job, and once they confirm that this is...what it is...then they're not going to need to be bothered with me any- more. It's going to be just fine. Matt will come home, and it'll be like before. *Before* before. Believe me, they're not interested in my little life."

It's not until a long time later, standing at my school locker, that I think, *But I was asking about me. Will the police call me?*
  But, Coach, what about me?

When we walk into school, Coach loops her arm in mine for a second, which she has never done and doesn't suit her. Still, I feel her strain and want to clinch her tighter, but I don't. Now we share something. At last. Except it's this.

I fall asleep in chem, my cheek on the tall tabletop of our lab sta- tion, a TV movie unreeling in my head: cheerleaders lined up at the police station in full uniform. On TV they always wear their uniforms all day long, and never stop smiling.

When I wake with a jolt to the sight of David Hemans flaring the Bunsen burner inches from my hair, I feel like I've just touched the tip of knowing, of realizing.

But then it goes away.

"You're the worst lab partner ever," he says, eyes on my Eagles letter jacket. "I hate all of you."

Second period, two minutes before the bell, and Beth slips into the seat next to me.

"Miss Cassidy," Mr. Feck says, hand on his hip like he does. "I don't believe I see you until fourth period. And not always then."

Full-on cheer-glamour mode, à la RiRi, Beth crinkles her nose with just a whiff of naughtiness and jiggles her index finger like a little inchworm, mouthing, *One second, Mr. Feck, please!!!*

Feck nearly bows his assent.

They are so weak. All of them.

Dragging my desk toward her, Beth whispers greedily in my ear. "Did she tell you about it? Spill, soldier, spill."

"Did who tell me what?" A routine that's getting old, even to me.

"Fuck me, Hanlon," she says, hand gripping my wrist until both our tan hands turn white.

"Yes," I say, clipping my voice. "She can't believe it. It's terrible."

"Suicide is *no* solution," she says, and she says it lightly, cruelly.

Then she seems to catch herself, and something tangles messily in her face. For a second.

Seeing that, I feel my chin wobble and heat rising to my eyes. Therein, somewhere, beats the heart of Beth.

"But, Addy," she says, looking at me low-eyed, like *c'mon, give it up, girlie,* "did she have any *more* information? How did she find out? Who told her?"

"I don't know," I say.

"Miss Cassidy . . . ," singsongs Mr. Feck, eager to reengage.

"Yes, m'lord," Beth says, and she curtsies. She really does.

Turning around at the door, her waist swiveling, she pokes two fingers out at me.

Later, be-yotch.

Later.

My finger poised over my phone, the text message screen blank and taunting.

UR nt gona tel abt Coach n Will ... I start to type.

But then I don't.

And I start thinking of all the text messages Beth must have about everything.

One by one, text by text, e-mail by e-mail, I delete everything on my phone, my breath loud in my own ear. But I know it doesn't matter.

You can't erase it all, not even half of it. Half my life surrendered to gray screens the size of my thumbnail, each flare carelessly shot from my phone to another now rocketing back, landing in my lap like a cartoon bomb, its wick lit.

The thing is, when this happens, you just have to give Beth the thing she wants.

But what does Beth want?

Yet Coach goes on, and I marvel at it.

At practice, she hustles us while Beth sits on the top bleacher deck.

Perched up near the rafters, black wings tucked tight, she's staring at her phone, her face lit by it.

Counting off our beats, Coach is focused, intense. She rides us hard.

"I've got to move things fast," she shouts. "I have to pick up my daughter. Don't drag on me, dollies."

At first, the hurting is not the good kind, and I can't pound my way to it. And when Mindy fishhooks me during a tumbling pass, knocking me to the mat, I'm embarrassed to feel hot tears popping from me. For the first time ever on the mat.

"God, Hanlon," Mindy says, surprised. "You *are* Lieutenant Hanlon, aren't you?"

But there's no time to feel the shame, and I make sure to hold nothing back when I jam my shoe into Mindy's hidebound shoulder next time around.

Soon enough, as we leap and tuck and jump, I start feeling better and my body starts doing astonishing things, tight and rockhard, nailing it.

But then Beth starts talking loudly on her phone. I see Coach looking up at her, again and again, and everything starts galloping back, hoofs up.

"Cap'n," Coach calls out to her, and I feel myself tense. "Can you run some tumbling?"

Beth looks up, a strand of hair slipping from her mouth.

We all look up.

She does not remove the phone from her face.

I feel like if I were closer, I'd see her baring her teeth.

"I'd like to, ma'am," Beth shouts, in her whiniest teen girl voice, "but I only have one tampon left and I've had it in *all day*, so I think if I do mat work, it'll come loose."

We all look at Coach now, and no one says anything.

Coach, oh, Coach, why did you ask?

"Then we'll see your blood on the mat," Coach says, planting a foot on the bottom bleacher.

Oh, Coach . . . these two, toe-to-toe, puffing their chests out, practically thumping them.

"I'd like to, Coach," she says. "Really, I would. But haven't we all seen enough blood lately? Shouldn't we really be thinking of our loss?"

Coach's face motionless, but I can see something in there, something caving in deep.

Look at her, Coach, I want to say. *Look at it. See how she is fearless now. See how long she has been waiting for her chance and now she has it.*

I have to make Coach see.

And I have to keep my eyes on Beth, ceaselessly.

We drive side by side down Curling Way, Beth play-gunning the gas. We're driving out to Sutton Ridge, where the red-scalped PFC, Jimmy Tibbs, agreed to meet with Beth.

She's pumping him or someone's pumping someone, and suddenly they are like comrades, passing briefcases and taping Xs on telephone poles.

The spooky rustlings of the ridge are spookier than ever now that the air's gone cold and everything's glass-bright. Or maybe it's the cryptic pause I feel in Beth. Like a thing arrested between coming and going. Like the second before a crouch becomes a bound.

We're to meet the PFC in a clearing up by the easternmost edge, and we walk in a hush, sneakers tramping, ankles twisting on strange clumps and roots and other things of nature. Why can't the world be as flat and smooth as a spring-loaded floor, as hard and certain as a gym's merciless wood?

We hear him before we see him because someone is whistling tinnily somewhere. It seems to put a little scare even in Beth, who doesn't suffer the red-tinted terrors behind my eyes.

But we get closer and the whistle sounds more like a young boy's. A whistle to ward off demons and night terrors.

He's whistling what I finally recognize as some quavering version of "Feliz Navidad."

Waving from the clearing, he heads toward us, jogging soldier-like and extending his hand as we nudge down the crest of our twining pathway, shoes skidding.

Beth gives him her golden hand and a look of great charm, the powerful illusion of delicate girlhood.

I see how this is with them.

Beth knows her mark.

"Listen, girls, I don't want to get anyone in trouble."

His freckle-rubbed face looking rubbed twice over, the PFC paces as he talks, scratching the back of his neck until it turns red.

"He was our Sarge," he says. "And he's still Sarge to me. And I got his back."

"Of course you do," I say. "None of us want any trouble."

"But the thing is, now our superiors are involved. The Army's doing their own investigation," he says. "And we have to cooperate fully."

He looks at us and it's then I realize he knows we know about Sarge and Coach, and I am guessing Beth told him.

"We understand," Beth says, all big-eyed sympathy. "It's your duty. What choice do you have?"

"We just want what's best for Sarge," he says, nobly. "And I want to protect your . . . sarge too."

Beth nods, slowly, her slowness a hint to him that maybe she has no "sarge" other than the truth.

"So they can't rule out anything yet?" she asks, fishing. I marvel at her big-eyed frail routine. It's like she can make her body smaller somehow just standing there. She can make her rough-skinned voice go soft and helpless.

"Well, the detective said that a lot of times the autopsy only tells you so much," he says, talking slowly so we can understand. "You have to look at the behavior the weeks, days, hours leading up to the death. That's how you figure out what was going on in a guy's mind. To figure out if it's a suicide or homicide."

"Homicide?" I blurt, almost a laugh. Then it is a laugh.

He's not laughing, though.

There is a long second when both of them look at me.

"What are you two talking about?" I ask, trying to keep the laugh going.

"A young guy, prime of his life," the PFC says, swapping a grave look with faux-grave Beth, the two of them admonishing me. "There wasn't any note. They have to look at all possibilities."

"But his wife . . . he . . ."

He bows his head, sighs, then looks at me intently. "The point is, they're trying to figure out what was going on with him, they're going to ask questions, and I've got to answer them."

I look at him, at Beth squirming delightedly beside him. These two. Who do they think they are, citizen soldier and good Samaritan?

"Just say it. You're going to tell them about how it was," I say. "With Coach."

"I have to."

I look at him, a bristling rising up in me.

"Sorry," I say, after a pause. "I was just thinking of the last time I saw you. Watching me knot this one's legs together in the parking lot of the Comfort Inn."

He looks at me, stricken.

"But back to your point," I say. "Yes, I guess you're going to tell him everything then. Like about all the booze you fed us, even fourteen-year-olds. You do know that JV is fourteen. And about Prine."

The PFC's face bursts redder than ever, a blaring siren.

Beth harrumphs like she's both annoyed and impressed. *My lieutenant, my lieutenant.*

"Girl looks out for her Coach, like she's a mama tit," Beth says to PFC, shrugging. "Point is, scrub, we all wanna protect our top dogs."

The PFC grates the back of his scarlet neck till it blazes, then nods, white at the mouth. White at the mouth like he's a little scared of both of us. Like he might need to start whistling again.

That word *homicide* snakes through my brain, its tail snapping back and forth.

Walking side by side back to the car, Beth twirls a finger through the bottom of my braid.

"Foul play," I say, eyes rolling.

"He's no JV runt, Hanlon," she says. "You get more honey from that hive if you buzz softly in his ear. You with your fucking chainsaw. Bringing up the Comfort Inn."

"I studied at the feet of the master lumberjack," I say, sounding like no one if not Beth.

"But our goal isn't to intimidate into silence," she says. "It's to find out what happened." She looks at me. "Isn't that right?"

Of course this is neither of our goals.

"And I'm sure Coach above all wants to know what happened to her man," she says, dipping her head closer to mine, so enjoying all this. "I'm sure she'll be grateful to know. I'm surprised you're not more eager to help her."

"I don't want him getting any of us in trouble," I say. "I'm looking out for the squad."

"Spoken like a born captain," she says, grinning. "I always knew you wanted to be captain."

"I never did," I say, turning from her to continue down the trail. It's so dark now, and I can hear her behind me.

"Of course not," she is saying, and I can hear a grin on her.

She's wrong, I never did. Not once. It was hard enough being lieutenant.

"Besides," she says, sidling next to me, "it *does* seem weird, now that I think of it. A man in the prime of his life. And *bang, bang,* puts a gun to his temple?"

"His mouth," I correct her.

As the words come out I feel myself go ice cold.

"His mouth?" Beth asks, lightning quick.

My whole life with Beth, under the hot lights. Standing beside her as she hotlights someone else.

"That's what I read, I think," I stumble. "Wasn't it his mouth?"

With her or against her, you better be on. Game on. Like when you're out there, grandstands thrumming, sneakers squeaking on polished floor, and you gotta fake-smile till it hurts. Till you want to die from it.

Ramrod that back, hoist those tits, be ready, always. Because she always is.

"I don't know, Addy," she says, her eyes on me. "Was it Sarge's mouth?"

"No," I say. "I've got it all wrong. I'm blood-sugar bottomed-out." I begin tugging my braid loose, bobby pins flying, scattering to the ground.

I can almost feel her disappointment at how poorly I've kept up with her, stayed in the game.

For hours after, I'm cursing myself for ever thinking I could run with Beth, for thinking I could keep up.

If you could have seen him, I want to say to Beth, you would know it was suicide. You would see. If you saw that dark smudge where his face was ... you would feel his desperation and surrender.

Wouldn't you?

Is that what I felt?

I'm not so sure.

I think briefly, darkly, of that apartment, legions deep now in my head. A glugging, boggy cove in the center of the earth.

Still, to me, it had felt like stepping in the marsh swirl of a man underwater, a man drowning.

Hadn't it?

It had felt bad. That's what I knew. It had felt like the worst place I'd ever been—and now that place, it was inside of me.

That night, at last, Coach calls.

"Addy, why don't you come over?" The warmth in her voice, and the desperation. "Stay at my place tonight. Matt's out of town, remember? It's so lonely."

I can't guess at the haunted feeling in her, given how it is with me. I'm glad to know she's feeling these things, because you'd never know it to look at her.

"I'll make us avocado shakes and we'll sing Caitlin to sleep and drag the velvet blankets out on the deck and wrap ourselves in them and look at the stars. Or something," she says, trying so hard.

I'd've dreamed of such courtship a month ago, and something about it does speak to me even amid all this, maybe even especially. It's a singular and troubling stake we share, but it binds us always, doesn't it? A stake that gives me new panics by the hour, yes, but now, for the first time, it warms me too.

So I go, but Caitlin's already asleep and Coach doesn't have any avocados, and it's raining slimily on the deck.

As I dangle on a kitchen island stool, without purpose, she makes a grocery list. She pays an electricity bill. She wrings out kitchen towels, twisting them across her hands and staring vaguely out the window over the sink.

It's almost like Coach doesn't want me there at all now that I'm here.

It's as if I remind her of bad things.

Once, I come back from the bathroom and see her looking at my phone, resting on the kitchen island.

"Can you just turn it off?" she says. "You didn't tell anyone you were here, right?"

I say no.

She pauses, fingertips still grazing the phone. Watching as I turn it all the way off, waiting for the screen to go blank.

"Oh, Addy," she finally says, "let's do something, anything."

And this is how we end up in the backyard close to midnight, doing backbends in the rain. Extended triangles. Dolphin plank poses.

There's a holiness to it, the wind chimes on the deck carrying us off to the deepest Himalayan climes, or wherever the world is peaceful and clear.

We sweat even in the cold, and I catch, amid a streak of light from some passing car out front, Coach's face looking untroubled and free.

The crying starts just after, when we're back in the house. Walking down the hallway, she bends over at the waist and sobs come hard and hurtful. I hold onto her shoulders, their tensile thew rocking in my hands.

She stops in the middle of the hall and I try to hold on and she cries for a very long time.

I sleep next to her that night, under that big dolloping duvet.

We face opposite directions and I think, this is where Matt

French sleeps, and I think how big the bed is and how far away Coach is, the duvet snowbanking in the middle, and if she's still crying, I wouldn't know.

It makes me feel lonely for both of them.

Sometime in the night, I hear her talking, her voice hard and strangled.

"How could you do this to me?" she snarls. "How?"

I glance over at her, and her eyes almost look open, her fists wrenching the covers.

I don't know who she's talking to.

People say all kinds of things when they're dreaming.

"I'm not doing anything," I whisper, as if she were talking to me.

22

Turning my phone on, seven a.m., I see our squad Facebook
page studded with new wall posts, from Brinnie, Mindy, RiRi:

Monday=FINAL GAME!

Go Eagles!

Slaussen, you better KICK ass! Our ticket to the tourney is on YOU!

I long to be a part of it. I long for it.

I find Coach in the kitchen, making toaster oven waffles for
Caitlin, who chews on the bottom of her pigtail and watches the
oven's orange glow, hypnotized.

"Did the phone wake you?" she asks, spoon in hand, slicing a
banana over Caitlin's pearly lavender plate.

It's then that I realize it did.

"I have to go talk to them at the station again," she says, her
eyes graying. "In a half hour."

"They're talking to the Guardsmen," I say quietly, as if Caitlin
might understand if I spoke more loudly. "The redhead PFC.
Tibbs."

The spoon, banana-slicked, slips from her grasp.

She pauses a beat, her hand still outstretched.

I go to reach for the spoon, but her hand shoots out to stop me. "They have to talk to his men," she says. "I figured on that."

"But, Coach," I say, with as much knowingness as I can impart. "No one wants to get anyone in trouble. *No one* does."

She looks at me, searchingly, and I'm not sure why I'm being so mysterious—something about Beth, eyes on the back of her ponytail, something about Caitlin's blinking stare.

"There's plenty of trouble to go around," she says, holding my gaze.

"Right," I say. "I'm sure that's what everyone realizes."

"Is that what PFC Tibbs realizes?" she says.

"I think so," I say.

But Coach must see something on me, some dread gathering under my skin.

"So what might make the PFC share such details with you?" she asks, her sticky hands still lifted in front of her, her body frozen.

"He shares them with Beth," I say, after the quickest of pauses. It still feels queasy to tell her, but it would feel queasy not to.

It takes her a second for this new bit of knowledge to descend.

"It's Beth," I repeat.

"Got it," she says, those slippery hands still raised up, like a doctor ready for surgery. Ready to lay his hands upon your heart.

In the first-floor corridor, after second period, after her visit to the police station:

"It's fine," Coach says, brisking by me. Her French braid is very tight, temple vein pulsing. "No problems. It's all good."

After lunch, Beth finds me in the school library, where I never go and where no one should ever have thought to look. But she looks.

"Back in my day, libraries had books," she says, as we internet surf side by side at tall terminals, "and we walked five miles in the snow to school."

"So that's how you got such thick ankles," I say, clicking aimlessly through sundry nothingness. Celebrity crotch shots, Thinspiration: Secrets to Fasting Only Anas Know.

"The PFC went in this morning," she says. "He told me his sad, sad song over malteds."

"And?" I say, twirling my finger in ballerina circles over the touch pad.

"He said they'd called Coach in."

"Yeah, she told me. It went fine." I don't look at her. I don't like the feeling that's coming, that prickling in my forehead.

"Ah...," she says, and though I'm not looking, I know she's smiling, can hear the gum clicking to the corner of her grinning mouth.

It reminds me of the time Beth's mother swore to me over her morning coffee that Beth was born with sharp teeth.

Better to drink the blood of JVs, Beth had said.

"So," Beth says now, "what has Coach told you about the hamsa bracelet?"

"What hamsa bracelet?" I say, fingers to my forehead.

"The one they found in Will's apartment."

I click on the ad for Wu Long Vanishing Tea.

"Wait a minute," she says, smacking her head. "Didn't you have one of those bracelets? The one you gave to Coach. Back in your puppy dog phase. To ward off the evil eyes of wronged husbands, I suppose."

I look at her. I hadn't even realized Beth knew about the bracelet.

"What about it?"

"Well, I guess she must have left it at Will's, at some point," Beth says. "During some ... encounter."

"Lots of people have those bracelets," I say.

She looks at me, and something pinches in my chest, a memory of something, a connection. But I can't hold on to it. She's watching me so closely, but I can't grab it.

"Do they think it's hers?" I say.

"*Is* it hers, Addy?" Beth asks, her left eyebrow lifting. "She must have told you they asked her about it. You two thick as thieves."

"We haven't really had a chance to talk," I say, holding tight to the edge of the terminal.

"Well, she's pretty busy," Beth says, with a slow nod. "Four days to the Big Game and all."

Turning away from the terminal, she flings one golden leg onto the nearest library tabletop.

"Look how tight I am," she says, surveying herself. "I'll grant Coach that. But you think Li'l Tacy Cottontail's up for Top Girl? The balance is all. One of her calves is bigger than the other. Did you ever notice that?"

"No."

"I bet you have. Your balance is impeccable. Four inches shorter, you would've been a perfect Top Girl."

I pause a second.

"The PFC doesn't know she has one, does he?" I ask.

"Has what?" Beth asks, maddeningly, surveying my legs now with her cold captain-appraisal gaze.

"A hamsa bracelet," I say, fighting a panicky tilt in my voice.

"Not now, Adelaide," she says. "Not yet."

I grab my books and start to walk away.

"You're going to have to forget how pretty and interested she is in you, Addy," she calls after me.

Walking out, I hear her all the way.

"Tighten that gut, Addy. Lock those legs. Smile, smile, smile!"

Everyone is looking at me, but I only look straight ahead.

"Remember what old Coach Templeton used to say, Addy!"

I push open the shuddering glass exit doors.

"A good cheerleader," she is calling out, "is not measured by the height of her jumps but by the span of her spirit."

23

"Four days, bitches!!" shouts Mindy.

RiRi is doing waist bends, flashing her panties, this time lined with sparkles.

The JV is clicking through YouTube on her laptop for the Celts squad's stunts.

Paige Shepherd is twanging— *"Ima go for the gold, heart is in control, I'm a go, I'm a go I'm a go getta"*—lifting one long leg into a Bow 'n' Arrow.

Cori Brisky shushes her hair up into her trademark extra-long white-blond pony whip, famous across three school districts.

Everything is as it ever was.

Still ground-bound since her spectacular fall, gimpy Emily is passing around the temporary tattoos she ordered for the squad. She has one on the apple of either cheek and she's dotted her knee brace with them. Which all seems sad to me, like she's our mascot. No one respects a mascot.

We all feel sorry for her. She can't even hall-stalk with us, can't keep up with that club boot, and has already become a recruiting target of lacrosse players and the golf team, which could not be sadder, and of the predatory courtship of the field hockey furies, promising to get her knees skinned.

I remember, sort of, being friends with her. Holding her hair back while she gagged herself pea-shoot thin. Even calling her at night instead of Beth, confiding things. But now I don't know what we'd talk about.

At three twenty Coach, chin high, strolls through the doors to the gym.

Beth, standing in front of the mirror, doesn't even look up, too busy oil-slicking her lashes with a mascara brush, no cares furrowing her face.

"I have some news, guys," she says.

I reach out to hold onto my locker door.

"I heard from my source at State Quals. There's gonna be a scout at Monday's game. We rock them, we're rocking Regionals next year."

Everyone whoops and woo-hoos, jumping on the bleachers, grabbing each other around the necks like the ball-ers do.

Poor boot-braced Emily bursts into tears.

"By next year you'll be flying again," RiRi says, hand to her shoulder.

"But not on Monday," she whimpers. "That won't be mine."

"Let's focus," Coach says, clapping her hands sharply.

We snap front.

Looking at her, I can't fathom it. I'd never guess anything else was going on at all. She is ready to ride us. She is sweatless and bolt-straight.

"We need to think about the Celts," Mindy says.

The Celts squad has serious game, famous for their facial expressions, head bobs and tongues stuck out and dropped jaws and wide eyes when their Flyers hit, when they spring back, the crowd gasping ah, ah, ah.

"They do two-girl Awesomes," Brinnie Cox says with a sigh, which is how she says everything. "A girl my size can catch both the Flyer's feet in one palm."

"Their facials are hot," RiRi admits.

"I don't care about their wiggling tongues or bouncing pony-tails," says Coach. "I don't care about the Celts at all. All I care about is that Regionals scout. The scout's gotta see our star power."

We all look uneasily at Tacy.

"Your Flyer isn't your key to the castle," Coach says. "It's about the squad. You gotta show you're the posse straight from hell. And there's only one way to do it. We're going to give that scout something that will guarantee our slot. We're going to show her a two-two-one."

The two-two-one.

It will be our shining achievement, if we nail it.

Three stories high of golden girls, two Bottom Bases holding up two Middle Bases in shoulder stands, the Flyer tossed through the center, Bottom Bases platforming her feet, the Middle Bases' arms lifted to hold her arms outstretched, crucifixion style. Spotters standing behind, waiting for the Flyer's death-defying Deadman fall.

It's illegal in competition, but not at a game.

And it's the kind of stunt you need to nail to make it to Regionals. To a tourney.

"Cap'n," Coach says, looking up at Beth, halfway up the bleachers again, her hovering black presence. "All yours today. Drill them hard."

She tosses Beth the whistle.

Beth, one eyebrow raised, catches it.

In an instant, a flare of energy seems to shoot up her body, that sullen slouch uncoiling for the first time in months, since... I can't even remember.

Coach has just handed her the Big Stick, and thank god she still seems to think it worth taking.

"Gimme some handsprings, bitches," Beth says, making her slow, willowy way down the stands, arms dangling, snapping her fingers low.

"Don't fuck with me, RiRi," she says. "Loose limbs may fly for your Saturday night specials, but I need you tight as a cherry. Time-travel me back."

So Beth wrangles us for a while, and it does feel good. And Beth is so on, so animated.

She is enthroned and magnificent.

At some point, I see Coach slink into her office.

Later, while Beth's busy trash-talking Tacy for a weak back tuck, calling her a sad little pussy, I slip over and peer in, see Coach on the phone, her hand over her eyes.

I think: it's the cops. It's the cops. What now?

An hour in, we're ready to run the two-two-one pyramid.

Because I'm not too big and not too small, I'm a Middle Base, one of the two shoulder stands in the middle.

Beneath me stands eagle-shouldered Mindy Coughlin, my feet curled around her collarbone, her body bracing.

But I think it's worse for me, no floor beneath me, and ninety-four pounds of quaking panic above.

Once we're up, Tacy will get rocketed between RiRi and me, and we will grab her legs and lock her body in place.

Then she'll wow them all, flipping backwards into a Deadman, falling into the waiting embrace of the cradle-armed spotters fifteen feet below.

Everyone will gasp, grip their bleacher seats.

The Deadman, that's our moment of shock and awe.

Despite what Coach says, it really is all about the Flyer.

We can hold her steady as she comes, but if Tacy wobbles, twists, turns the wrong way: snap, crackle, pop.

Which is probably why she looks like a doomed tail gunner waiting to be wedged into a quaking turret.

"You all need to man up for Slaussen," Beth tells us. "Or she'll be mat-kill. Two years ago, at the Viking game, I saw a girl jiggle just an inch up there. Her girls didn't have her. Smack! Her neck hit the ground, skidded so hard that a piece of her blond ponytail ripped from her scalp."

Tacy's face goes from green to white to gray. Beth, with that power to annihilate with a single breath. Two months ago, Tacy galloped hard at Beth's side, lackey under her mighty sway. Oh, the turns of fortune...

Eyes on Tacy's toned legs, which look like mini-butterfingers, Beth shakes her head.

I realize she's right. One calf is bigger than the other.

"You always were such a hoodrat," Beth says, shaking her head. "Always quick to hoist your legs in the air for my sloppy seconds. But I guess you were only hoisting the left one."

Beth kneels down on the mat in front of Tacy's dainty body.

Then, she wets her finger and runs it along Tacy's thigh and calf.

We all observe, like watching a gang recruit get jumped in.

"I thought so," Beth says, rising and wiggling her index finger, smudged with what looks to me like Mystic Island Radiance. "All the spray tan in the world won't give you what you don't have. You either have muscle or you have twig. Or, in your case, Q-tip."

"I can do it, Beth," Tacy says, voice pitching high. "Coach knows. I've earned my spot."

"Then let's see it, meat," she says, standing back. "Make a believer out of me."

Stepping back, she turns the speakers up and our game music, bawdy pop with baby-doll vocals cut through with a molasses-throated rap, *"Get down, girl, go 'head get down."*

I swing up to Middle Base, above Mindy's ramming shoulder, her hand foisting up, palm spreading over my bottom.

At that moment, Coach walks back into the gym.

"You got it, Slaussen," Coach nods, strolling past Beth to the back of the pyramid. Hearing her, such a relief. "You nailed it once, you'll nail it again."

Coach inexplicably becoming the good cop in this strange new world.

But RiRi, the other Middle Base, and I feel a joint twinge, our eyes on Tacy's legs, like little cinnamon sticks that might snap.

When we raise her up, air-puff light, she is shaking like a bob-blehead doll, like Emily was. I can feel her try to make herself tight, can feel it radiating through me, but the cartoon terror eyes put a chill in me.

"Ride that bitch," Beth's voice booms at us. "Ride it."

Our arms shaking, we've got to lock it in place, but it's not locking. It's like trying to make a pair of gummy worms stand straight.

We bring her back down for a second.

"She can't do it," Beth pronounces. "Either no two-two-one or we need a new Flyer."

We are all quiet.

Suddenly, RiRi's voice rises from behind me. "What about Addy?"

I turn around and look at her, my heart speeding up. She smiles and winks.

"What if Addy were Top Girl?"

Coach looks over at me, eyebrows raised. I feel Beth's gaze on me too.

"Addy doesn't like to be on top," Beth says, poker-faced.

"Hey!" Tacy cries. "I've been flying all season."

Coach nods. "It's something to think about, long haul," she says. "But for now we need Addy right where she is, in the middle. She's our spine."

I don't like all the eyes on me. I wish RiRi had never said anything.

It doesn't matter anyway because, a second later, everyone is just looking at Tacy again.

"She can't, Coach," says Beth, as simply as she's ever said anything.

My hands fresh off Tacy's kindling hipbone, I feel certain Beth is right.

"Look at her," Beth scoffs. "She's not trained up."

These are fighting words and we all know it. It's spit in the eye to any coach.

"She just wants my spot, Coach," Tacy nearly whimpers. "I can do it. Elevator me up again."

"Slaussen?" Coach looks over at Tacy. "Are you ready?"

"Yes!"

Beth sighs loudly. "What happens," she practically sings, "when a pretty young coach takes a ragtag team of misfits and feebs under her wing? Why, they fly, fly, fly."

Coach looks at her.

"We just needed someone to believe in us," Beth finishes.

"Stop gaming her, Cassidy," Coach says, staring her down, duel-at-dawn, but her tone still flat, toneless, "or I'm gonna ground-bound you instead."

"Look at her leg," Beth says, "like a wishbone twanging."

"Cassidy," Coach says, like she's forgotten the caution she's supposed to use with Beth, or she's just stopped caring. "When you start showing me you can do more than flash your tits and treat your mouth like a sewer, then maybe we'll have something to talk about."

Don't, Coach, I think. *Don't.*

"You heard the coach," Beth says, turning to us with a smile. "Load her up and let her fall."

The music thumping again, Beth counting off, Mindy and Cori line up, Bottom Bases. Spotters Paige and a JV stand behind them and load up the second level, RiRi and me, our bodies springing up to shoulder stands, their palms cradling our calves.

Facing each other, we lift Tacy between us, throwing her above us into a stand, our arms lifted high, hands tight on her wrists. Her arms outstretched, Jesus-style, her left leg knee-bent in front of her, the girls beneath grasping her right foot to hold her in place.

For a second, she is solid.

Seven, eight, Beth counting off until the Deadman and it is time. Time for us to drop her backwards into a stiff-spined horizontal fall. Ready for Paige, the JV, all her spotters to catch her down below.

We let go.

Her eyes wild, Tacy drops, but her body seems to rubberize, limbs like spaghetti. As her hand grapples for me, I feel myself sliding down with her, Paige and Cori, on the ground, shouting, "Slaus, here, here, here. Hold it!"

But she plunges, our hands empty.

The sickly sound as Tacy, still half in Paige's sloping arms, hits the mat, face first.

RiRi and I still on high, I think my knees might give, but I hear Coach's voice, iron smooth, "Hanlon, slow down that dismount," as RiRi and I sink down.

I feel something clamping on me, and Beth is right there, her hand gripping my arm all the way down. Depositing me safely on the mat, feet first.

Coach is on the floor with Tacy, strewn from the spotters' tangled arms, her feet still in their grip even as her head, neck tilted, her chin split wide open, swabs the mat.

"At least she can fall well," RiRi mutters.

Her mouth opening in a strangled sob, Tacy's teeth blare bright red.

"You come at the king," Beth says, "you best not miss."

RiRi and I take Tacy to Nurse Vance, who slaps on the butterfly bandages and tells me to take Tacy to the hospital for stitches, which sends her into a new round of sobs.

"Your modeling career is over," I say.

Walking to her locker, Tacy is purple-lipped and cotton-tufted, crying about the Game and the scouts and how she's *got* to do the two-two-one, she's the only one light enough, which isn't even true, and Coach damn well better let her cheer, no matter what she looks like.

Then, a new sob choking in her, she takes a deep breath.

"But it should be Beth anyway," she whispers, dramatically. "Beth's Top Girl."

For a second, I hear RiRi. *What about Addy? What if Addy were Top Girl?*

But it never has been me, has it? I never wanted it to. I was never a stunter, I was a spotter, a hoister. That's what I am.

And Top Girls were different from the rest of us.

I think of Beth last year, after the Norsemen game, all of us drinking with the players up on the ridge, and Brian Brun thrusting her above his head, hands gripping around her ankles, her feet tucked in his palms, then one leg flung behind her, rendering her celebrated Bow 'n' Arrow, as she spun and lifted her right leg straight in the air, slipping it behind her glossy head, making one beautiful line of Bethness, all of us gasping.

It's all we could talk about, dream about, for days, weeks.

"It's always been Beth," she slurs, grazing her temple with the back of her wrist. "And the squad is what counts. Cheer, I never knew it mattered so much. Not until Coach picked me. She changed my life. Now it's all I can think about, Addy. I hear the counts in my sleep. Don't you? I don't ever want them to end."

I tell her to stop talking.

"Don't you see, Addy?" she says, words tumbling in her mouth, eyes shiny and crazed. "When we go out there Monday night, we need to show them what we can do. What we are. We need to make them know it. We need to give them more than awesomeness.

"We need to give them greatness."

It hurts to turn the steering wheel. I can still feel Tacy's grasping fingers, the fear my arm socket might pop. The sound of Beth saying, "Ride that bitch ... ride her."

And Beth, the way her hand fastened on me, stopping my fall.

And after, Coach saying, as I walked the limping Tacy across the gym, "Next time, Hanlon, when you let her go, keep those arms to the side. Don't let her see your hands are there. If she does, she'll grab for them. Wouldn't you?"

Wouldn't you? I want to ask.

I think of injured Emily again, withering up in the stands. And I remember how, last week, she posted on my Facebook wall: "U never call me anymore. None of U." And I decided it was a joke, one of Emily's endless LOLs.

I couldn't be bothered.

At the games she sits, just barely separated from the bleacher crowd—in the borderland, the nowhere zone between our bronzed glory and the gray blur of everything, everyone else in this sad world.

At home later:

U put a hex on Slaus, I text Beth.

U shoulda given *her* the hamsa, she replies.

Like at a hypnotist's cue, my head floods with the image of my bracelet in Will's apartment. A crimson ring on his carpet.

But I keep hearing Beth's words in my head: . . . *Coach must've told you they asked her about the bracelet. You two thick as thieves.*

Why hasn't Coach told me?

I think I should just call her and ask her about it. But I don't.

I want her to tell me.

It doesn't mean anything if I have to ask her.

A blipping text message comes hours later, but it's from Beth: **Guess who's flying Mon nite?**

Tacy's out, Beth's in. A peculiar mix of terror and relief floods through me—and then the taunting mystery of what kind of conversation transpired between Beth and Coach during those hours after practice to lead to this.

R U happy now? I text back.

But there's no reply.

It's the dark muddle of the night when I feel the phone hissing in my hand.

Come outside.

I flick my blinds with a finger and see a car out front, Coach behind the wheel.

The cold grass crunching under my feet, I bound across the lawn.

We sit in the car, which is Matt French's and isn't as nice as Coach's car. It smells like cigarettes, though I've never seen Matt French smoke.

The cup holder is stained with three, four coffee rings like the center of an old tree.

Something's wreathing my ankle, maybe the hand loops of a plastic bag, or the curled edges of an old receipt, some stray Matt Frenchness left behind.

Something about how messy the car is makes me feel things, like that time I saw him, after midnight, drooped over a bowl of cereal, and understood it was his dinner, that gritty bowl of Coach's special holistic blend of organic gravel, soot, and matches, and Matt French hunched over it by himself on the kitchen island, socked feet dangling, headphones on, tuning out all our hysteria and gum chewing.

And now. Poor Matt, in some airport or office tower in Georgia, some conference room someplace where men like Matt French go to do whatever it is they do, which is not interesting to any of us, but maybe it would be if we knew. Though I doubt it.

Except sometimes I think of him, and the soulful clutter in his eyes, which is not like Will's eyes were because Will's eyes always seemed about Will. And Matt French's seem only about Coach.

"He's still gone?" I ask.

"Gone?" she asks, looking at me quizzically.

"Matt," I say.

She pauses. "Oh," she says, turning her face away for a second. "Yeah."

As if he were an afterthought.

Hands curling around the steering wheel, she says, "There's something new, Addy."

The bracelet, she's going to tell me at last.

"The police," she says. "I think they're hearing things. They asked me what the nature of our relationship was. That's how they put it."

"Oh," I say.

"I told them again that we were friends. They're probably just trying to understand his state of mind."

"Oh," I repeat.

"They had a lot of new questions about the last contact I'd had with him. I think they—and the Guard—they want to understand how he might have come to this," she says.

The words don't feel like hers, exactly. So formal, her mouth moving slowly around them like they don't fit.

"I'm sure it's fine, Addy," she says, her fingers clenching tighter. "But it seemed like I should tell you."

"I'm glad you told me," I say. But she hasn't told me anything. "Is that all?"

As if sensing my disappointment, she pats me on the shoulder.

"Addy, nothing can really happen if we keep tight," she says, resting her fingers there. I don't remember her ever touching me like that. "Keep strong. Focus. After all, it's just you and me who know everything."

"Right," I say. And I want to feel the dazey warmth of sharing things with her, but she's not sharing, not really, and so all I feel is Beth, the way she seems now, crouched, watchful, hovering.

"So we're good?" she asks.

Part of me wants to tell her everything, all the ways she needs to watch for Beth, knives out. But she's telling me only what she wants to. So I don't say any more.

"I gave it to Beth," Coach says, reading my thoughts, like she can. Like they both can. "She's Top Girl. She's flying at the final game."

Coach, I want to say, what makes you think you can stop there? You have to give her everything until we figure out what she wants. Until she does.

"First I made her captain. Now I've made her Top Girl," she says, eyes on me, searching.

She didn't make me Top Girl, I can hear Beth saying. *I made me Top Girl. I made myself.*

She loops her fingers around the gearshift.

"I don't know what else to do," she says, a slightly stunned look on her face. "Jesus, she's just a seventeen-year-old kid. Why should I..."

There's a pause.

"She'll get bored with it all," she says, as if trying to convince herself. "They always do."

At home that night I spend an hour, forehead nearly pressed to my laptop screen, reading the news.

No Answers Yet: Guardsman Cause of Death Still Under Investigation.

What would it mean if it were murder? What does it have to do with Coach, with me?

Coach, Coach, like my very own sergeant, who took me straight into the fog of war...

I wanted to be a part of your world, but I didn't know your world was this.

That night, I dream about that time with Beth, the first drunk I ever had, both of us climbing up Black Ash Ridge. She kept saying, *Are you sure you're ready, Addy. Are you?* And I promised I was, our heads schnapps-fuzzed and our bodies ecstatic. She said, *But you're not afraid, Addy, are you? Show me that lion heart.*

Later, I remember falling back, great big Xs for eyes and half delirious, and Beth crawling over to me, her shirt off and flaming red bra. She says she will stop me from log-rolling to my death. She promises she will save me, us.

Just don't look down, Addy, just never look down.

...and her voice, like it was coming from a deep gorge inside me, vibrating through my chest, my throat, my head, my heart.

When you gaze into the Abyss, Addy, she says, her eyes glowing above me like two blazing stars, laughing or even crying, *the Abyss gazes into you.*

24

"Guess what I'm doing?" Beth asks, calling me crack-o-dawn, while I'm standing at the mirror, trying to make my face over candy-clean. Streaming petal pink across my cheeks, my eyelids, slashing it across my trembling lips.

I don't say anything. I don't like the way her voice sounds. Cat-and-canary-like.

"I'm reading the newspaper. I thought the old lady would faint. She said, 'Do you even know what that *is,* darling daughter?' Oh, the morning wit in the Cassidy household."

"Mmm."

"'A National Guard source indicated increasing doubt that the Sergeant's death was suicide,'" she reads. "'Results from a gunshot residue test on the victim's hands showed only trace amounts.'"

I don't say anything.

"Oh, and turns out you were right," she says, pausing as if taking a bite. I have a sudden image of raw meat shearing between her teeth. "It was a gunshot to the mouth, not the temple. You said you were confused, but it turns out you weren't confused at all, Addy."

★   ★   ★

The dying fluorescent lights buzz above me mercilessly.

I'm in the first-floor girls' room, second stall, having just thrown up, my right cheekbone resting on the porcelain. I'd forgotten what that kind of throwing up could be like, the kind where you're not, Emily-style, nuzzling your finger down your fishtailing throat, begging for release from the dreaded sluice of cupcakes or from the acidic sludge of too many Stoli Citronas—cheer beer, they call it, we call it. No, this is throwing up like coming off the tilt-a-whirl at age seven, like discovering that dead rat under the porch, like finding out someone you loved never loved you at all.

Now I'm sitting on the floor of the stall, damp newspaper still folded in my hands, the smeary sentences:

"...While police would not comment on reports of conflicting evidence at the scene, a source close to the investigation questioned the position of the weapon near the body. Recoil will usually cause a handgun to land behind the body, the source noted, not next to his head where it was found."

I feel my stomach turn again.

Suddenly, Beth is there, standing above me, handing me a long sheaf of paper towels, still billowing, untorn, from the dispenser.

At first, I think I'm hallucinating.

"You wait your whole life for something to happen," she's saying, her face virtuous, princess-like, under the rimy fluorescents. "Then, suddenly, it's all the terrors of the earth all at once. Is that how it feels to you, Addy?"

She winds the trail of paper towel around me, leans down, dangling one edge into my sick-moist mouth.

"I'm just sick," I say. "It's nothing."

She smiles, tapping the newspaper in my blackened hands.

"I keep waiting for them to write about that hamsa bracelet," she says. "Put a picture of it to see if anyone recognizes it."

"They don't write about it because it's not important," I say. "They know it could've been left there anytime."

"It could've been. Except it wasn't," she says.

"How do you know?" I say, a fresh round of dread rising in me.

"Because of where they found it," she says. "Or didn't our fearless leader tell you?"

"Where they found it . . . ?" I say, fighting the moan in my voice.

"Under Sarge's body," she says. "PFC told me. Riddle me that."

Her smile is so faint and yet so piercing, I feel I may go blind.

And the picture in my head, that nubbed carpet, Will's spent body, head black like a mussel's glistening shell.

Under his body.

"It doesn't matter," I say, shaking my head quickly, my words coming faster and faster. "Maybe it was lying there from before, kicked there."

"Hanlon," she says, bending down, a waft of coconut and sweet vanilla, her girliest perfume, worn only on days of biggest trouble and mayhem. "You should be careful here. After all, you may have given it to her, but it is *your* bracelet."

"Everyone knows I gave it to her," I blurt. Which is true, but I realize I've given Beth a new gift. Shown her a crack in the armor.

I'm ashamed of myself.

Smiling down at me, she extends her hand, but I don't take it.

"I know what she means to you, Addy," she says, hand dropping. "But this is bigger than your virgin crush. You best watch your back."

My head jerks up, smacking the wall tile.

"This is epic," she continues. "This is too big to girl out on me. Sack up."

She starts telling me about a show she saw on truTV about a man whose wife killed herself, or so it seemed. It turned out he'd murdered her.

"You know how they knew? Her teeth. They were all fucked up, like the gun had been forced in there."

The blade through the center of me is sharp and exacting.

"What's that got to do with anything?" I whisper.

"PFC and his captain ID'd the body. They said Sarge's top front teeth were shattered. Caps, by the way. In case you want to know."

I don't say anything. I'm picturing Will confiding in us at Lanvers Peak, showing us his counterfeit smile, like taking off a beautiful mask and revealing a more beautiful one underneath.

"So someone jammed a gun in Will's mouth," she says, tapping her own front teeth, I can hear the clack, "against those ivory tusks of his and went... *POW.*"

Sliding back against the wall, I am too weary for her.

"That's not right, Beth," I say. "He jammed it there himself."

"How do you know?" she says, laughing with a kind of giddiness rare and unnerving in Beth. "Were you there?"

In class, in the hallways, trying to shake off Beth's sly hustle, the way she can whip me up into it with her, the way it can sweep through my body, like a fever.

What does she know? I think. She's just guessing. Wanting.

But the bracelet, the bracelet. *Under* his body.

There are a million explanations, I tell myself. And Coach will tell me, she will.

This isn't like before, when the boom of Beth's voice in my head could drown everything else out.

Once it was, and I did what she said. Even last summer, at cheer camp, when she told me about Casey Jaye and how Casey was lying about me behind my back. Finally I believed her. I surrendered to it.

But not this time. There's things I've seen that she hasn't. Lanvers Peak, the three of us there, Coach, Will, and me. The way the two of them nestled around me, knowing I'd take care of them. The smell of burning leaves, the way we shared it, that sense of a lost world of beauty and wonder.

The three of us, what we shared. It was a fleeting thing, but it has a radiant power. It is something just mine, and I won't have her take it from me.

And the boom of Beth's voice isn't enough to make me give it up.

Because Coach would never let anything happen to me.

You can, she told us, *fall eleven feet and still land safely on a spring floor.*

Except later that day, in English class, Beth's text popping up in my phone. The link to the second article, *Hunt for Answers at The Towers.*

It will not stop now.

It talks about police going door-to-door, interviewing every resident in the apartment building.

And about how lab technicians are going through everything found in the apartment, pulling up carpet samples.

My flip-flops, did they leave a print?

But I remember Coach, with what I now recognize as a stunning presence of mind, had us both remove our shoes. Staggering presence of mind, really.

But then the article says, in a throwaway line, the last in the piece:

"Detectives will be reviewing security camera footage of the lobby."

Security camera footage of the lobby.
Coach and I padding out, her sneakers in hand, at two thirty a.m.
I feel a curtain fall over me.
A second text from Beth, just three words this time:
Truth will out!

In Coach's office, blinds pulled tight.
She's behind her desk, my phone lying on the blotter in front of her.
I have never cried in Coach's office and I don't intend to now.
"Beth sent this article to you?" she says, nodding to herself.
"Yes, yes," I say, waving my finger at the phone screen. "Security camera, Coach."
"What about it," she says. "If they'd seen me on that camera, don't you think they would have said so?"
What about *me,* I want to say. But don't.
"Coach," I say, trying again. "They think it's murder."
"It's not murder," Coach says, with such firmness, flicking my phone with her fingers, swatting at it like a fly. "You can't let them scare you, Addy. The Guard's looking out for themselves. It's all about bad publicity."
I don't say anything.
"Addy," Coach says. "Look at me."
I do.
"Don't you think I'd like to believe more than anything that Will didn't do that to himself? To me?"
I nod.
Something creaks open in her, a place she does not want to go.
"We saw him, Addy," she says, her fingertips to her mouth, her face sheeting white. "We saw what he did."

I want to hold tight to her hand and say soft things.

"Addy," she says feverishly, her fingers fisting. "You have to understand. People will always try to scare you into things. Scare you away from things. Scare you into not wanting things you can't help wanting. You can't be afraid."

"Three days left!" shouts Mindy. "I hear scouts *always* sit high left in the bleachers. We gotta work toward that corner."

My chest lifts. Our weird little universe where a word from Mindy Coughlin, her face red and brutish, can suddenly make me care again about the Big Game. Our qualifying shot.

But Coach is nowhere to be found.

"Why does she keep going away?" Tacy asks, mouth muffled with bandages. She's standing next to Cori, who's rotating her left wrist anxiously, taped tight where wavering Tacy's foot lodged.

And Emily. Gimpy Emily, still boot-braced, near forgotten.

This array of casualties, and I wonder how I'm still standing.

We happy few, we band of bitches, Beth used to say. Don't you forget it.

As if on cue, Beth strolls in front of us, hip-slinging gangsta.

"Let's get started, kitties," Beth says. "The Celts wait for no sad-ass chicken hearts."

This, I think, is good for her. I think, *Yes. Yes, Beth. Take it and let it feed you. Feed off this for a while, please.*

"The way to win is to sell it," Beth shouts, her voice rising high and thrumming in all our ears.

"Whip your heads," she says, and we do.

"Make your claps sharp," she says, and we do.

"Make your faces like you're wired for pleasure," she says, and we gleam ecstatic.

"Give 'em the best blow-job smiles you got," she says, and if she had a bullwhip, she'd be slapping it against our thighs. "Turn it on, on, on."

We ride rough and work hard for her. We have three days until the final game and we have to call up another JV whippoorwill and we will work hard for Beth because we want to show our hot stuff, our epic impudence, our unholy awesomeness in front of the sneering Celts masses on Monday night.

But most of all, we work hard because it raises a din, a rabid, high-pitched din that can nearly drown out the sound of the current and coming chaos. The sense that everything is changing in ways we can't guess and that nothing can stop it.

Or maybe that's not it at all. Maybe all we're trying to drown out is the terrifying quiet, the sense that all there is to hear is our own thin echoes. Our sense that Coach is slipping from our clasping hands, that maybe she is already gone. That there is no center anymore and maybe there never was.

All we have is Beth. But that is something, her thunder filling up all the silence.

In the locker room, the din dissolving, girls scattered and then gone, I find myself alone, or nearly so.

With no Coach, everyone leaves a mess. This is how it was under Beth before. Flair strewn about, rolling empties of zero-carb rockstar and sugar-free monster, tampon wrappers and crushed goji berries. Even one cobwebby thong.

Bobby pins crunching under my feet, I walk through, surveying the damaged girlness.

My heart still hammering from the practice, I'm thinking of how hardcore Beth was out there today, like I haven't seen her since sophomore year, when it still beat in her so hard. When she hadn't gotten distracted by petty grievances and her own miseries of life, her own creeping boredom.

Maybe she has never been this good, cared so much.

This is what Coach has done for her, I think. *She helps us all.*

Then, lurking in the open doorway of Coach's office, she is there. The shadow she throws seems so large that her five feet swallow the office hall. Beth.

"Cap," I say, wanting to help sate her, "you bled us today."

Her back to me, I can't see her face.

I walk closer.

I'm hoping, praying for elation.

I mean, isn't she the Coach Itself now, for the moment at least?

"Beth," I say again. "Return of the King."

The sunfall flooding everything, her whole body lit darkly gold, I stop a few feet from her ambered back.

"Beth," I say, "you got everything."

Finally, slowly, a half turn of her head. A whisper of her profile, darkened by her shudder of black hair.

That's when I see that nothing's been had at all, nothing's been saved. She thought this would be it, and it wasn't.

"The sun's down and the moon's pretty," she says, her voice hushed. "It's time to ramble."

And I say yes. Of course I say yes.

25

Sprawled on the hood of my car, we are high up on the south face of the ridge, right where it drops a thousand miles or more, into the deepest part of the earth.

We have been drinking cough-syrupy wine that clings to the tongue. Beth calls it hobo wine, and it feels like we are hobos now. Wanderers. Midnight ramblers.

I forget everything and think that, hidden up here behind the sparkly granite of a thousand gorges and knobs, I am safe from all hazard.

But there is Beth beside me, breathing wildly and talking in ragged lopes that seem to streak around my head, across the sky above us.

At some point I stop listening and instead focus on the loveliness of my own white hands, bending and canting them above me, against the black sky.

"Do you hear what I'm saying, Addy?" she asks.

"You were speaking of dark forces," I tell her, guessing, because this is usually what Beth is speaking of.

"You know who I thought I saw yesterday," she says, "driving her whorey Kia over by St. Reggie's?"

"Who?"

"Casey Jaye. All last summer, cheer buddies in your camp bunk, giggling together in your matching sports bras, and that love knot she gave you."

"It wasn't anything," I say, feeling an unaccountable blush. "It didn't mean anything."

"Opening her thighs to show you her tight quads. I knew her wormy heart. But I shot my wad too soon and you weren't ready to believe me. You didn't want to."

She will never let it go. She will never forget it.

But then she jerks up suddenly and I nearly slide from the car hood, hands gripping her jacket.

"Look out there," she says, pointing into the distance, the place where Sutton Grove would be if it weren't just nightness out there.

I peer off into the black, but I can't see anything, just a shimmer of some town somewhere that's mostly, if not fully, asleep.

A lush wino haze upon me, I guess I've been hoping, with colossal naïveté, that Beth will determine she has won, that she is Captain, that Coach is barely even a coach these days, ceding more and more power, and now she will let it go . . . she will let it go and Coach will be free.

It's all over, or nearly so.

The police will realize the truth, and it will all be over.

And Beth will be done.

Or nearly so.

I am drunk.

"With her private jokes and her yoga orgies and her backyard jamborees," Beth is saying. "All of you curled at her feet. Cleopatra in a hoodie. I never fell for any of it."

"You never fell for it once," I agree, trying to fight off the feeling of menace piercing the haze.

"But when I look out there," she says, sweeping her hand across the lightless horizon, "all I can think is that she's *getting away with it*. Getting away with everything."

"Beth," I warn. My eyes on the velvety dark below. The expanse of nothingness that suddenly seems to be throbbing, nervous, alive.

What does lie down there?

In this state, the unruly despair of Will's life, the battered end of it, comes to me freshly.

I want sparkled cheeks, high laughter, and good times, and I never asked for any of this. Except I did.

"Addy," she says, kicking her feet in the air. "I've got that fever in my blood. I'm ready for some trouble. Are you?"

I am not. Oh, I am not. But who would leave Beth alone when she's like this?

"Let's go look the devil in the eye, girlfriend," she says, tilting that wine bottle to my lips, to my open mouth, and I drink, drink, drink.

Beth now at the wheel, we are looping endlessly, in curling figure eights, and the streetlamps overhead are popping over my eyes.

Then we're climbing upward again and there's a pause between songs and I hear a roar in my ears. Face to the window, I see the crashing interstate is newly below us.

We're nearly there before I realize where she's taken me.

"I don't want to be here," I whisper.

She stops the car in front of the lightboxed sign, The Towers.

We sit, the light greening our faces.

"This is not a place I want to be," I say again, louder now.

"Can you feel the energy here?" she says, putting lip gloss on with her finger, like we are readying for our dates. "It's some black mojo."

"What are you talking about?"

"Our great captain's captain, the she–wolf. The li–o–ness. I can feel her here," she smiles spookily. "How it was for her that night."

I don't say anything.

"The night she done shot her lover dead," Beth says, crooking her fingers into little guns.

Bang-bang, she whispers in my ear, *bang-bang!*

And there it is. She has said it.

"You have lost your mind," I say, the words heavy in my mouth. "You have lost it."

"Hey, Coach," Beth sings, her grin wider and wider, *"where you goin' with that gun in your hand?"*

"Shut up," I say, my hand leaping out and shoving at her, a strange half laugh coming from me.

But then I'm shoving harder and I'm not laughing, and Beth grabs my hands and locks them together. *When did she get so sober?*

"He killed himself," I say, so loud it hurts me to hear. "She didn't do anything. She'd never do anything like that."

My hands in hers, she leans toward me, very close, her wine-thick breath in my face, my hands knotted in hers so tight I feel a hot tear in my eye corner.

"She would never do anything like that," she repeats back to me, nodding.

"She loved him," I say, the words sounding small and ridiculous.

"Right," Beth says, smiling, pressing my hands against her own hard ribcage, like clutching in the backseat with a boy, "because no one's ever killed the person they love."

"You're drunk, you're drunk and awful," I say, and I'm trying to get my hands free, and we're rocking, our faces so close. "An awful bitch, the worst I ever knew."

She drops my hands at last, tilting her head and watching me.

Suddenly, the alcohol heaving in me, my hands palsied, I have to get out of the car.

Feet on the smooth, freshly poured asphalt of the lot, I breathe deep.

But this is what she wants because she gets out too.

I look at her, face shot through not with moonlight but with the wan blue of the bank of parking lot lights.

"Let's go," I say. "I don't need this——"

"Do you smell something?" Beth asks, suddenly. "Like flowers or something. Honeysuckle."

"I don't smell anything," I say.

I smell all kinds of things, most of all chlorine. Bleach. Blood.

"Did you know the government is studying the possibility that people might give off these scents when they're lying?" Beth says, and I must be dreaming. "And each smell is very individual. Like a fingerprint."

I've dreamed my way into one of Beth's nightmares, the one where we're standing above the gorge, like an open throat.

"I wonder if yours is honeysuckle," she says.

"I'm not lying about anything," I say.

"Honeysuckle so sweet I can taste it. You're good enough to eat, Addy-Faddy," she says, and I feel she's monstrous now.

"He killed himself," I say, my voice almost too low to hear. "It's the truth, if you want to know."

"You lie and lie, and I keep lapping it up," she says, clucking her tongue. "Not anymore."

"He did. He shot himself in the mouth on his carpet," I say, and it's not even my voice, not even my words, but they come so fast and so sure. "It's the truth."

Beth is watching me, and there's no stopping me now.

"He shot himself," I say. I wish I could stop, but I can't stop until I convince her. "He fell on the carpet and his head was black. And he died there."

With those security floodlights glaring, her face like marble, she says nothing.

And I keep going.

"You don't know," I say, the wind whipping my hair into my face, my mouth. "Because you didn't see. *But I know.*"

"How do you know?" she darts back, and repeats her question from the girls' restroom. "Were you there?"

"Of course I was," I say, almost a howl, my breath sliding from me.

"Of course you were," she says, fingers reaching out, lacing through my blowing hair.

"So that's how I know," I say, tightening my voice. "That's how I know more than you. I saw his body. I saw it lying there."

She is quiet for a moment.

"You saw him kill himself."

"No, after."

"Ah, so you saw him after he was already dead. After Coach shot him dead."

"No," I say, my voice loud. "We found him together. We got to his apartment and there he was."

There is a pause.

"I see," she says, an unspeakably lewd leer rising. "So what exactly was going on that Coach would bring you to the Sarge's apartment, at all hours of the night. Were you some virgin prize—"

"No," I nearly shout, feeling stomach-sick. "She found him and she called me. I went and got her."

She smiles faintly. "Huh," she says.

My stomach turning, I lean against the open car door, breathing in.

"Wait," I say, heeling back, dropping into the front seat. "You saw us that night. You saw me come home after."

"I didn't need to see you," she says, toe-kicking at my ankles. It's not really an answer, though. "I know all your beats, Addy."

"You know everything," I mutter.

"I know you, Addy," she says. "Better than you ever could. You've never been able to look at anything about yourself. You count on me to do it for you."

I press my face into the car headrest.

"And what you've just told me," she continues, "I'm glad you finally fessed up, but it doesn't change anything."

Turning my head slowly toward her, my mouth drifting open...

"What?"

"All it proves, Addy, is that you lied to me. But I knew that already."

Later, in bed, the alcohol leaching from me, I cannot make my head stop.

Drunk and weak, I gave her everything.

I feel outmaneuvered, outflanked.

Because I was.

Don't you believe me now? I'd said, whining like a little JV, all the way home.

Don't you get it? she'd said, shaking her head. *He was done with her. And now she's done with him. And now she's sunk you down in it with her. And soon she'll be done with you too.*

She made you her accomplice.

She made you her bitch—but then again, weren't you already?

I think I will never sleep and then, finally, I do.

26

I wake up with a start, and a picture flashes there.

Last Monday night, Coach opening Will's apartment door to me. The alarm in her eyes like she'd forgotten she'd called me. The shimmery dampness clinging to her thick hair.

The picture so vivid, it aches. My heart rocketing in my chest, I feel my T-shirt sticking to me, my hung-over body blazing.

Grasping for the warm water bottle by my bed, I know something suddenly. Something I'd forgotten.

The dew on her.

Faint. Like someone who'd showered maybe a half hour before.

And Will, lying on the floor in his towel.

I can't quite piece it together, but it reminds me of something.

It reminds me of another time.

It reminds me of this:

Will, waving through the lobby doors, his hair wet and seal-slick.

Coach, slipping from behind him, walking toward me, her hair hanging in damp loops to her shoulders, darkening her T-shirt.

The first time I drove to The Towers, the time I came and picked her up. And I knew what they'd been doing before I arrived, because it was all over them.

Their clothes on but they seemed so naked, all their pleasure in each other streaked across their faces.

Fresh from their shower, their shared shower I'd imagined.

I imagine now.

Monday night, Coach and Will, both shower damp, but Will is dead.

She didn't find his body, Beth said. *She was there when it happened. She was already there.*

The phone rings and rings and rings. I turn it off and stuff it under my mattress.

The thoughts that come are rough and relentless.

The days leading up to Will's death, the way Coach had been acting, missing practices, the car accident, and now I wonder if she'd lied about all of it. If she had felt Will slipping away and had been calling, had been begging him to come over, like that day at her house, when she finally lured him there. When she had me wait in the backyard with Caitlin.

And that night. The faintly damp hair. The bleachy tennis shoes. What had that been about, really?

And how did she get to Will's?

I took a cab, she'd said. *I snuck out of the house. Matt was asleep. He took two pills. I had to see Will, Addy.* That strangely robotic voice. *So I called a cab. But I couldn't call a cab to take me back, could I?*

Snuck out at two in the morning, and Matt French didn't hear her? It made so much more sense that she'd gone over earlier, made some excuse to Matt, or gone because Matt wasn't home yet.

Could Will have been done with her, and she . . .

Suddenly, I think of last week, that sleeping snarl in the night as I lay beside Coach:

How could you do this to me? How?

Pow-pow, I can hear Beth say. *Pow-pow.*

A Post-it left for me on the kitchen island:

"A, Debbie says someone from PD called for you. Someone steal mascot again? Love, D."

Yes, Dad, I think, holding the edge of the counter. *That's exactly it.*

I'm running on Royston Road when the car pulls up.

I never run. Beth says runners are uncreative masturbators. I didn't know what that meant, but it made me never want to run.

But this morning, my stepmother's klonopin still sticky on my tongue, running seems right.

Like at practice, like at games, I can forget everything but the special talents of my special girl body, which does everything I ask it to, which is unravaged and pure, baby-oil soft and fluttered only with the bruises of girl sport.

The feel of the concrete pulsing up my shins is near-exquisite and when the release comes, it's like hitting a stunt but better because it's just me and no one can even see, but I'm doing it, doing it anyway and without peering out waiting for anyone to tell me I hit it, because I know I did. I know it.

So I keep running. Until all I feel is nothing.

And no one can touch me. My phone shut off, far from me, and no one even knows where I am, if I'm anywhere at all.

Except the detectives.

It's just like on TV. They pull up to the curb, and one of them is leaning on the doorframe.

"Adelaide Hanlon?"

I stop, earbuds slipping from my ears.

"Can we ask you a few questions?"

*   *   *

The man gives me a bottle of water. It gives me something to do with my hands, my mouth.

We sit in an office, and when the woman sees my sweated legs puckering a little on the seat, she offers me the desk chair, and she doesn't seem to care that I sweat on it.

"If you'd feel more comfortable with your parents present," the man says, "we can call them."

"No," I say, shaking my head. "That's okay."

They both look at me and nod, as if I am being very wise.

Then they exchange a quick look. He leaves, and the woman stays.

In my head, I start doing my cheer counts. One–two, three–four. I count them until my heart finally slows down. Until I can empty my face, teen-girl bored.

"We're just trying to confirm a few details about last Monday night," she says.

She has a tight ponytail that reminds me of Coach's, and a dimple on one side of her mouth. She doesn't really smile, but she speaks softly.

Somehow I start to feel okay, like having to talk to the assistant principal about something you know about but had nothing to do with. If you just say as little as possible, they really can't do anything.

The questions start generally, more like a conversation. What do I like about school? How long have I been a cheerleader? Aren't some of the stunts dangerous?

When the questions turn, it's a gentle turn, or she renders it gently.

"So you and Coach French spend time together outside of school?"

The question seems strange. I think I've misheard it.

"She's my coach," I say.

"And last Monday night, did you see your coach?"

I don't know what to say. I have no idea what she told them.

"Last Monday?" I say. "I don't know."

"Try to remember, okay? Were you at her house last Monday?"

That second part, a gift. *At her house.* If Coach didn't tell them that, who would have?

"I guess I was," I say. "Sometimes I help her with her little girl."

"Like a babysitter while she goes out?"

"No, no," I say, calm as I can. Besides, who is she to call me a babysitter? "I don't babysit."

"So just pitching in?"

I look at her, at her bare lips and badly plucked eyebrows.

"I hang out there a lot," I say. "She helps me through stuff. I like being over there."

"So last Monday you were there with your coach and her husband?"

And her husband. "Yes," I say, because doesn't this have to be Coach's story and don't our stories have to be straight for both our sakes? "I was."

"And you knew the sergeant?"

"I'd see him in school."

"Was your coach friends with him?"

"I don't know," I say. "She never said anything to me."

"You never saw them together?"

"No."

I have no idea what I've done or undone.

"And you like being at Coach's house. You like spending time there." She's watching me closely, but I can't get over the stitch of stray eyebrow hair to the side of her overgroomed right brow.

How could she miss something like that? That detail, like spotting a slack move in another squad's routine.

It makes me feel strong.

Deputy Hanlon, stone-cold lieutenant, my old guise—I'd forgotten how good they felt.

"That's what I said, yes, ma'am."

I lean back, stretch my legs long, and adjust my ponytail.

"It was a comfortable place to be? They seemed to get along?"

"Yeah," I say.

"Seem like a happy marriage?"

I look at her with my head tilted, like a dog. Like I can't guess what she might mean. Who thought about the happiness of marriages?

"Yeah, sure," I say, and my voice clicks into something else, the way I talk when I have to talk to people who could never understand anything at all but who think they get me, think they get everything about girls like me.

"We like Coach," I say. "She's a nice lady."

And I say, "Sometimes she shows us yoga moves. It's really fun. She's awesome. The Big Game is Monday, you should come."

I lean close, like I'm telling her a secret.

"We kick ass Monday, we're going to Regionals next year."

"We may have some more questions," the detective says, as she walks me out.

"Okay," I say. "Cool." Which is a word I never use.

Walking past all the cops, all the detectives, I raise my runner's shirt a few inches, like I'm shaking it loose from my damp skin.

I let them all see my stomach, its tautness.

I let everyone see I'm not afraid, and that I'm not anything but a silly cheerleader, a feather-bodied sixteen-year-old with no more sense than a marshmallow peep.

I let them see I'm not anything.

Least of all what I am.

27

At home, I drag my phone from under my mattress.

There are seven voicemails from Coach, and sixteen texts. They all say some variation on this: *Call me before anything. Call me NOW.*

But first, I decide to do some stretches, like Coach showed us.

Cat tilt. Puppy dog. Triangle pose.

She can wait.

I turn the shower on and stand under it a long time.

Then I blow-dry my hair, stretching each strand out languorously, my mind doing various twists and turns.

Somewhere in the back of my head some old cheer motivational words sputter forth: *Time comes, you have to listen to yourself.*

That seems like something old Coach Templeton—Fish— would've said, or printed out from the internet, or typed in scroll font at the bottom of our squad sheets.

As if listening to yourself was just something you could do. As if there were something there to listen to. A self inside you with all kinds of smart things to say.

My fingers touch my open computer screen, our squad Facebook page, all the cheer photos from three years of death defiance and bright ribbons.

Cheerlebrities!!!

There's one shot of Beth and me in the foreground, our faces glitter-crusted, our mouths open, tongues out, our fingers curled into the devil hand sign.

We look terrifying.

The picture was from last year. At first, I don't recognize myself. With all the paint, we are impossible to tell apart. Not just Beth and me, but all of us.

The front windows of Coach's house are still rimy from last night's frost, and Caitlin's paper snowflakes scatter across. A lamp glows inside.

It has the feel of a fairy-tale cottage, like one of those paintings at the mall.

Caitlin stands inside the front door, two fingers punched in her mouth. Usually so tidily groomed, her hair looking oddly knotted, like an uncared-for doll. Breadcrumbs scatter up her cheek.

She doesn't say anything, but then she never does, and I twist past her, my legs brushing against the barbs of her ruffled jumper, which seems more suited for July.

She likes to look pretty, Coach always says, like that is the only thing she really knows about her.

"I didn't think they'd get to you so fast," Coach says. She's washing the windows in the den, wielding a long pole with a squeegee at the end, and a soft duster beneath it. "I was calling and calling. I thought for sure I'd get to you before they did."

There's a sheen of sweat on her face.

I don't say anything because I want that sweat there, at least for now. She's made me sweat enough.

"It just seemed easiest to tell them you were here that night," she says. "If you were at my house, then I couldn't possibly have been at Will's."

She looks at me, from under her extended arm, elegant muscles spun tight.

"And you couldn't have been there either," she adds. "So we're both covered."

"What about Matt?" I say, dropping my voice.

"Oh, he's back," she says, gesturing out the window. "He's outside."

In the far corner of the lawn, I spot him sitting on the brick edging of an empty flowerbed.

I can't figure out what he's doing, but he's very still.

I've never seen him like that, or outside at all. I wonder if he feels peaceful.

"No," I say, regaining my focus. "I mean he told the cops you were home asleep, right? Which is what he thought anyway?"

Why did you need me as your alibi, I want to say, *when you had him.*

"This is better, Addy," she says, the words just tripping from her tongue. "They never believe the spouse. And he was asleep, that's not much corroboration..."

She stops for a second, eyes fixed on something on the windowpane. A smudge I can't see.

"I used to use newspapers," she says. "Then Matt bought me this thing." She touches her fingers to the duster at the end of the pole. "It's lamb's wool."

I keep waiting for her to say sorry, *sorry I didn't warn you, sorry I didn't prepare you, sorry I didn't protect you from all of this.* But she's never been a sorry kind of person.

"Coach," I say. "Don't you want to know what I said to the cops?"

She looks at me.

"But I know what you said," she says.

"How do you know?" I say, kneeling on the sofa where she stands, barefoot. "I might have blown it without even realizing it."

"I know because you're smart. I know because I trust you," she says, and lifts the pole again, telescoping it higher. "I wouldn't have gotten you into this otherwise."

"Gotten me into what?" I say, my voice scraping up my throat. "Coach, what am I in?"

She will not look at me. She's looking out the window.

"My mess," she says, her voice smaller. "Don't think I don't know that."

I follow her gaze.

Far back on the lawn, Matt French has turned and seems to be looking toward us. Toward me.

I can't make out his face, but it's as though I can.

"Coach," I say, "why was your hair wet?"

"What," she says, swooping the squeegee back up the window.

"When I got to Will's apartment that night," I say, my eyes still on Matt French in the backyard, his rounded-over shoulders. "Why was your hair wet?"

"My hair wet? What kind of... it wasn't wet."

"Yes it was," I say. "It was damp."

She sets the pole down.

"Oh," she says, looking at me at last. "So it's you who doesn't trust me."

"No, I..."

"Did the police... did they...?"

"No," I say. "I just remembered it. I'd forgotten it and I remembered it. I'm just trying... Coach, he was wearing a towel, and your hair..."

Something is happening, that vacant, efficient expression slip-

216

ping away, revealing something raw, bruised. It's like I've done something powerfully cruel. "I took a bath before I went over there," she replies. "I always did."

"But, Coach..."

"Addy," she says, looking down at me, the pole piercing the cushion, like a staff, or sword, "you need to stop talking to Beth."

A burr rises up under my skin.

"Because she just wants her pretty doll back," Coach says quietly, lifting the pole again, pressing the squeegee against the window, making it squeak.

I feel something tighten in me and have a picture suddenly of Beth's fingers circling my wrist.

Then at last, I say it. "You never told me about the bracelet."

"The bracelet?" she says, finally releasing the pole and descending from her perch.

"My hamsa bracelet."

"Your what?"

"To ward off the evil eye. The one I gave you."

She pauses a second. "Oh, that, right. What about it?"

"Why didn't you tell me the police found it?" I say, then wait a beat before adding, "under Will's body."

She looks at me. "Addy, I don't know what you're talking about."

"You mean they didn't ask you about it? They found the bracelet under Will's body."

"They told you that?" her voice bounds.

"No," I say. "Beth did."

I start to feel like my feet are going to slip out from under me, even though I'm sitting down.

*   *   *

We're standing in front of Coach's bureau, her smooth mahogany jewelry box before us.

She sets her hands on either side and lifts the top with a shushing sound.

We look at the tidily arranged bracelets woven into the soft ridges. Her tennis bracelet, a few neon sports bracelets, a delicate silver-linked one.

"It's got to be in here," she says, fingertip stroking the velvet. "I haven't worn it in weeks."

But it's not.

I look at the box, and at her, at the way her face looks both tight and loose at the same time, veins wriggling at her temples, but her mouth slack, wounded.

"It's here," she says, sliding the box off her bureau, everything tumbling radiantly to the carpet.

"It's not," I say.

She looks at me, so helpless.

For a long time, maybe, we are both kneeling on the floor, fingers nuzzling into the carpet weave, shaking loose those filmy bracelets, tugging them from the caramel-colored loops.

That beautiful carpet with its dense pile. At least five twists per inch.

"Addy, you've listened to Beth, now you need to listen to me. If they found that bracelet, a girl's bracelet like that, like one of yours," she says, pointing to my arms, ringed with friendship flosses, neon jellies, a leather braid, "don't you think they'd have asked you too?"

There's nothing I can say. I watch her as she walks into the bathroom and shuts the door.

Neither of us wants to reckon openly with how deep Beth's

trickery may go and neither of us wants to reckon with why I have believed her.

I hear the shower start and know I'm meant to leave.

Being part of a pyramid, you never see the pyramid at all.

Later, watching ourselves, it never feels real. Flickering YouTube images of bumblebees swarming, assembling themselves into tall hives.

It's nothing like it is on the floor. There, you have to bolt your gaze to the bodies in your care, the ones right above you.

Your only focus should be your girl, the one you're responsible for, the one whose leg, hip, arm you're bracing. The one who is counting on you.

Left spot, keep your focus on the left flank. Don't look right.

Right spot, keep your focus on the right flank. Don't look left.

Eyes on the Flyer's eyes, shoulders, hips, vigilant for any sign of misalignment, instability, doubt.

This is how you stop falls.

This is how you keep everything from collapsing.

You never get to see the stunt at all.

Eyes on your girl.

And it's only ever a partial vision, because that's the only way to keep everyone up in the air.

On my way out, I see Matt French still roaming around the backyard. It strikes me how few times I've seen him without his laptop in front of him, or his headset on. He looks lost.

I stop at the kitchen window, wondering what Coach has told him. What he believes.

Matt French reaches out to a branch spoking from a tall hawthorn bush, the one Caitlin is always cutting herself on, its hooks curling under her feet.

He looks no sadder than usual, which is sad enough.

Suddenly, he looks up and it's like he sees me, but I think I must be too far, too small behind the paned window.

But I think he sees me.

"You made it up," I say.

I'm at Beth's house, in her bathroom. She has her leg propped up on the toilet seat, where she's examining it with care.

"The Asian girl did the sugar wax on me, and she is comprehensive in her approach," she says, shaking a flame-colored bottle of Our Desire, her mother's perfume. "Except now I reek of poptart. Frosted. With sprinkles."

"You made it up," I repeat, smacking her leg off the toilet seat. "The cops never asked her about any bracelet. You made all that up."

"The hot fuzz called you in, eh?" she says, standing up straight, still shaking the perfume bottle, shaking it side to side like some dirty boy gesture. "They called me in too. I go right after practice today."

"They never found any bracelet at all, did they?"

"You'd best stay right, girl," she says, lifting her leg back up, sending a fine mist of bitter orange and ylang-ylang over it.

This I don't like. She can't batter at me like I'm Tacy, like I'm some JV.

"What made you finally ask her?" she says.

I knock her foot off the toilet seat again and sit down on its furred lid.

"You made it up," I say. "If the detectives found a bracelet, they would've asked me about it."

"Addy, I can't make you believe me," she says, looking down at me. "And as for you and Coach . . ."

She lays her hand on my head, like a benediction.

"We are never deceived," she says, her voice deep and ringing. "We deceive ourselves."

We are lying on Beth's deep blue bedroom carpet, as we've done a hundred, a thousand times, collapsing from our labors, the wages of war, one kind or another. Adrift on that speckless ultramarine, Beth would lay out all her martial machinations for me, her attaché, her envoy. Sometimes her mouthpiece. Whatever was required.

In some ways, Beth was almost never wrong in her judgments.

Paper-thin, master cleansed Emily was not, in fact, strong enough to do the stunt.

Tacy didn't have the head game or the strong legs of a true Flyer.

With Beth, so full of lies, you have to push past the lie to see the deeper truth that drives it. Because Beth is almost always lying about something, but the lying is her way of rendering something else, something tucked away or confounded, manifest.

And you have to keep playing, and maybe the truth will reveal itself, maybe Beth will get tired and finally show her hand. Or maybe it'll stop being fun for her, and she'll just hurl that truth in your face, and make you cry.

I never liked you anyway.

You're just so goddamned fat it depresses me.

I saw your dad at the mall buying lingerie with a strange woman.

Casey Jaye said you can't throw a back handspring for shit, and she told RiRi there's something weird about you, but she wouldn't say what.

Oh, and I only pretended to care.

"It can't be easy," she says, surveying her lotioned legs, "knowing you were an accessory to a crime, even if it's *after the fact*. It's not really a position a red-blooded All-American teenage girl expects to be put in, especially given everything you've done for your Coach."

"Like the things I've done for you?" I say. "Did you think I was going to be your lieutenant forever?"

"What have you ever done for me," she replies, her eyes snake-slitted, "that you didn't want to do?"

Flipping over on her stomach, she props her tanned chin on one palm and reaches out to me with her other.

"Oh, Addy. You can't even see it, you're so love-blind. I'm sorry about that. And sorry to have to do this to you. Really, I am."

"I'm not . . . love-blind," I stutter, the word throwing me. Which I guess it's meant to, but—

"But you're bringing a knife to a gunfight," she continues. "You can't see the facts, even laid out plain. Even when the *po-lice* department, Addy, calls you in to the station to investigate her lover's murder. What will it take?"

I feel a sob creep into my chest, she's just so damned good and I can't breathe.

"You keep saying these things," I say, "but you've never given me any real reason to believe why you think she would ever . . ."

Beth slants her head. "Why she would ever?" she repeats, singsongy. "Why *wouldn't* she?"

My head throbs, not knowing what to believe now, ever, except I believe them both—Beth and Coach, in different ways—when their words wormhole into my brain. They make everything seem real. Dark. Painful. True.

"It kills me, I tell you," Beth says, "the way you all fawn over her. The way you, Addy, the way *you* fawned over them both. She isn't what you think, and neither was he. They were not star-crossed. He was just a guy, like all of them. They fucked each other and he got tired of her before she got tired of him. She gets everything she wants, and she couldn't stand not getting him anymore."

The throbbing becoming something else, something worse and more insistent.

I lift myself up to sitting position, my head light and everything lifting lightly in me. The edge of hysteria sliding into her voice, it can come to no good.

"And none of us gets away with anything," she says, climbing up onto her knees in front of me. "None of us."

"You don't know anything," I say. "Neither of us knows."

She looks at me, and for a second I almost see all the misery and rage, centuries of it, tumbling across her face.

"She's not a killer," I say, trying to make my voice bore-thick.

She looks down at me, her eyes depthful and ruinous.

"Love is a kind of killing, Addy," she says. "Don't you know that?"

There are three hours before practice, the Big Practice before the Big Game.

I can't live in Beth's head a moment longer, so I spend a few hours at the mall, wandering, hands knotted around my jug of kombucha, its fermented threads swirling around the bottom of the bottle.

Coach, my Coach. I think of that pearl-smooth face of hers and wonder if I can ever imagine it, try to picture her hard, ordered body doing the thing Beth says she's done.

It's impossible and I keep trying but the image that comes instead is of her, legs hooked hard around Will in the teachers' lounge, the elation, everything in her unpinned, untucked, unveiled. No one looking, no one watching, and everything hers.

He is mine, he is mine, and I will do anything to feel this always.

Anything.

Feeling Will slipping from her, might she find herself doing something she never thought she'd do?

Maybe it's a feeling I know.

It's the feeling that sends me out to The Towers again, second time in as many days, some magnetic stroke tickling inside me, summoning me there.

Pulling into the lot, I see no sign of police. There are even fewer cars than usual on this blustery day, the wind whistling under my windshield wipers and the sky raw and melancholy.

I sit for a long time, punching radio presets, then turning my car off, putting my earbuds in, drowning in the plaintive songs of adolescent heartache, then quickly becoming disgusted by them and flinging my player to the floor of my car.

Then, the flinging seems to be part of the same counterfeit world of those tinny teenbox songs, and I hate myself too.

But that's when I realize that I've been on a stakeout, without even knowing it.

Because there, walking across the parking lot into Building A, is Corporal Gregory Prine.

I'd know that bullet head anywhere.

I watch him enter the building and then, without even thinking, I follow him, sneakers squeaking across the wet parking lot.

Stopped short by the locked lobby doors, I can't guess why he has a key and wonder if it's Will's key. I stand at the big buzzer board where I stood five days ago, and I try to be Beth-bold, my dayglo nails dancing over the silver buttons, pressing them all, waiting for any crackling voice, the ringing wail of entry.

"Sorry, I live in Fourteen-B and forgot my keys. My mom's not home, can you buzz me in?"

Someone does, and before I know it, I'm in the elevator, a slick sweat on me now, and the fluorescent light hissing, and then I'm in the empty hallway on Will's empty floor.

I'm not scared at all but seem to be fueled by the same kind of chemical rush like at a game, like when there's just been too much slim-FX and nothing to eat but sugar-free jell-o so you can get back the space between your upper thighs, it's a feeling most spectacular.

I have it now and it's so strong in me I can't stop myself from charging forward, my foot accidentally punting a piece of crime-scene tape, catching it on the tip of my puma.

And there I am, standing in front of number 27-G, a lone strip of tape still curled around its handle.

But before I can decide what I plan to do—ring the bell, burst in like some gangbanger—I stop myself, tripping backwards against the stairwell door, inhaling deeply three times.

Prine, what if he . . .

That's when I notice that the door to the neighboring apartment is just slightly ajar, and a whoosh from the heating unit has nudged it farther open.

I walk slowly toward it, peeking in.

Inside, it's the mirror image of Will's apartment but spartan-bare.

The same parquet entry, the same sandy carpet.

The only difference seems to be the plastic lazy susan perched on the table in the entryway. Stuffed with brochures: *Luxury Living on Nature's Edge.*

Were I to step closer, to step inside, I'm sure I'd see the same leather sofa slashed across the center of the room.

But I don't step closer. Somehow, I feel if it were an inch closer, this sofa will become that sofa, and there on the carpet, I will see it. Him.

But mostly, the place just feels empty.

Except it's not.

A door thumps, then the sound of feet skimming across the carpet, and heading toward me is the bullet head himself, a plastic grocery store bag clutched in that ham-hock hand.

It all happens so fast. Spotting me, he stops short in front of the open door.

Gorilla-puffed chest, sunglasses perched on his crew-cut head, he blinks spasmodically, red rushing up his thick neck and face.

It's as if he can't believe his eyes, and I nearly can't either.

"Oh," he says, "it's one of you."

Back in the near-empty parking lot, we sit together in my car.

"Listen," he says, the plastic grocery bag hooked daintily around his wrist. "I haven't said anything. So don't worry."

"What do you mean?" I say, marveling still at the idea of Prine in my car, us both here. Everything.

"I have some priors. I had a substance problem," he says, fingers crackling noisily at the bag. "So I'm not saying a goddamn thing to those cops. You can tell her not to worry. And you can tell her to leave me the hell out of this."

I don't know who "she" is, but I don't ask.

There is a palpable sense of revelation coming and I want to tread carefully. Finally someone not smart enough to lie to me, or even to know why he should.

Though, as I'm sitting there with him, his left foot ensnared by the cheetah-print sports bra on my car floor, it strikes me he might be thinking the same thing.

"So you live here or something?" I ask, fingering my gearshift.

"No," he says, watching my hand. He takes a breath. "Sarge let me crash in that apartment. He knew no one was living there. The realtors are always just leaving it open. He gave me the building key. For when things get tough at home."

He looks over at me, sheepish.

"My old man and me don't always see eye to eye," he explains. "Sarge understood . . . Sarge, he was such a good guy."

Suddenly, Prine's eyes fill. I try to hide my surprise. He turns away and looks out the window, flipping his sunglasses down.

"So why are you here now?" I ask.

"I had to see what I left behind," he says. Looking down, he opens his plastic bag, showing me a travel-size mouthwash, a single-blade razor, a dusty bar of soap.

He lowers his voice to a whisper, even though there's no sign of life anywhere. *Luxury Living on Nature's Edge.*

"Listen, the cops don't know I was here that night," he says.

I try not to let him see my flinch.

"Okay," I say.

"It doesn't matter anyway," he says. "I left before any gunshot. I don't know what the hell happened. But I did hear the two of them headboard banging for a good fifteen minutes before midnight and I couldn't get any sleep."

Coach, there, that night. When Will was still alive.

I take this fact, this staggering and harrowing fact, and put it in a far corner in my head. For now. I can't look at it. It is there for safekeeping.

"That's how it always was with them," he says. "I don't like hearing other people's private business. And, to be honest, the two of them, it made me sad."

He looks at me, fingers plucking at the bag loop.

"I mean, that was a messed-up situation, right?" he looks at me, raising his eyebrows. "You could see something bad was going to happen. Something was going to go down."

I know he's waiting for some kind of confirmation, but I don't say anything.

"The point is," he goes on, "like I promised her, I'm not saying a goddamned word."

"Her?" I ask, measuring my voice. Hiding everything.

"Your friend," he says, a little impatiently now. "The brunette."

"Beth?"

"Beth," he says. "The one with the tits. I mean, you seem nice, but so did she at first. Girl like that, she could make trouble for me."

Craning his neck, he looks up at the apartment building, ominously.

"All of you, you're a whole lot of trouble," he says, softly. "I don't need that kind of trouble."

A whole lot of trouble, I think.

"Guess Sarge found out, didn't he?" he looks at me, grimly. "Queen of the hive. Don't mess with the queen."

I look at him and wonder which queen he means.

Driving away, I can't begin to unravel it all. Why would Beth want Prine to keep quiet about hearing Coach in Will's apartment that night? And why didn't she tell me, at least, if her aim is to convince me of Coach's guilt?

But the pulsing center is this: Coach was there with Will that night, Will alive. She and Will in bed.

The picture in my head now, Coach standing before me, bleached sneakers in hand.

Coach.

Tilting pyramid-top, reaching for me, bucking for my arm, knowing what it will mean. Where it would take both of us.

*   *   *

"Two days, four hours," RiRi says, fingers tapping on her thighs anxiously. "Fifty-two hours till the game, hollaback girls. Where *is* she?"

We are all standing in the gym, waiting for Coach.

I haven't figured out what I will do when she does arrive, if I will let my face betray anything.

I slide two Tylenol with codeine, leftovers from last year's thumb jam, under my tongue and wait.

But Coach doesn't show.

And Beth, well, she's not there either.

"I don't understand how Coach could do this to us," Tacy yowls, her battered lip now a frosted lavender. "Two days before the big game."

"It must be some kind of test," Paige Shepherd says, chin-nodding with unsure surety. "To show us we can do it on our own."

RiRi is doing a straddle stretch against the wall, which usually calms her down.

"No," she says. "Something's wrong. Really wrong. I've been hearing things. What if this is all about Sarge Stud?"

Oh, this causes quite a conflagration.

"My brother—listen to this!" Brinnie Cox gasps through those big chiclet teeth of hers. "My brother works at the sub shop next to the police station where the cops come in for lunch and he heard them mention Coach. And I don't know what they said, but..."

There's scurrying and speculations spun like long sticky gum strands, but I am out of it.

Instead, I work it. I pound that mat. I'm doing my tucks, over and over, curling my body sharklike upon itself.

"You are so fucking tight," RiRi murmurs, strolling by.

I slap her thigh hard and grin.

"You're better than you ever were with Beth," she says.

"I'm working harder," I say.

"You were kicking it with Casey Jaye last summer," RiRi says. "You were so good."

"Why are you bringing that up?" I say. "Why does everyone always want to talk about that?"

It's the thing no one can let go of. But I can. I'd like to never think of any of it again.

"I was glad when you two got together," she says. "That's all I'm saying."

I think suddenly of Casey, the ease of her light hands on me, flipping my hips up, laughing.

"You know," RiRi says, "Casey told me she thought you were the bravest, best cheerleader she ever knew and she's cheered her whole life."

"She meant Beth," I say. "She must have meant Beth."

Addy, Casey whispered one night, hanging from the bunk above me. *She's never going to let it be you. Fuck your four inches. You're light as air. You could be Top Girl. You're a badass and beautiful. You should be captain.*

"And that fight between you and Beth, we all knew it was coming," RiRi says, shaking her head. "Four of us to pull you two off each other."

"It was an accident," I say, but no one ever believed me. "My hand got caught."

One day, tumbling class by the lake, I was spotting Beth's handspring. When my arm flung up, my fingers caught her hoop earring, pulling it clean through.

I was trying to catch you, I'd told her, the hoop still hooked through my fingers. *You were bending.*

But she'd just stood there, holding the side of her head, a brick red trickle between tan fingers.

Everyone whispered that it was about Casey, but it wasn't. It was an accident. Beth and her big door-knocker earrings. It just happened.

Sometimes now, when she's not looking, I stare at her earlobe and want to touch it, to understand something.

I never thought you'd be friends again after that, RiRi said later. But we were. No one understands. They never have.

"I stood with her when they stitched up her ear," RiRi says now. "I never saw her cry before. I never knew she had tear ducts. Hell, I never knew she had blood in her."

"It was just a fight," I say, remembering the two of us tangled up, someone screaming.

"I thought," RiRi says, " 'Addy's finally manning up to Beth.' None of us ever had the guts."

"A stupid fight, like girls do," I say.

"And, for what it's worth, Beth talked all kinds of trash about Casey," RiRi says, "but I never believed it."

I had, though. And I stripped my bunk of sheets and walked down to the end of the cabin, to the bunk Beth had already vacated for me. And I never talked to Casey again.

"Addy, you could still do it," RiRi says now. "You could be captain, anything."

"Shut the fuck up," I say.

RiRi brushes back, like I've hit her.

"That was a long time ago," I add, setting my arms up for another tuck. "That was last summer."

A half hour passes, everyone doing lazy tuck jumps and stretches, before we hear the sound.

Coach Templeton's ancient boom box sliding across the gym floor, blasting bratty girl rap: *"Take me low, where my girlies go, where we hit it till they're kneeling, till there's glitter on the ceiling . . ."*

All our heads turn, and there is Beth, white-socked and whistle swinging.

"Bitches," Beth hollahs, ringingly. "Front and center and show me your badass selves. I'm self-deputized."

"What do you mean?" demands Tacy. "Where's Coach?" Our now perpetual lament.

"Didn't you hear?" Beth says, turning the music up louder, the rattle in it sending a few girls to their feet, bouncily. "She got hauled in by the po-po."

"What are you talking about?" I say.

"She's at the station house. The cops picked her up in the squad car. Her ball-and-chain went with her."

I don't let her catch my eye.

"How do you know?" RiRi says, cocking an eyebrow.

"I went over there to see if Coach needed a ride. Barbara-the-Babysitter told me. She looked scared pantless. She said the cops came in with trash bags. Started hauling off stuff."

Everyone exchanges wide-eyed glances.

"But I'm not here for idle gossip," she says. "Show me you got something other than chicken hearts behind those padded bras."

Everyone starts forming their lines, I can't even believe how quickly.

Clapping tight and shaking their legs out and faces tomato-bursting.

Like they're eager for it.

Like anyone will do, if they're hard enough.

"And no more tantric chants and bullshit," Beth says. "I want to see blood on the floor. And remember what old Coach Temp used to say..."

She steps back as everyone but me assembles for their back tucks.

"Cheer, cheer, have no fear!" they all chant. Some of them are even smiling.

Grinning, Beth gives the response: "When you're flying high, look to the sky, and scream Eagles, Eagles, Eagles!"

An hour later, we hit the two-two-one, Beth our Flyer.

Tossed up between RiRi and me, already six feet up, our legs braced by Mindy and Cori beneath us. Tossed up, our ponytailed apex.

My arms lifted above, I have her right side, her right wrist, her arm like a batten, hard and motionless, and RiRi her left.

She, spine so straight, the line of her neck, her body still, tight, perfect.

I have her, we have her, and Beth is higher than I've ever seen anyone.

After everyone has scattered to the locker room, I spot a lone figure watching practice from high up in the stands.

No tan for her, no nothing, but thinner than ever, a bobby pin, and she seems to be saying something to me.

That mammoth brace on her knee and her mouth open, a big O, straining to rise.

It's Emily. And she's saying something.

"What?" I call up. "What do you want, Royce?"

Slowly, she gimps her way down the stands, each step meaning a wide swing of her leg.

It never occurs to me to climb up and meet her.

"Addy," she is saying, breathless. "I never saw it before."

"Saw what?"

"I never saw the stunts. From back there," she says. "I never saw us."

"What do you mean?" I say, a slight ripple in my chest.

"Did you ever really think about it? About what we're doing?" she says, holding tight to the railing.

She starts talking, breathless and high, about the way we are stacked, like toothpicks, like pixy stix, our bodies like feathers, light and tensile. Our minds focused, unnourished, possessed. The entire structure bounding to life by our elastic bodies vaulting into each other, sticking, and then...

A pyramid isn't a stationary object. It's a living thing.... The only moment it's still is when you make it still, all your bodies one body, until... we blow it all apart.

"I had to cover my eyes," she says. "I couldn't look. I never knew what we were doing before. I never knew because I was doing it. Now I see."

I am not listening at all, her voice getting more shrill, but I can't hear. A month on the DL, a month stateside, this is what happens.

I just look hard into her baby blue eyes.

"Standing back," she says, mouth hanging in horror, "it's like you're trying to kill each other and yourself."

I look at her, folding my arms.

"You were never one of us," I say.

28

I drive by the police station and see Matt French's car. An hour later, it's still there.

Prine heard Coach there that night. Which means Coach lied, which means Coach was there when whatever happened to Will...

These words still hang, sentence unfinished. I just can't finish the sentence.

I remind myself that, hard as she is, I have seen her grief blast apart her stony self. At least once I did, holding her by the waist in her bedroom hallway Wednesday night. Feeling the bed shake with it while we slept. How is that a killing soul?

But does anyone ever seem like a killer? I can hear Beth's voice squirming in my head.

To Beth, of course, everyone does.

I believe both of them and neither of them. All their stories poured in my ear, maybe it's time to start finding out on my own.

At ten o'clock, I drive by Statler's. I'm remembering Beth's texts.

Teddy saw Coach @ Statlers last week

Drinking, talking on cell all nite, crying @ jukebox.
Said she ran outside + hit post in parking lot, peeled off

The shaggy guy at the door won't let me in with my premium Tiffany Rue, age twenty-three, driver's license, but I don't need to go inside.

Instead, I walk from parking lot post to post, hands on the peeling silver paint.

On the farthest one from the door of the bar, I spot the chewy dent, paint glittering the asphalt.

"What happened here?" I call over to the door guy.

He squints at me.

"Life is hard," he says, "and you're too young for the parking lot too, little miss."

"Who did it?" I ask, walking toward him. "Who hit the post?"

"A woman wronged," he says, shrugging.

"Was she late twenties, brown hair, ponytail?"

"I don't know," he says, pointing with one long delicate finger at the Eagles patch on my arm. "But she had a coat just like yours."

I sit and tally the lies, but there are so many and they don't quite line up.

Why would Coach tell me she hit a post in Buckingham Park instead of Statler's? One small lie, but there've been so many. Add them all together and they seem to teeter five miles above me.

It's eleven when I drive by Coach's house again.

At last, the car is there.

I find her on the deck, smoking clove cigarettes. One knee hunched up, her chin resting on it, she seems to hear me before I've even made a sound.

"Hanlon," she says. "How'd practice go?"

Have you lost your mind? I want to say. *Have you?*

"Awesome," I say, teeth gritted. "We're tight in the fight. You should've seen us rock the two-two-one."

"Make sure you don't lean down to pull your Flyer up," she says. "Bend your legs to reach her, otherwise you could pull the whole stunt down."

"I've never done that once," I say, wincing. "You weren't there."

"I'm sorry I missed it," she says, moving her ashtray from the deck chair beside her.

If it weren't for the slight tremble to her hands this might be any other night at all.

"Well, you had a pretty good excuse." I sit down, our matching twin letter jackets zipped tight up over our chins.

"I'm guessing my captain ran the show?" she asks. "Or maybe you don't want to talk about that."

All the cold and loneliness of the night sinking into me, all I want is to hammer through that stony perfection. Hand heel to chisel, that's all I want.

"You were there," I say. "You were at Will's that night."

She doesn't say anything.

"You didn't hit a post in Buckingham Park," I say. "You had a fight with him. You ran into a post at Statler's. Everything was falling apart with you two, or something. He was breaking up with you, he was done with you."

She remains statue-still.

"And you didn't find Will's body," I say, throwing myself into it, hammer, hammer, hammer. "You were with him. You were in his bed. You're a liar. You've lied about everything."

Jumping forward in my chair, I'm nearly shouting in her ear. "You're a liar. So what else are you?"

She doesn't move, doesn't even turn her head to face me.

A moment passes, my heart suspended.

"Yes," she says, finally. "I was at Will's earlier than I said. And I did hit a post at Buckingham. And I hit another post at Statler's. I've hit posts, curbs, streetlamps all over town. I've forgotten to feed my daughter dinner. I've forgotten to brush my hair. I've lost eleven pounds and haven't slept, really *slept,* in weeks. I've lost my daughter in stores, and slapped her little face. I've been a bad influence and a bad wife. I've haven't known my mind in months.

"What's the difference, Addy? The thing that matters is this. Will's dead and everything's over."

She turns and looks at me, the porch light catching her for the first time. Her face swollen, soft.

"Is that what you wanted?" she asks. "Does that help you, Addy? Because making you feel better is what matters, right?"

I flinch at that. The rest is too painful to look at.

"You," I say, my voice rising, "*you* called me that night. You dragged me into this."

"I did, Addy," she says. "But don't you know I'd tell you more if I could?"

"Why can't you?"

"Addy, I called you that night because I knew you'd help me. You understood how it was with Will and me. You were a part of it."

I was. I was.

"So, yes, I was at Will's that whole night, Addy," she says. "But I didn't do anything. I was with him, but I found him too. It's all true. Everything is."

I think about this a second, this riddle. But I can't decipher it, not with everything else happening, not with the hammer and chisel still trembling in my hand.

"So why can't you tell me?" I say, a pleading in my voice I can't stop. "I'm trying to help you. I am."

Suddenly, a band of light streams from the kitchen. I hear Caitlin's fretful weep.

Coach turns her head, glancing through the patio doors.

"You better go home," she says, rising, her cigarette dangling from her fingertips.

"Not yet," I say. "Why can't you tell me? I need to know more than this. I need..."

Caitlin's weep squalls up into a sob, something about bad dreams. What about my bad dreams?

"But Coach," I say, my mind scattering madly. "Beth says she's going to the cops tomorrow."

She stops at the patio door, one hand on the handle. "To say what?"

"To say all this. The parts she's figured out. The parts she's guessing at."

She takes one last drag on her cigarette, staring out into the black murk of the back lawn.

"She thinks you did it," I say. "She thinks you killed Will."

The first time such words come from my mouth, and they sound more monstrous than anything ever.

"Well, I didn't," she says, dropping her cigarette to the deck, letting one foot tap it out, with infinite grace.

In bed, late, I'm whispering into my phone, to Beth.

"You didn't go today? To the cops?"

"You're a freaking broken record, Addy Hanlon," she says.

"If you're so sure you know everything," I say, squinting my eyes tight, trying to figure my way into her, "why haven't you gone already?"

"I'm still collecting the final pieces," she says. I swear I can hear her tongue churning in her mouth like a vampire. "I'm working on my deployments and flanking maneuvers."

I picture her, on the other end of the phone, plucking her marked lobe, the crescent scar, but then I realize it's me, fingers gnarled around my own ear.

"Beth, I have to ask you something," I say, my tone gliding elsewhere.

"I'm waiting," she says.

"Beth," I say. Without even planning on it, my voice slips into something from our past, the Addy who needs things from Beth—her skinny stretch jeans, the ephedra tea you have to mail order, the questions for the chem exam, someone to tell her what to do to make it all bearable.

The voice, it's not an act, it isn't, it never was, and it's like a message to her, to both of us, to remember things, because she needs to remember too. I need to make her step back and see.

"Beth, I could get in trouble here," I say. "I helped her. Can you give me one more day? Just one more day to see what I can find out. To see if you're right."

"You mean one more day for her to save her own skin."

"One more day, Beth," I say. "Wait until Tuesday. Monday's the game. Tomorrow you're Top Girl."

There's a pause.

"One more day, Beth," I say, softly. "For me."

There's another pause and its quiet feels dangerous.

"Sure," she says. "You take your day."

29

She's given me one day and I have no plan for it, no idea.

All the voices from recent days, all the threats and calamity, and I can't think my way through any of it, least of all those words from Coach: *I was there, Addy, but I didn't do anything. I was with him, but I found him too.*

It's all true.

Everything is.

Crawling under the covers Sunday morning, three a.m., I take more codeine-dosed Tylenol, and the dreams that come are muddled and grotesque.

Finally twisting myself into a trembling sleep, I dream of Will.

He comes to me, his arm outstretched, palm closed. When he opens it, it's filled with shark teeth, the kind they show you in science class.

"Those are Beth's," I say, and he smiles, his mouth black as a hole.

"No," he says, "they're yours."

When I wake up, there's a newfound energy in me that boosts me from bed, that feels like the day before a Big Game. That feels powerful. It's the day of readying.

Standing in front of the mirror, toothbrush frothing, I feel certain things will happen and this time maybe I will be ready for them.

I try to find a way to reach PFC Tibbs. I think he might share more with me, reveal something, as Prine did. But I can't find a number for him, and there's no answer at the regional Guard office, so I have no way to reach him without Beth.

I drive to the police station, park in the back. Wait for an hour, door-watching.

I think about going inside, but I'm afraid the detectives will see me.

I was there, but I didn't do anything. I was with him, but I found him too. It's all true.

Beth or Coach, who do I believe when one never tells the truth and one gives me nothing but riddles?

Something about it reminds me of pre-calc. Permutations and combinations. *Consider any situation in which there are exactly two possibilities: Succeed or Fail. Yes or No. In or Out. Boy or Girl.*

Left or right. You're the Left Base, you know your only job is to strut that left side of the pyramid, hold that weight and keep your girl up.

But am I on the right side, or the left?

Watching the back door of the police station, I ponder a third way. I imagine going inside, telling them everything, letting them sort it all out.

But it's not the soldier heart in me.

I'm just about to start my car when my phone rings.

I don't recognize the number, but I answer.

"Addy?" A man says.

"Yes?"

"This is Mr. French," he says. "Matt French."

I turn off my car.

"Hey, Mr. French, how are you?" I say, on babysitter autopilot, like during those long three-minute rides home with the fathers wanting to know all about cheerleading and what it does to our bodies.

Except it's not one of our dads, it's Matt French and he's calling me and I've been a party to his family's ruin.

"I'm sorry to bother you," he says.

"How did you . . . ?" I say. "So you got my number from Coach? You . . ."

"This isn't weird, okay?" he says quickly. "It's not."

"No, I know," I say, but how is this not weird?

Matt French. I picture him standing in his yard, this forlorn figure. I picture him always like he's looking at us through glass — windshields, sliding patio doors. I don't know if I could even picture his face if I tried, but the sight of that sad slump in his shoulders is with me now.

"Can I ask you a question, Addy?" his voice muffled, like his mouth is pressed close to the phone.

"Yes."

"I'm trying to figure something out. If I tell you a phone number off my call log, do you think you could tell me if you recognize it?"

"Yes," I say before I can even think.

"Okay," he says, and he reads off a phone number. I type it in and a name comes up.

Tacy.

I say her name out loud.

"Tacy," he repeats. "Tacy who? Is she your friend?"

"Tacy Slaussen. She's on the squad," I say. "She's our Flyer. Was our Flyer."

There's a pause, a heavy one. I get the feeling something monumental is occurring. At first I think he's processing what I'm saying, but then I realize he's the one waiting for me to process something.

He wants me to remember something, mark something, know something.

It's like he's the one giving something to me.

I just don't know what.

"I was glad it wasn't your phone number," he says. "I was glad it wasn't you."

"What wasn't me?" I ask. "Mr. French, I—"

"Good-bye, Addy," he says, soft and toneless. And there's a click.

The phone call knifes its way through my head.

Matt French has found out something, or everything. It's all blown apart and he's going through her e-mails, her phone calls, everything. He's amassing all the pieces, pieces that will damn us all, will damn us both.

Adulteress, Murderer, and *Accessory to.*

But that doesn't fit with the call. With what he asked and what he didn't. And there's the way he sounded too. Unsteady but reserved, troubled but strangely calm.

I tap Tacy's number. I almost never call her, maybe I never have, but we all have each other's numbers in our phone. And Coach has them all in hers. Squad rules.

Which is how Matt French might have Tacy's number.

Except I don't think he was looking at Coach's phone when he read off the number. If he were looking at Coach's phone, it would say "Tacy" or "Slaussen." It would say something.

My call log, that's what he said. His phone.

His phone.

But why would Tacy call Mr. French? And if she did, why wouldn't he know who she was?

So I call Tacy's number, but it goes straight to voicemail.

Hey, beyotch, I'm out somewhere, lookin sick n sexified. Leave a message. If this is Brinnie, I never called you a bore. I called you a whore.

I'm glad it wasn't your phone number, he'd said. *I'm glad it wasn't you.*

Matt French, what is it you want me to know?

I drive to Tacy's house, but she's not there. Her jug-jawed sister is, the one who I always hear in the speech lab droning on about Intelligent Design when the Forensic League meets after school.

"Oh," she says, eyeing me. "You're one of those."

Slouched against the doorframe, she's eating wrinkly raisins from a small baggie, which is just the kind of thing those kinds of girls are always doing.

"She's not here," she says. "She borrowed my car to go to the school. To practice her hip rolling and pelvis thrusts."

Looking at the cloudy Ziploc in her hand, at the sad gray sweater and peace sign nose ring, I say, "We don't need to practice those."

I see the ice blue hatchback in the parking lot, and pull in next to it.

The gym backdoor is propped open with a rubber-banded

wedge of dry erasers, like we do when we want a place to drink Malibu before a party. And now some of us use it to practice weekends, off-hours, or we have since Coach drove our bodies to perfection, elevated our squad into sublimity.

I hear her first, her wheezy grunts and the soft push of pumas on airy mats.

Cheek still puffed from Thursday's fall, she's running tumbles. Throwing roundoff back handsprings, one after another. She should have a spotter because her technique, as ever, is pussy-weak.

"Stop throwing head," I shout. "Arms against your ears."

She stutters to a stop, nearly crashing into the padded wall at the far end.

"Fire, form, control, perfection," I count off, like Coach always did.

"Who cares," moans Tacy, breathlessly. "I'm ground-bound anyway. With Beth back, my life is practically over."

She slides down the wall and collapses onto the floor, pulling cotton wisps from her glossed mouth. God love Tacy, full makeup on a Sunday morning, by herself, in the school gym.

"It's only one game," I say, even as I know it's the Big Game, the Biggest Ever, and who cares about cheering spring baseball?

"Besides," I add, "how long do you really think Beth can possibly last as captain?"

"I don't know," Tacy says, now picking cotton from under her grape-lacquered fingernails. "I think she might be captain forever."

"Why would you think that?"

"Because of what's happening," she says. "Coach French was the only one who could ever stop her. And now Coach is gone."

"She's not gone, she just——"

"She's not coming back. Face it, Addy, it's all over for Coach." She looks at me, that swollen face of hers, lapin-jowled. "Which sucks because Coach was the only one who ever saw it in me. My *potential,* my *promise.*"

"Slaus, the only reason Coach put you up there is because you're ninety-four pounds and you're Beth's pigeon," I say, wanting to wring her little-girl neck. "If you care so goddamned much about Coach, why do you keep helping Beth?"

She looks startled but too dumb to be startled enough.

"I'm not helping Beth. Not anymore."

"But you were."

She takes a deep breath.

"Well, you don't know what's happened, Addy. Coach maybe did something really bad," she says, shaking her head. "It's Beth's fault, sort of. But that's no excuse. My dad says we're an excuse society now."

"Tacy," I say, my voice grinding, "tell me what you mean. Tell me what you know."

I press my foot against her bendy-straw leg, press it hard.

She looks at me, rabbit scared, and I know I need to slather some honey but keep that foot pressed too. That's what she loves. Both those things at once.

"Tacy, I'm the only one who can help you now," I say. "I'm the only one who can help."

Her tears come and I fight off the urge to slap those swollen dewlaps of hers. I fight it off because she's about to give me gold, and she doesn't even know it. She thinks her gossip, her petty grievances are significant, but they are tiny pinholes. The things around them, though, the fabric of Beth's lies and fictions, they are the gold.

"Coach was sleeping with the Sarge," she says, eyes saucering up at me. "And she loved him. And then Coach found out. About Beth. About Sarge and Beth."

$\star$ $\star$ $\star$

I'm leaning against the padded gym wall and Tacy's still on the floor, legs tucked tight, looking up at me, and talking, talking, talking.

She isn't what you think, and neither was he. That's what Beth said. *He was just a guy, like all of them.*

But Will, Will and Beth? I just can't make my head believe it.

"This was right when he first started coming to the school," she says. I'm relieved for that. Before Coach, before all that. Lost, wandering, wondering Will. "And they had that bet, her and RiRi. She wanted to beat RiRi. She said RiRi was all tits and eyeliner and she would eat her heart whole.

"So one day after school she was waiting by his truck for him. You know how he'd park in the back, behind the school lot, on Ness Street?"

I used to walk Coach there. Coach, whose face would flush at the sight of his SUV shadowed under the oak tree, its leathery leaves hovering, the shadows of them across her face as she turned to look at me, to say, *Here he is, Addy, here is my man.*

"My job was to wait by the tree with my phone," Tacy is saying, "so I could take a picture to prove she'd done it."

I don't know what's coming, but I feel a churning in my gut.

"So she's out there, waiting for him in her miniskirt," Tacy says, her fingers carelessly grazing my ankle as I stand above her. "Well, Beth, she's a hot bitch, and Sarge was a guy, right?"

He's a guy, right.

"But he couldn't go through with it," she sighs, resting her fingers on my ankle bone. "Just kid stuff. And I only got one half-decent shot, but you couldn't see much."

I don't say anything.

"But here was the thing," Tacy says, shaking one of her fingers. "Beth never did show it to RiRi. Maybe she knew it wouldn't be good enough to win the bet. Finally I asked her about it and she had me text it to her. She said she was saving it. She just kept it on her phone. She loved to flash it at me."

This seems like Beth and I wonder why she never flashed it at me. But I guess I know. Once we found out about Coach and Will, she couldn't be sure where I'd stand. She couldn't be sure I'd play for her side. She was right.

"Then all of a sudden she tells me something happened to her phone," Tacy says, "and she lost the picture and she needed me to send it again."

The memory comes to me: Coach torpedoing Beth's twizzler-red phone down the toilet.

"So I say, tell me what you need it for first," Tacy says, looking up at me, her smile coming and going as she tries to read me, read how I'm taking this, and if I want to play with her, to relish all this just a little.

"So she *had* to tell me," she, rocking in her seat, so eager to recount it, to relive the moment. "And that's when she said she was going to use it so Coach would stop giving her such a hard time."

I rest my back against the wall, not looking down at Tacy, sliding away from her, her hot breath on my legs.

"So that's when she told me about Coach and Will," she says. "She had to."

I look down at her, that lapin face squinting with conspiratorial pleasure, and I say nothing.

"So, after three years of hustling for that queen bitch, now I had something Beth wanted," Tacy says, her voice sharpening in a way that's almost impressive. "Beth had lost the goods. She didn't even e-mail the picture to herself or save it on her computer. She thinks she's so goddamned smart. How smart is that? But it was *me*. I saved the picture. And now she needed something from me."

That's a feeling I know so well it's like she's stuck her fingernail to my own beating heart. But it doesn't warm me to her.

You and me, Tacy? We share nothing.

"By then, I was Flyer, I was Top Girl," Tacy says. "But Beth warned me I'd better do what she said, or she'd make it bad for me."

Tacy's voice goes baleful, the panic spiraling back through her eyes.

"She said I'd better not make her unhappy because I oughta know that she's never unhappy alone."

No, she's not, is she.

"So I gave in," Tacy says, sighing. "But I felt sorry for Coach. And then when the Sarge died, I felt rotten. I thought maybe Beth used that picture in some evil way. And that Sarge killed himself on account of it. Is that what happened, Addy?"

"I don't know what happened," I say, finally.

She stares up at me, glassy-eyed.

"Tacy," I say, "you better show me that picture."

"I deleted it," she says, too quickly.

"You did not," I say.

Sighing again, she reaches into the pocket of her yoga pants and pulls out her tiny phone, a searing purple.

The image on the screen looks like it was shot through a fuzzed screen door.

You can see Will's uniform, the green suit coat, the gold buttons shimmering, the braid on the lifted sleeve, and part of his face, the rest concealed by the back of a female head, a swamp of dark hair and bare shoulderblades.

For a second, I think it's Coach. It looks so much like Coach.

But then I recognize Beth's green hoodie, the one slipping down, his palm spread across her back.

The look on Will's face, how could I really name it, everything so pixilated into blurred nothingnesss.

His face, though, seems to me the saddest I've ever seen.

Both stricken and despairing.

Like the pictures you see of people standing in front of their burning houses, like one I saw once of a dad holding his night-gowned little girl in his arms, trying to put on her shoe, watching his house burn to the ground.

And I know, just like that, if Tacy had been standing on the other side of the truck, if her camera lens captured Beth's eyes instead, it would show the same thing.

The picture, I can't stop looking at it. Because it seems to me suddenly filled with truth. Because it seems so beautiful.

"I never wanted to get anyone into trouble," Tacy says. "But Beth, she scares me. I mean, she's always been scary. But since all this, it's been different. It's like she's gone up three levels of scary."

I stop looking at the photo and look at Tacy instead.

Things begin to shimmer into view.

"So you just gave Beth the photo and that was it?"

"That's what I said," Tacy says, flipping over, lying back on the mat beneath her. "Isn't it?"

Resting on elbows, she stretches her skinny little toothpick legs, observing them, admiring herself.

Looking down at her, all I can think of is the time she's cost me, these collusions, her weakness. The fact that this little tinkerbell got to be Top Girl.

Something in that puffball face of hers and I can't stop myself, my foot pressing against her face. Pushing into her blighted chin, still vein-mottled from her fall. I push it hard, harder than I meant to, its softness giving way.

"Addy," Tacy moans, scratching at me with her fingers. "Addy, what are you—"

"You sent that picture to Mr. French, didn't you?" I say, my voice husky and surprising.

Hands flinging up, she tries to shove my leg away, but she can't.

"Yes, yes," she whimpers, tears coming in long syrupy strands.

I drop my foot back to the floor. And she tells me the rest.

How Beth got Matt French's number from Coach's phone and made Tacy send it, claiming she didn't have a new phone yet.

And that Beth wrote the text herself: Look at the kind of woman you're married to. Look at the trash she opens her legs for.

Beth was always good with words. And knowing the times when simplest was best.

"But the picture didn't mean anything," Tacy insists. "A dumb prank. I guess Beth probably thought Mr. French would make her quit, or Coach would get fired. But wouldn't it have made more sense to send it to Principal Sheehan?"

I shake my head at this stupid girl.

Heels of hands to her mascaraed eyes, she whispers, "Do you think that blurry little picture could have had something to do with all this? With Sarge and everything?"

I'm thinking of Matt French reading the text and looking at that picture. I'm guessing what he really thought:

Not, *There's some man with one of my wife's cheerleaders.*

No, instead, There's some man with *my wife.*

"And now Beth won't back off," she says, her hand back on my ankle, holding on to it, but eyes fixed straight ahead, at the locker room doors. "She keeps saying I better not tell anyone what we did. At practice the other day, when I fell, it was like she was showing me what she could do to me."

Her gaze locked on the doors, fiercely vibrating from the school furnace's blast, she doesn't even see me click a button on her phone and text the picture to myself.

"She showed me all right," Tacy says. "But I still told you, didn't I? I told Addy Hanlon. I guess I'm not such a cottontail. I guess I'm not the little pussy she says I am."

Her head dipping, as if from the weight of her ponytail slinging forward, she lets her body go lax.

"I was always afraid of you," she says, touching her cheek lightly, the tread of my shoe dancing faintly there. "Even more than Beth. I heard what you did to her. That scar on her ear."

This time, I don't correct it. What I'd done to Beth. What *I* had done to Beth, the scariest badass we ever knew.

I fold my arms and glance down at Tacy. She looks so small.

"I just wanted to be Flyer," she says. "I'm going to be again."

"Sure you are," I say, handing her phone back to her.

She looks up at me as she takes it, and something passes over her face.

Dropping her phone into her pocket, she flings her hand upward, as if I should help her to her feet.

"Sure I am," she repeats, brightening. "I mean, you're gonna bust Beth now, right?"

A smile wiggling there, she adds, "Then I'll be Flyer again."

I was there, but I didn't do anything. That's what Coach had said.

I was with him, but I found him too. It's all true.

Matt French's phone blips, he looks at the screen, he sees that picture, reads those words:

Look at the kind of woman you're married to. Look at the trash she opens her legs for.

A mistake that also happens to be true.

So Matt French, he sees the military uniform and goes hunting. Finds out who the recruiter is. Or he just checks his wife's phone, her e-mails, something. Anything.

He finds out where this recruiter lives, and he drives out there, to that empty steel tower on the edge of nothing, and he finds his wife and her lover.

And . . . and . . .

And he wants me to know.

And then there's Coach, the alibi she built for me.

"So last Monday you were there with your coach and her husband?" the detective had asked.

"Yes," I said.

Coach protecting Matt French, Matt French protecting Coach. The things between them, their webbed history and hidden hearts, and so instead of turning on each other, they are raising the ramparts high. The two of them locked in something blood-deep. Who knows what lies between them now? Wrists crossed, head to head, they are closing so tight, but they need me.

They do.

And Beth. There is Beth.

30

Work hard and believe in yourself. That's what they always tell you. But that's not really it at all. It's the things you can't say aloud, the knowledge that what you're doing, climbing high, jumping, hurling yourself into the air, hooking arms, legs around each other to create something that will collapse with the bobble of one knee, a twist of a wrist.

Standing back, Emily said, saying the thing you're never supposed to say, *it's like you're trying to kill each other and yourself.*

The knowing that what you are all doing, together, is the most delicate thing, fragile as spun glass, and driven by magic and abandon, your body doing things your head knows it can't, your bodies locking together to defy gravity, logic, death itself.

If they told you these things, you would never join cheer. Or maybe you would.

In the morning, it takes a long time under the showerhead to get my blood moving. To pinprick my skin to life. To get my head game.

I stand under the bracing gush for so long, looking at my body, counting every bruise. Touching every tender place. Watching the swirl at my feet.

I'm really just trying to jack up my heart.

I think, *This is my body, and I can make it do things. I can make it move, flip, fly.*

After the squall of a blow-dryer, I gather my hair, sliding in bobby pin after bobby pin, pulling it all into place.

I stand in front of the mirror, my face bare, flushed, taut.

Slowly, my hands lifting, the sticky nozzle, dusty brushes, oily wands waving in front of my face, fuchsia streaking up my cheeks, my lashes stiffened to brilliant black, my hair stiff, gleaming, pin-tucked.

The perfumed mist, thick in my throat, settling.

I look in the mirror.

And it's finally me there, and I look like no one I've ever seen before.

"Game Day—Kill Celts!!" shrieks the banner across the school entrance, a tissue paper eagle, wings stiff and high, rising behind it.

I let my heart rise to it.

The morning passes, I don't see Beth at all, and Coach has called in sick. That's all anyone can talk about.

She's abandoned us twice, three times over. We are losing count.

She doesn't care about us at all.

She hates us.

"What did we do wrong?" the JV girl sobs, pressing her face against her locker door. "What did we do?"

School skitters by without touching me, and Tacy, face bleach-white, will not meet my gaze.

I am thinking of things, of the Abyss and its greasy stare and how I won't blink. I can't.

*   *   *

At three fifteen we are in the gym, jumping high.

"Scout's a-coming!" RiRi hollers. "Wait till she sees what we got!"

Everyone screams.

And it feels like God touching me. What would I do without this, because here I am, propelling to heaven itself, soles resting on Mindy's knotty shoulders—or on the floor, knees sponging, lifting Brinnie Cox, nimble feet in my palm, surging her straight to God.

That feeling, it is God's greatest gift.

Just like that adderall. Found that morning in the corner of my hoodie pocket from a long ago act of Beth's generosity, it gallops through me, and I know I can do anything.

When you have nothing inside you, you feel everything more, and feel you can control all of it.

With Jesus in my heart, and with that seismic blast, who could stop my ascent? Any of ours?

In the locker room, forty minutes to game time, we are Vegas showgirl–spangled. The air thick with biofreeze and tiger balm and hairspray and the sugared coconut of tawny body sprays, it is like being in a soft cocoon of sugar and love.

There's RiRi, slinging her curling iron like a gunfighter, shaping the spring-shot ponytail, its helix curls.

There's Paige Shepherd, temp tattoo blazing across her tan face, kicking her leg high and twisting, tumbling into Mindy's arms, her wrists black duct-taped like Roman gladiator cuffs.

See Cori Brisky, rubbing flexall on her numbing wrists, her smile showing all her teeth, and how sharp they are, and I know that there's a jungle princess in there who's ready for hot blood.

See even shell-shocked Emily, our fallen comrade, fingers glazed with icy hot, running it across Mindy's armor shoulder blades, whispering in her ear.

And there I am. If you could see me — tall, tight, lightsome, and powerful, flipping my back tucks on the slippery tile, afraid of nothing, no one. Just try to stop me.

That's what people never understand: They see us hard little pretty things, brightly lacquered and sequin-studded, and they laugh, they mock, they arouse themselves. They miss everything.

You see, these glitters and sparkle dusts and magicks? It's war paint, it's feathers and claws, it's blood sacrifice.

But where's our fearsome leader? Either of them?

We need somebody to gather all this hectic energy, to link these pulsing organs into one powerful, unstoppable body.

What if that somebody were me?

Moving girl to girl, I start back-stroking, French-braiding, tiger-balming, offering rallying words, *C'mon girls, let's show them what we got.*

I even talk, for the first time ever, to that poor yellow peep JV, the one who will have to fly tonight if Beth doesn't show, the one shivering like a downy chick.

I know I can lift her, I can.

She's not a girl but a butterfly resting on my fingertips.

But then there's a clatter from the backdoors, and a flurry of whoops and bratty squeals and, baby lamb JV tucked under my arm, I turn and know I will see her.

Beth.

Leaping up on the locker room bench, eyelids scorched with blue glitter, she heaves her throaty voice to the drop ceiling.

"Hella, bitches!" she bellows, rocking her feet on the bench so it shudders. "Our scout, that Regionals scout, I can feel her out there, waiting. And, bitches, she is so ready to be fucked."

The gasp from us is loud and exultant.

"I've just trawled through that gym to check out the Celt squad and I've never seen anything so appalling. Ana girls with accordion ribs, a coupla dykey ringers with treebark legs and Charlie Brown faces. And those Celt ballers, skidding and squeaking, tossing that baby's ball around like they're kings of the world? Pathetic."

Everyone, so eager, twirling near her, just like the old days when she'd preen and twist and flash her blue Eagles tatts and we'd clamor, *Give it to us, Captain, rise up, rise up!* . . .

"You know who the stars are? We are. Why? Because we don't throw around a fucking rubber ball. You know what *we* throw around? Live girls. Do you know who flies? We do. You know what we hurl to the rafters? Each other."

I hear Emily's tender gasp behind me, her boot brace clacking, and the muffled squeal of the JV Flyer.

"Tonight, you've got to spill their blood," she says, her raised arm, her temples, her neck pulsing, "or I promise you they will spill yours."

There's a dark roiling on Beth and it's starting to sweep through us. We are letting it, all of us.

"Brace those arms. Bolt those knees. Look at that crowd like you're about to give them the best piece of ass they ever had. Sell it."

The feelings charging through the room, they're complicated and incendiary and none of us, not even me, can name them all. Everything in Beth, in her swarthy energy, so repulsive and so captivating—

"Bases, eyes on your Flyer, she is yours. You lock her to your heart. You lose her, blood on the mat. She is yours. Make her."

All the swirling ponytails nod in unison, as if they know, as if any of us know what Beth, veins tight on her upstretched arms, means or could ever mean.

"JV," Beth says, pointing her witching finger at the yearling under my arm, and because none of us really know her name. "You fail, you fail all of us. So you will not fail."

The JV shakes her head back and forth, looking like she might cry.

"Girlie, you've been a chick long enough. I need you to show me that egg tooth," she says, slipping her fingers under JV's tank top, heaving her up on the bench with her. "Tonight's the night, you're gonna pip through the shell."

Beth tugs the girl under her own bronzed arm, stares her down and nearly laps her face. "So stiffen the sinews, summon up the blood. We've come to bury them. We've come to plow their bones by the final bell."

She pounds her pumas until that bench rattles, our bodies shake.

"It's harvest day, girlies," she says, her voice like crackling lightning. "Get busy when the corn is ripe."

I almost fall for it, for Beth's hoodoo grandiosity.

Our captain, like Beth from before, our noble, proud, heartstrong Beth, and this Beth too, a warrior nearly vanquished but not quite, never quite.

We few, we happy few, she might say, *we band of sistuhs, for she today that sheds her blood with me, shall be my sistuh always.*

Couldn't I just let that be enough for these two hours?

But then Tacy sputters in, late, her face still bruise-dappled and her eyes lightless, damned.

And I'm reminded of everything.

Including the feel of my foot pressed against her face, what she made me do.

This feeling, this high, it's not real. It's that Jesus-love flooding through me, by which I mean the adderall and the pro clinical hydroxy-hot with green tea extract and the eating-nothing-but-hoodia-lollipops-all-day.

And most of all the high that comes from Beth's dark supply.

I don't want it.

Ten minutes to game time, and no Coach to stop the squad, everyone's breaking rules and whirring through the back bleachers, scout-spotting.

Back in the locker room, I sit, trying to get my game head on.

SCOUT! 3 row frm top, lft — lady w. cap + mirror shades! RiRi texts.

I hear a rustling one row over and there's Beth, hands in her locker, tugging off her rows of friendship bracelets, tightening her pin-straight ponytail. Eyes on herself in her stick-on mirror, face blue and frightening.

Were it not for the angle of her locker door, the way the parking lot lights slant through the high windows, I might never have seen it.

But I did.

The hot glow of an evil eye, lurking between a pile of hair ties and toe socks.

A hamsa bracelet. Coach's hamsa bracelet. My hamsa bracelet.

Hands to her slick shea-buttered arms, I catch her by surprise, flipping her around.

"What, did you think I wouldn't show?" she says, and her blood all up in her cheeks and temples. "I'd never let the squad down."

My chest lurching, I grab the bracelet with one hand and, with the other, shove her into the shower stalls.

"You did it. You took it. You lied about all of it," I shout raggedly, my voice echoing to the slimy ceiling of the showers. "It was never in Will's apartment, was it?"

"No," she says, with an odd stuttering laugh, "of course not."

"Why did you tell me the police found it?"

"I wanted you to see," she says. "She was hiding everything from you. She never cared about you."

"But you stole it. You were going to try to plant it, something," I say, squeezing her so hard I feel one of my nails start to give. "My god, Beth."

"Oh, Addy," she says, still laughing, her head shaking back and forth. "I took it a long time ago. That time we slept at her house."

I think of it now. That long-ago night of the Comfort Inn party. Beth, the wounded kitty. Those hours I'd abandoned her to Coach's sofa, left her free to prowl the house, her viper's crawl. Shadows flitting by all night.

"But that was before everything," I say. "Why?"

"She didn't deserve it," Beth says, her voice rising, throaty, the laughing gone. "She'd tossed it on the kitchen window ledge, like an old sponge. She didn't deserve it."

Wrestling away from me, she shoves hard, her face a blue smear.

"And now her time is up," she says, husky-voiced and deadly grave. "Now she'll see what I can do."

Face so close, painted shooting stars slashing up her temples, she's heated up on her own words. But I can smell something dank and musky on her, like she has been clawing hard through loamy earth. Like she has very little left.

Which means it's my time.

"You're not going to the cops," I say, voice as cold and hard as I can manage. "You never were. You don't want them to find out what you did."

Maybe I thought I'd never see surprise on her face again, but there it is. It almost frightens me.

"What *I* did?" she says. "I gave you your goddamned day, and you used it to let her spit more venom in your ear. When I think of the yogi hold that cheer bitch has over you, I wanna puke."

"Beth, I know it all now," I say, pushing myself close to her, towering over her. "You used Tacy to send that picture of you and Will to Coach's husband. Tacy told me everything."

A stitch of panic rises over that high brow, her back rustling against the vinyl curtain, and here I am, I suddenly realize, five inches taller than the little shrub, the little Napoleon. I just never felt it before.

"Slaussen. I should've guessed it," she says, grinning wryly. "I never saw a fox eat a rabbit before. I'd like to. How did she taste?"

"Did you hope Matt French would look at the picture and think you were Coach?"

"I didn't care what he thought," she says, chin jutting high, graveling her voice. "All I cared about was getting her out. Someone had to get us out—"

Somehow my hand has a hold of the bottom of her ponytail, fingers slapping against her scarred ear.

It's like how it sometimes is with me and Beth, the closeness that comes from being hand to hand, arm to arm, body to body, and always spotting each other. I know her body and the way it turns, the way it moves, and what makes her shake.

"You started all this," I say, fingers gripping tight. "It was you."

Snaking her fingers between mine, she swipes my hand from her hair and rolls her eyes with comic book magnitude.

"For fuck's sake, fuck me if Coach's husband mistakenly thought his wife was fucking the National Guard recruiter. Oh, wait," she says. "She *was.*"

"You set it all in motion," I say. Then wielding another hidden card, "You knew Coach was with Sarge that night. Prine told me everything."

She doesn't say anything, just stares at me, the angry blue war paint blaring.

"If you wanted me to believe Coach killed Will," I say, "why didn't you tell me she was there?"

And then I realize it. "You were afraid I'd tell Coach. Warn her."

"I wasn't *afraid* you would warn her," she says. "I *knew* you would. You're just her little pussy, and always were."

I shove her shoulder, and she laughs, an aching laugh, a laugh I remember most from the worst times for Beth, the scariest times after bad nights with boys or her mother, and I'd try to say tender things and she would laugh, which was her way of crying.

"Prine's gonna do what I say, Addy," she says, curling her hand on top of mine, pressing it into her own sharp shoulder. "He thinks I might statutory him, or worse."

"You knew all along," I say, feeling her veins pulsing under my grip. "All your lies—"

"My lies?" she says. "All you've done is lie to me. All you've ever done. But you've always been the fox. Stone cold."

"I'm telling everything, Beth," I say.

Like there's a fever in my brain, or Jesus in my heart, my hands are on her again, hurling both her shoulders back against the shower tiles, her eyes flashing and her mouth a tight grin.

She's trying to smile, yes, but there's a horror in it. *Push harder, push harder. Ride that bitch.*

"What can you tell? All you have is Slaussen," she says. "You think I can't win back that rabbit heart of hers? I have my two front teeth sunk in it. I have things I can tell about her, about Coach, about you—"

My hand whips across her face so fast I gasp.

But she doesn't flinch. Instead, eyes darkening, she slides back against the wall, tilting her face so it smears against the damp tiles, her spangled mask blurring blue.

She doesn't say anything for a second and the silence feels heavy, epic. I don't know what to do with myself except listen to my own breathing.

"He said he was sick with himself over it," she says, quietly, darkly.

It takes me a second to realize she's talking about Will.

"Like I was this dirty thing he'd done," she says.

She puts a hand to the back of her head, rubbing it with an eerie softness, like she's in slow motion. "Who is he to call me dirty?" she asks, her eyelashes slipping glitter.

I'm thinking of the snapshot of the two of them, the look on his face.

"You should've seen how he looked at me after," she says. "Like you're looking at me now."

I don't know what to say to this.

"Then I saw him and Coach together," she says, "the way they just gloated in their fucking. So freaking enthralled with themselves, and you just so enthralled with them. With her."

There is the secret song in me of an old Beth, schoolyard Beth, playground and sleeping bag and bikes with streamers Beth. The Beth who never wanted me to sleep over at Katie Lerner's house, and would always wait in front of my house the night I got back from summer vacation. The Beth who always, chin to my shoulder, looked out for me, and I for her. Our bodies interlocked.

"But, Beth, you can stop now," I say, shaking my head. "You can stop all this."

Something stirs in her face and she's looking down at my clenched, glitter-crusted hands on her arms.

"I did it for all of us," she says. "I did it for you, Addy. Somebody had to. And it's always been me."

I let my hands go, staring, not sure what to do or what she means.

"The funny thing is, Addy, it turns out you were the dangerous one," she says, voice steadying now, drawing strength.

She walks past me and, her palm clasped over her scarred left ear, adds, "You were the tough one, the cruel one. The fox. You just couldn't admit it. You've always done whatever you wanted. It was always you."

And she's gone.

I hear her whistling through the locker room, and her voice, mournful but resonant now.

"Arrow in the quiver," she sings. "At daggers drawn."

31

We are phalanx-spread four deep across the floor. Oh, the roaring, if you only knew. Like being crest-deep in a wave and all the pounding to go through you.

We are assembled soldiers. My eyes flashing past us, it's like looking at fifteen duplicates of one shiny-eyed girl, midnight blue halters and silver-lined minis, spoking legs and bleached white sneaks, hair slicked back into uniform ponys, shimmer-blue foiled bows.

We all have our eyes on the woman in the red hat and mirrored shades, high up on the left flank. Whether she's the scout or not, we're giving everything to her.

RiRi, superstitious, singing softly, *"Jesus on my necklace, glitter on my eyes,"* knuckles rapping against mine.

The pounding of our thirty assembled feet, pounding so it thunders all through us, as we undulate into a V.

There is Beth at the diamond tip, her face streaked indigo and, from afar, never looking more like the savage princess she is, like she might have a necklace of human tongues.

"Split the 'V,'" she shouts, and forking her fingers at her hips, "Dot the 'i,'" and sliding her finger down low, shimmying, legs vibrating, "Rock that C-T-O-R-Y!"

Seeing her like that. Seeing her, bright white sneaks on the gym floor, legs and arms together, chin up proud to the crowd, their howling and foot-thundering frenzy, I feel all kinds of things I can't name.

Her face is so lovely, a perfect spritely smile carved there, lightning bolt tattoo streaked across one high cheekbone.

And on her wrist, the hamsa, plucked from the shower stall floor.

Marching in formation, our heads snapping, feet thumping, four-five-six across, the diamond splitting.

"Beat those Celts, slaughter that ball.

"We will die for you above all."

"That's not how it goes," mewls Brinnie Cox, as if Beth has just flubbed the line.

"We will die for you above all," Beth repeats.

Those words, I know them, but I don't know how and there's no time.

RiRi, Paige, and I darting to the mat's far corners to spring across with our tumbling passes, everyone whipping past me and the noise like an ocean in my ear.

And I land it and Beth is there and I am spotting, Mindy and Cori popping her into the air, tick-tocking one leg to the other, her feet in their hands, her arms V-ed.

And Beth is shouting, and I am looking up at her, her chin trembling, her neck pulsing.

She is crying, but only I can see that. I'm the only one who's seen it before. Her face like something precious split in two. A diamond cracked, a web spreading.

"It's Coach," comes Tacy's squealing shout. "It's Coach."

My head whipping to one side, I can't believe it, but I see her

there, soft hoodie and hemp yoga pants, and her hair knotted tight
on her head.

Coach.

Oh, my Coach.

And she is saying something, or she isn't saying anything at all,
but we know what to do and we do our back tucks in perfect unison, symmetric soldiers all in a line, then the whistle blows and the
bounding boys come and we run to her.

We run to her.

And I see Beth, and her broken face, and I can't help her at all.
I can't.

It's all a heady blur, the floorboard-pounding mayhem of the game,
and Coach there, placing her hand gently on the backs of our
heads, pulling, even, so un-Coach-like, on Mindy's golden braids,
and by the time the halftime horn thunders, I've lost Beth entirely.

In the locker room, the air clear from the tall windows lifted open
by Coach with that long iron stick.

We are not actually on our knees, but it feels that way. It feels as
if we're on our knees, like prayerful Southern football players.

We are all bowing inside, to her.

Coach, you've not forsaken us.

"I'm glad to be here right now," she says, and she's speaking so
low but somehow even amid the bumptious din coming from the
gym we can hear her, hear every beat.

"I'm lucky to be in your company," she says. "And I'm talking
about all of you. You mighty women."

Something catches in my throat. *Coach.*

I feel a hand twist around my arm, and it's RiRi, her curls
shaking, and beside her Emily, half leaning, still casted, against the

lockers, and all of us standing, craning our necks, huddling toward Coach's clear eyes, clear face, clear voice.

How could the things we would laugh at out there, scoff at and eye roll and dismiss, move us so much in here? Because it is Coach.

"For all kinds of reasons," she says, her voice wobbling so slightly I feel sure only I can hear, "we're all going to remember tonight."

All of us circling forward, wanting to warm our hands, our bodies to it.

"It's the last game of the season, after all these months of sweat and blood. And, after all this, I want you to be able to speak proudly, to strip your sleeves and show your scars, and talk about what you did tonight."

Her words are vibrating through me, touching my very center.

"After the night's over," she says, her voice lifting higher, "after you graduate, and you're off to college or wherever you girls go—ten years from now, your little girl's going to pull your dusty Eagles yearbook off the shelf and ask what you were like in high school.

"You won't have to cough, look the other way, and say, 'Well, sweetie, your mom was in the French Club and sang in the choir.' You won't even have to say, 'Your mom waved pom-poms and shook her ass.' Because you will know what you were, what you are forever.

"Squad, *take this moment,* seal it over your heart."

The quiet among us, the devotional silence starts to break apart as we feel ourselves lifted, feelings and gasps and eager squeaks and throatier yeas and rustling and rumbling and most of all the sense of greatness rising from within us and hoisted high.

"You're going to look your girl straight in the eye and say, 'Baby, your mom rode to the rafters. Your mom lifted three girls in her hands, grinning all the way,'" she says, our voices rising to a baying now, all together.

"'Your mom built pyramids and flew high in the sky, and back in Sutton Grove, they're still talking about the wonders they saw that night, still talking about how they watched us all reach to the heavens.'

"Don't you want to be able to say that?"

Our innermost selves, in some magnificent ascent, and a clattering as some girls leap onto the benches, crying out, overtaken.

But not me—me who wants to bathe in the moment's sacredness forever.

"You may have the bodies of young girls," she says, her voice deep and holy, "but you have the hearts of warriors. Tonight, show me your warrior hearts.

"That's all."

And she turns and pushes through the locker room doors into the brightly lit hallway.

But instead of turning in to the clanging gym, its frenzy pitched to madness, she walks straight out the loading dock doors, into the starred night.

It's like when a fever breaks, and you don't know what's happened, or what all those voices in your head meant, but the Celts squad does their halftime routine and all I see are flying bodies and cries and the greater and greater sense of a battlefield of fallen enemies on which we will march.

And I realize, Beth gone again, I don't even know who Top Girl is.

"It's gotta be the JV, right?" whispers RiRi. "We're tossing her up, right?"

But there is no time, and there we are, running out on that gym floor, and I feel my body flipping into my handspring, and Brinnie Cox's legs spiraling next to me, and suddenly we're twenty seconds in and I can hear myself shouting:

> . . . said shah shah shah shah booty
> Got that rhythm feelin' tight
> Let your body rock SNAP-SNAP
> Let your hips show some might STOMP-STOMP-STOMP
> shah shah shah shah booty

I'm looking for the JV Flyer, but I don't see her.

> We don't need no music
> We don't need no bands.
> All we need are Eagles fans jammin in the stands!
> Oh wait, stop a minute, WAIT
> shah shah shah shah booty

I feel her before I see her.

Dark hair shimmering, the thunderbolt seared to her face.

Beth, in the JV's place. Lining up in the top Flyer spot for the two-two-one.

And if you could understand how time can stop, it did for me.

Mindy has her hands on my waist, my hands gripping soft shoulders, my toe slipping into the pocket of her bent knee, pushing off with my right foot and lifting my other knee as high as I can, planting it on her shoulder, front-spotting Paige below, propelling up my other foot.

RiRi and I face each other, feet fixed on Mindy's and Cori's shoulders, their hands tight on our ankles.

"Who's counting?" I shout.

shah shah shah shah booty

Emily, swinging her boot brace across the front row, her eyes avid, her fear gone.

"I'll do it," she cries. "I'll count. No one knows better than me. No one knows—"

We are now ten and a half feet high, my eyes fixed on RiRi's wild green ones, her face cobalt-brushed, ecstatic, mouthing, *"B-E-T-H!"*

shah shah shah shah booty

"One-two, three-four," Emily's fierce counting like a pulse in my brain, like a hammer over my heart.

The whole pyramid sponging, rubber-banding as it should, the living thing, the beating heart.

Below I see Beth's black hair, and she flings her head back, her eyes squeezed shut.

I will die only for you above all.

That's what she'd said, and I remembered it now, from long ago. Age nine or ten, poring over a Time-Life book in my dad's library, an old picture of a Japanese pilot tying his headband, eyes determined, jaw set.

And the caption: "I will die only for you above all."

Beth loved that picture and tore the page out and pasted it in her locker with rubber cement, and at year's end, we tried to claw it free, but it came off in shreds and there was nothing she could do.

I will die only for you above all.

Six hands on her and she's propelled up between RiRi and me.

Lying flat, her arms outstretched, and we pop her up so she is standing.

Blocking out Emily's dire warnings of what it's like from out there, from the stands, as they see all of us spring-loaded into the air, defying gravity, logic, the laws of physics itself, I know all I must think of is Beth's wrist in my tight-clawed—

One

shah shah shah shah booty

and loading her forward, slingshotting her back to life, pitching her higher, locking her in place, holding her widespread arms like points on a star,

Two

shah shah shah shah booty

I can feel, fingers to Beth's wrist, the veins pulsing, the beat slower than it should be, and I think—

Three

you ain't got

—her pumas balancing on the gathered hands below, a pinched tightrope and she is cheering, oh, is she cheering.

Waiting for Emily to count EIGHT, then *DEADMAN,* we drop Beth's wrists, she falls backwards, limbs outspread, into the waiting arms below . . . that is what she is to—

Four

you ain't got it, you ain't got it, ain't got it

She is so high, fifteen feet, sixteen, seventeen, a thousand—and the whole gym shaking victorious, her body still like a fierce arrow—when I feel her suddenly yank her wrist from my clasp.

My body pitches forward, but terror-eyed Mindy has hold of me, and RiRi bobbles to keep hold of Beth's other wrist.

I have my eyes on Beth, I think I am calling out to her, her name choked in my chest, but she won't turn, she couldn't or she'd—

Five

...and I know and I'm not going to stop her, there is no stopping her.

This is what she wants, after all.

Six-and—and two beats too soon, she propels herself backwards with such force.

The gasp from the bleachers lashes through the air.

The power with which she thrusts her body backwards.

The force with which she twists her body, spinning it, and then kicking backwards

RiRi and I teetering on our Bases, nearly falling forward toward each other—

—and all our hands grabbing for her, and the will with which Beth pitches her body, legs kicking so far back, so far back.

All the way back.

The air sucked from me, the sounds gone from the world.

The way, for a second, her body seems to lift, dance to the rafters, then the way everything shifts, all our bodies tilting in space as I feel myself falling, as I feel Beth falling.

It's like she doesn't weigh anything at all, and she might never hit the floor, until she does.

Then the sickening crack and seeing her head click backwards, like a doll's.

But you must see:

She never really wanted anything but this.

The Abyss, Addy, it gazes back into you.

32

I'm sitting in the hospital's east corridor, a waiting room behind a wall of glass bricks.

Beth's mom appears in the doorway just past nine, flinging her camel Coach bag onto the sofa and bursting into inky tears that seem to come in gaping spurts for hours.

She talks mournfully of her failures, her weaknesses, and most of all the harshness of life for pretty girls who never know how good they have it.

Finally, she cries herself to sleep, sinking into her coat like a slumbering bat.

I move three seats away.

The TV, pitched high in a corner, scrolls footage of Beth being wheeled out on the gurney, one arm dangling limply.

Then the on-camera interviews, and there's Tacy Slaussen's rabbit face.

"I just want everyone to know that our stunts usually hit," she says, tightening her ponytail and showing all her teeth. "But let's face it. Cheer can be dangerous. I got injured just the other day. It was supposed to be me out there."

Behind her, Emily sobbing in the background. "I didn't mess up the count, I didn't."

I reach up and switch the channel, but Tacy's on that one too.

"But Beth always told us, life is about taking risks, and you can die at any moment," she says, with those pointy teeth of hers, forehead shining.

"It's what we sign up for."

And then Brinnie Cox, crying just as she cried a few hours before when she flunked a chemistry quiz, and a few hours before that, when Greg Lurie called her Bitty Titty.

"She is such a talented girl," she wails, raccoon-eyed, "and we all feed off her positiveness."

Not long after, I see the news of the arrest.

The closed caption reads: *Cheerleading coach husband to be charged in slaying.*

Which is such a simple way to say what is anything but simple.

The snapshot they show on the news seems to be from some other world I don't know, Coach and Matt French, faces giddy, a great custardy wedding veil whipping around her.

I think of him out there in the backyard the other day, his stillness. But wasn't he always so still, a shadow drifting past all our antic energy? So strange to think how much was roiling in him. The thing we mistook for blankness, for boringness, for a Big Nothing, turned out to be everything. A battered heart, a raging one.

"What is this, the all-cheerleading network?" brays a tired expectant father in the chair next to me, until he sees my uniform, the sequins matted to my leg.

Later, Beth's mom comes back from talking to the doctor and smoking twelve cigarettes in the parking lot.

She says it's a skull fracture in three places.

★   ★   ★

"I was waiting for her." That's what Beth kept saying, lying on the gym floor, her eyes black. "Where did she go?"

All the way out, like on some continuous loop. "When will she come back? I was waiting for her."

There seems no point in sitting, so I drive to the police station at two a.m. and sit.

It's an hour before I see Coach, holed up in the back lot with a pack of Kools—these are not times for clove cigarettes—her breath making dragony swirls.

"Hey," she says, when she spots me.

We sit in my car, her eyes darting over and over to the back door, like she's waiting for the cops to realize she shouldn't be out here alone.

I don't tell her about Beth, don't ask if she knows.

It's her time to talk, and she does.

That night, like any other night, she tells me, Matt was working late and she still had no car.

Will wants to see her, needs to, really.

Says he'll drive her back and forth if she'll come. He never wants to be alone.

No one ever needed her half as much, not even her daughter. She is sure of it.

At his apartment, everything feels different. It's been that way lately. The feeling that it's all too much, and even scary, the way he holds her hard enough to hurt, talking the whole time about how she is all that keeps him from the way he feels, which is like his heart is pumping water and drowning him to death.

These are the ways he talks lately, and the only thing to do is to hold on to him. Some nights she's held him so hard, she has bruises on the heels of her hands.

They are in the bedroom a long time, and nothing is made better for more than one tight minute. The look on his face after frightens her.

She takes a long shower to give him time to pull himself together, to shake off the night horrors of his dark room.

But when she turns off the faucet she hears a man talking loudly. Saying something over and over. At first she thinks it's Will, but it isn't Will.

Over and over, the same rhythm and the same feeling of panicky anger, like her dad after things started to go wrong for him, at work, with her mom, with the world, and sometimes it was like he would tear the whole house down with him, raze it, incinerate it.

She guesses she is hearing it through the ceiling, the floor. Doesn't that happen in apartments, where nothing is private or secret?

For a few seconds she doesn't even call out to Will, figures she is being silly, all the noises that rattle through these big buildings, the way sound carries in the gorges.

But then the sound flies up fast and is now familiar to her, feels close enough to touch. That's when she pulls on her T-shirt, her body still so wet it fuses to her in an instant, and starts walking out of the bathroom.

"Will," she says. "Will."

And she is shaking the water from her hair. Her head is down and so she doesn't see how it started.

"Listen, please, calm down and—"

Will, towel wrapped around him, is talking to someone in the tone she sometimes uses with Caitlin when Caitlin scares herself at night, seeing ghosts slipping under her closet door.

And another voice, one she knows:

"—think you can do whatever you want. Another man's wife—"

And it is Matt, and how can Matt be here? She wonders if she is still asleep and this is like a soap opera when you walk out of the shower and learn everything has been a dream.

Matt.

At first she thinks it's his phone in his hand, that black curve always like a dark beetle in his palm.

She remembers hearing Will say, "How did you get my gun—"

Will had shown her the gun the week before. He'd taken it from his top bureau drawer and said, *Is this what life is supposed to be about?*

He'd held it in his lap as he told her he hated the Guard, hated everything except her.

Because that was how he talked lately, which wasn't a way she wanted anyone to talk, not after Dad.

In bed with him, it was all she could think about.

When he was sleeping, she opened the bureau drawer again, took the gun, and put it in her purse.

She hid it in her file cabinet at home, far in the back behind the hundreds and hundreds of Xeroxed cheer routines. She tried not to think about it. But it was there and, trying to sleep at night, she could think of nothing else.

But now her husband has the gun, holding it funny, like it's this thing in his hand he doesn't recognize.

It happens so fast, Will saying to Matt, "Do you think I care? Do you think I'd stop you?"

And Will grabbing for the gun, and Matt's eyes seizing on her at last, spotting her standing there, and abruptly gaining focus, gaining balance.

Matt, suddenly realizing, but not fast enough to stop it.

The two men pressed together, almost like they are embracing. It is as though they are embracing.

And then suddenly the gun is shoved up between their faces, and Will tipping back, the gun tilting—like the way you'd feed a bottle to a baby.

"This is it," he says. Will says.

She'll always remember that.

And the pop.

The flash from Will's mouth.

Like a cherry bomb.

Like Will's face lit from within.

Candescent.

And Will sliding to the floor.

It is so graceful, like a dance.

If it hadn't been what it was, it would've been beautiful.

After that, she loses time.

Mostly, she remembers the high, sharp whistling sound that she finally realizes is coming from her.

And Matt crying. She'd never ever seen him cry, except when Caitlin was born and he'd sat in the chair next to her hospital bed and told her that he had never been so happy and nothing could ever be bad again, he wouldn't let it be.

After that, everything is a red blur, Matt smearing the gun on the sofa cushions, smearing his fingerprints away.

She remembers thinking, *How does he know to do that?* And then thinking, *Everyone in the world would know to do that.*

She remembers him holding her in his arms and telling her things, and the red-wrung way of his face, and how she felt sorry for him, she just did.

She remembers how she looked down and his shirt cuffs were misted red.

He tried to get her to leave with him, but she refused. Maybe he tried. That part she doesn't really remember.

She remembers sitting on the leather sofa for a minute, staring out the big windows, night-blackened.

She couldn't have, but she thinks she heard Matt driving away, twenty-seven floors down.

She doesn't remember calling me.

She never looked down at the floor.

When she finishes telling me, we're sitting on a back curb and it's so cold but neither of us wants to go inside.

"After, I remember shouting, 'How could you do this to me?'" she says with almost a wry laugh. "But which one of them was I saying it to?"

How could you do this to me? I wonder if she knows she's still saying it in her sleep.

"When I came home that night, all the drawers were open, the file cabinet dumped on the floor. He'd gone through everything," Coach says. "But I don't know what started it."

I don't say anything.

"I don't think he ever meant to use that gun at all," she says. "That's not how he is."

"But if Matt explains how it was, if you both do," I say, my voice rising up, "maybe they'll let him go."

She looks at me wearily, as if to say, *And then what, Addy? Then what?*

"I saw his face right before," she says. "Will's face. I saw the way he was looking at Matt."

She turns to me.

"He never looked at me at all."

Picturing Will, I think I finally see what it was. I could never name it before, the way his eyes were always drifting, never connecting. There was the feeling with him always of a room everybody had left.

"Tonight, just before they came to arrest him," she says, "Matt said, 'What they'll never believe is that he wanted to die.' He said, 'Colette, it doesn't seem fair that I get to know that. That I get that. But it's true.'"

She looks at me, smiling sadly. "But you know what? He's right. It really isn't fair that he gets to know that."

Her smile turning grim. "Because that doesn't help me."

We sit quietly for a long time.

"Coach," I say, my voice surprising me. Then I ask something because I have the feeling it's my last chance to ever ask it. "I never knew why you love it. Cheer. How you came to love it."

She runs a finger along her upper lip. "I never loved it," she says, shaking her head. "It was just a thing. I never cared about it at all."

I don't believe her.

"What happens now?" I say.

She looks at me and laughs.

A few days later, I'm watching the news, my new habit, when I see the latest report.

"The break came when a witness identified Matthew French as the man he had spotted running from The Towers apartment building the night of the murder. Sources say the witness reported that, under the parking lot lights, it looked like French's clothes were covered in blood."

You can't keep secrets long, and it's RiRi who tells me who the witness was.

Jordy Brennan, crooked nose and high-tops.

One of his late-night runs, he made it nearly all the way to Wick Park. Spotting the bright lights of The Towers parking lot, he stopped to look for just the right song for the run home.

I wonder what it must have been like to see Matt French tearing through those front doors. If Jordy was really close enough to see any blood. If he was close enough to see the expression on Matt French's face. Sometimes I feel like I can.

Jordy Brennan. I picture him up there, taking long, dragging breaths in the frosted air, during the moments before he saw Matt French. Just a few hundred yards from the spot where he once kissed me messily for a half hour or more, those vacant eyes of his shut tight. Believing something was beginning.

Those moments when he stood up there, catching his breath, looking for his song, I wonder if he thought about me.

I visit Beth in the hospital once. It's very late and past visiting hours, but I don't want to see her mom again or all the squad girls teeming there, at first as if on deathwatch and then as if on a healing prayer vigil. Oh, to see them and to watch their paroxysms, like Salem witches tearing their hair out, lolling their tongues.

Then, when the Reaper no longer lurked and there was no more talk of intracranial bleeding and cognitive impairment, they turned to epic poems on the We Miss You Beth! Facebook page, where everyone wishes their ♥♥ and *get well soon, sistuhs!* and to hourly deliveries, cookie bouquets, pluming gift baskets stuffed with smiley-face cupcakes, teddy bears donning nurse's hats. Everything Beth would just love.

So I come late, the hospital blue and lonesome.

I stand at her bed, my hands on the side rails.

There's a start in my chest when I see she's awake, her eyes bright in the moonlight, as if waiting for me.

She tells me she didn't think I'd come, that everyone has come but me.

"Even my dad," she says, smiling faintly. "He wants to talk about a lawsuit. Can you figure?"

I tell her Coach has left town, has taken Caitlin to her mother's, will only come back for the trial.

But she doesn't say anything and it's a while before she talks again.

When she does, she starts in the dreamy middle of something, her words caught in her lips.

"I'll never forget seeing it. How she came in one day and I saw her wearing it," she says, her voice wool-thick and plaintive. "I couldn't believe it when I saw it. It was the worst part, worse than anything."

I don't know what she means, and wonder about the things happening in her brain.

"I couldn't believe it," she said. "You gave it to her, the very same one, the very same."

She keeps looking at me, a barely banked fire there, hovering behind her eyes.

"How could you give her that bracelet, Addy?" she asks.

The bracelet. I can't believe we're back on the hamsa bracelet after everything that's happened. The fluid pressing on Beth's skull, that's what it is, like when it happened, the black blood pooling in her ear.

I shake my head. "It was just a bracelet, Beth. I don't even re-member where I got it—"

"I mean, that was the worst part," she says. "It really was."

That's when I remember.

A present for you, Beth had said when she gave it to me a year ago, or more. *Wear it forever.* Which I think is the same thing I'd hoped for Coach.

"I forgot," I say. Which must be a lie, but it's one of the pieces I don't look at. Like Beth says, I choose what to look at. I choose what to remember. Beth is my memory, remembering for me.

"You've given me lots of bracelets. We all do that," I say. "It's what we do."

It's a terrible thing to say, but I'm ashamed.

"I shouldn't have kept it," she says. "I should have thrown it down the gorge. Down at the bottom of the gorge with the Apache maidens."

"I can't believe I forgot," I say, softer now.

Her eyes glassing, she turns away.

"It was you and me, Addy," she says.

Something plucks inside of me, something deep and near for-gotten.

"Addy, are we going to pretend forever? I know you remem-ber," she says, her back to me.

But of course I remember. I know precisely what she is holding tight.

A year ago, early spring, drunken sky-searching at midnight up on the ridge, cold enough to see our breath, but Beth, stripped to streaky-white, and the way I leaped after her, foot sliding in wet leaves, and my hand on her back, hot to the touch.

Collapsing to mossy soil, our backs sinking into it, our faces pitched up to the sky. Just back from two weeks with her mother in Baja, she has something for me, and asks me to lay my hand across her belly and close my eyes. The feeling of the soft leather on my wrist, the cold amulet, the Hand of Fatima charm.

And she told me the story of Fatima, how she was stirring a pot when her husband came home with a new wife. Brokenhearted, she let the ladle slip from her fingers and kept stirring with her own hand, not noticing the pain.

"The hand protects you," she said. "Nothing can hurt it now. Nothing can touch us now."

We raised our arms in the air and let our wrists touch, the beam from its mirrored hand, its promise of protection.

Wearing it, it made me feel strong and safe. Powerful. It made me feel like her.

Lying there, our shorts riding up, we compared the plummy bruises that marked both our right hips, matching thumbprints from where Mindy, Cori, and other girls would press hard to spin into their stunts.

She pushed at mine and I poked hers, and, wincing, we kept pushing on each other's, the pain mysterious and soothing and strange.

How did it happen, us tangled upon each other?

My breath on her neck, my mouth on her ear. I started it, but I don't even remember why or how. We never tugged our shorts all the way off, and we never did what things we might do, but if I let myself, I can still feel my cheek on her knee bone, still feel the pressure of her hands on my thighs. My mouth on her mouth, her laughing.

We never talked about it, and things were maybe different after. Maybe I felt different.

Then the season ended and there was a boy or another boy, and cheer camp, and I bunked with Casey Jaye and wore the love knot

Casey gave me, and things got bad and were never the same again. And when she saw Casey and me, legs swinging from the upper bunk, laughing—the look on her face, and the look on mine. I can guess what mine looked like.

No, I don't think about it ever, that night with Beth up high on the ridge.

There was a wonder in it, and who needs to talk of such wonders? We nestle them away, deep in the fury at the center of us, where things can be held tightly, protected, and secretly cherished as a special notion we once held, then had to stow away.

"You never could look at yourself, Addy," she says. "What you wanted, what you'd do to get it. But here you are."

Here I am.

"You wanted it. It's yours now," she says. "It was always you."

33

AUGUST CHEERLEADER TRYOUTS

"The one shining thing about high school for me has been cheer."

Pacing in front of the fifteen soon-to-be JV girls in the epically hot gym, first day of summer cheer camp, that's me, offering it up. The words, true and real.

"There are people who say it isn't cool," I say, "who make fun of it, but I've never cared. I know they don't have what I have."

Sitting on the long mats, their fluffy faces, eyes cartoon-wide, they gaze up at me as though I were passing along all the wisdom of the world, which I am.

"Cheer has given me a purpose. It has given me a hard body and a strong mind. And I've made friends for life."

RiRi at my side, I walk the length of the mat, back straight, chin high.

"Don't you want to be able to say that?" I say. "If you do, you have to hang tight and tough with your girls."

They all nod, soundless.

"If you don't trust each other," I say, "this mat becomes your gangplank."

The hush falls even greater now. I'm swinging my whistle and all you can hear is the faint scratch of it as it brushes against my sweats.

Emily marches up beside me, her wounded leg back in fighting form, her mind swept clean of her Cassandra-like horrors. She is finished with all that. I know. I showed her how.

Lifting her elbow, she rests it on my shoulder, jaw up. She and RiRi, my deputies, my bad lieutenants.

"We've got five weeks before the new coach begins," I say, "but I choose not to waste those weeks. Do you?"

Clicking jaws, flipping ponytails, rocking in their Indian-style poses, their jelly legs waiting to be molded. Rescued from mediocrity. Saved.

"I choose to excel, not compete—do you?

"I choose to make changes, not excuses—do you?

"To be motivated, not manipulated.

"To be useful, not used."

Beth could come back this fall, couldn't she? Emily keeps asking. *She's at home, she took her finals, I even saw her in her car.*

But I know she never will. She never will and I took something from her and I won't even look at it. I won't—

"I choose to live by choice," I say, "not by chance—do you?"

Their fingers twisting into each other's linking hands, looking up at me, at RiRi and her magnificent body, and Emily and her beatific grin. All of us.

"Cheer taught me to trust my girls to catch me when I fall," I say, *and it's Beth's face I see when I gaze past them, into the empty stands, not Coach's. It's Beth's face, all the darkness and mischief and mayhem and, beneath it, that beating heart.*

Turning from the stands, facing my girls, I gather everything in my chest. I hold it there. I have to hold it tight. These things I've learned.

"It showed me," I say, pulling in my breath, "how to be a leader."

Acknowledgments

With tremendous gratitude and ongoing debt to the inestimable Reagan Arthur and her brilliant team, especially Miriam Parker, Theresa Giacopasi, Peggy Freudenthal, and Sarah Murphy.

Deepest thanks are also owed to the wonderful Kate Harvey and Emma Bravo at Picador UK, and to Angharad Kowal, Maja Nikolic, and Stephen Barr at Writers House. And most of all to Dan Conaway, without whom.

For ongoing and bottomless support and love: Phil and Patti Abbott; Josh, Julie, and Kevin; Jeff, Ruth, and Steve; Darcy Lockman; Christine Wilkinson—and my blood sisters, Alison Quinn and Sara Gran.

About the Author

Megan Abbott is the Edgar Award–winning author of five previous novels. She received her PhD in English and American literature from New York University and has taught literature, writing, and film studies at New York University, the New School, and the State University of New York at Oswego. She lives in New York City.

READING GROUP GUIDE

DARE ME

A Novel by

MEGAN ABBOTT

A CONVERSATION WITH MEGAN ABBOTT

Give us some insight into the choices you made for telling this story: it's in the present tense, narrated in the first person by a sort of Nick Carraway–like character who (at least initially) doesn't seem to have a direct stake in the central conflict.

I've always been interested in the lieutenant/second-in-command figure—whether it's a war movie, a gangster tale, a Shakespeare play. What is their stake? Do they hold their own ambitions? What is it like being the always–beta girl? Also, since most of us are not "alphas," it seemed like a useful perch from which to tell the story. I had, however, initially intended her to be more of a fly-on-the-wall narrator. But, like Lizzie in *The End of Everything,* she just kept inserting herself.

"Cheer," a short story you wrote prior to Dare Me, *has some similar characters and themes, but is actually quite different. What were your goals for the novel versus the short story?*

That story was meant to be a nasty little slice of noir, but I couldn't picture living with those characters for the duration of the book. I have to love all my characters in a novel, and so they all transformed. I always think of that line from the French movie *The Rules of the Game:* "The awful thing about life is this: everyone has their reasons." And as the novel unfurled for me, I found the heart of all the characters. I felt for all of them, even when they did bad things.

I read an interview you did for your previous book, The End of Everything, *in which you said that part of the idea behind writing* Dare Me

was to set Shakespeare's Richard III *in the world of high school cheerleaders. I can see the power struggle for leadership of the cheerleading squad
being like Richard's struggle for the throne, but I'm not sure I could say
which character in* Dare Me *would be Richard, especially by the end. In
your mind, is there a Richard, or are all of the central characters tainted or
corrupted in some way by the struggle?*

Originally, I suspect I had a clearer match-up in mind, but it
fell apart quickly. Mostly, I wanted to absorb the atmosphere of
the play, the feeling of drive, desperation, treachery. And the way
Richard, despite his bad behavior, draws us in. He is our guide,
our vantage point, and we are his confidantes, so as much as his
actions alarm us, we find ourselves linked to him.

*When I went to high school, cheerleaders were more like "cheerlebrities,"
to borrow a term used by Addy. They were all about looking good and
rallying support for the school's (male) athletes at high school games and
matches. The cheerleaders in* Dare Me, *on the other hand, pretty much
view the high school games as a venue for their performances. They don't
talk or think about the athletes on the school teams, and are not even con-
cerned whether the team wins or loses. Why is it so different for them?*

This is, foremost, a change in cheerleading over the past twenty
years. It's now a competitive sport (even if it can't quite garner
that particular designation) that girls train from a young age to
take part in. Shaping their bodies, taking tumbling and gymnastics classes, going to cheer camp. Their focus is tournaments,
beating other squads. In many ways, it would be like expecting
gymnasts to rally for football players. But our long-burnished
image of the cheerleader as the peppy rally girl for her team

persists. I recently wrote a piece about this—I think it's hard for us to let that image go. There's a nostalgia for it. For the America that originated it.

Having characterized the cheerleaders of my generation as cheerlebrities, as I did, I will also mention that the head cheerleader, homecoming queen, and girl voted most respected in our class later joined the Marines. It strikes me that there is something almost martial about the squad in Dare Me. *Coach Colette French could be viewed as a drill sergeant come to whip her recruits into shape, and the girls' performances as the "battles" they do against other schools' squads. There's also the requirement to have each other's backs in the stunts they perform, like soldiers have to protect their buddies. Is that taking things too far?*

Not too far at all. The book sprang from a sense that these girls were, in many ways, like hardcore Marines, bad-ass warriors. Squads, after all, are martial by nature. And the book was framed around these captain and lieutenant characters. It quickly spilled over into the language the girls use (which is only a slight exaggeration, if that, of the language in use among the more serious squads I observed). I found myself riffing on famous military speeches (MacArthur, Patton) for Coach. It was a huge influence on the way I wrote the book. And one of the pleasures in writing it; I really got to explore the power of military rhetoric.

I made the mistake of installing the Facebook Messenger application on my cell phone, and during the early morning hours of my birthday not long ago, was subjected to an almost constant barrage of notification buzzes and beeps as friends waking up around the world left birthday wishes on my wall. I was too sleepy/lazy to get up and shut the phone off, but for the first time I realized how connected I had become to other people via my phone. It also made me think about how much worse it must be for today's teenagers, given the volume of texts and phone calls they are constantly exchanging. Can you talk about the electronic "connectedness" of the characters in Dare Me *and how that informs the plot?*

It felt to me that texts, Facebook, and Twitter are the contemporary equivalents of notes passed in class in my day. Except then, your reputation could take until the end of the day to be ruined, as the note passed from hand to hand, period after period. Today, it only takes an instant. It struck me as very powerful, both intimate and treacherous.

Also, in my teen years, you could, as long as you didn't pick up the family phone, leave the terrors and heartache of the school day behind when you got home. Now that's very hard. Your experience with your birthday wishes—that's the part I mean. I feel that in my life too. My phone has become this virtual appendage, a live thing buzzing in my hand. All of this felt like exciting tools for suspense.

For a fifty-something male, reading Dare Me *is probably as close as I will ever get to experiencing life as a teenage girl. A lot of that comes from the verisimilitude of Addy's voice, and the language you chose to narrate the story. Her interior dialogue feels a lot like a fever dream at points—so body conscious, so tied to real time, with little emotional distancing. Is that an effect you consciously sought?*

I'm so glad it reads that way. I can't say I sought it out consciously. It seemed to come once I found her voice, which took a while. At first she was a far more tentative and distant narrator. It was on the advice of my first reader, Dan Conaway, that I gave her more breathing room, more room to feel things. As soon as he suggested I do that, I knew she wanted something. And once I knew that, she became very strong in my head and grew to surprise me.

Without giving away any key plot points, can you say which character you have the most empathy for, and why? Do you expect the reader will share that empathy?

Beth. I had an idea about her when the book began and it changed dramatically. She is the putative troublemaker here, but I grew to love her. Her bruised and dented heart. The more I fell for her, the more space I gave her, the more I granted her. I definitely get that she can come across as a "mean girl," or as a villain (she behaves very badly in the book), but I don't see her that way myself. She's my girl.

In past interviews, you've expressed admiration for the writing of Raymond Chandler. To your credit, your admiration hasn't assumed the form of forced mimicry. If you think he's had any direct influence on you, how would you characterize it?

I think he will always be my biggest influence in terms of style. The way, to him, mood mattered above all. Sights, scents, colors, pressures in the air, the way sound can travel. The way it can feel like everything around you is part of you, part of your own longing or fear or trepidation. That if you can strike a mood, it's far more than a mood. It's a world you've given your reader.

In your nonfiction study of hard-boiled fiction, The Street Was Mine, *you point out that Dashiell Hammett's protagonists, as opposed to Chandler's and James M. Cain's, are less introspective and more self-contained.*

Does that make them less interesting to you? Are you less influenced by Hammett's writing as a result?

Boy, I don't remember writing that (ha!), but it feels true. I am a Hammett lover, but I do have a weakness for damaged, unreliable narrators whose neuroses can't help but peek through. Hammett's are harder nuts to crack. He feels more removed from his pro- tagonists. Which is one of the gifts of his books. They are less constricted by point of view, for one thing. And that distance makes the books whip-smart, so incisive. But Chandler and Cain can't help but love their protagonists/narrators and that leads to a certain messiness I love. They identify with them and want to pro- tect them, which makes their books much crazier than Hammett's (and not as jewel-perfect) but so openhearted.

Can you give us any details about your next novel?

It's called *The Fever* and it's about a mysterious outbreak in a small town.

And will you confirm for Rap Sheet *readers that the red-lipsticked lips on the cover of* Dare Me *are yours?*

As someone who has admitted a predilection for unreliable narra- tors, I can wholeheartedly say: Of course.

This interview was conducted by author Mark Coggins and originally appeared on the *Rap Sheet* at therapsheet.blogspot.com/2012/08/dare-me.html.

MEGAN ABBOTT'S PLAYLIST FOR
DARE ME

I'll start out with a confession: I was never a cheerleader. In high school, I was distinctly the school newspaper type.

But somehow, all these years later, I have found myself writing a novel set firmly in the dark heart of a high school cheerleading squad. Of course, the cheerleader of my era—all pom-poms and ponytails and a few high kicks—bears little resemblance to the cheerleader of today. Battle hardened by gymnastics training and a sneaky kind of girl power, the cheerleader of 2013 is a hard-core warrior, putting herself at risk and devoting everything to an increasingly dangerous, thrilling experience.

So, in doing the research for the book, what I found was a fundamental and fascinating contradiction. Cheerleading remains the most quintessential experience of all-American girlness. At the same time, however, it's this rich terrain on which all the big emotions and dramas of teen girlhood are enacted: ambition, competitiveness, aggression, rivalries, fear, loyalty, achievement, and power.

As I wrote the book, a whole world emerged for me, one filled with confusion, mystery, longing, the fight for power and dominance. In short: high school, times ten, which is already life times ten.

This playlist, then, is my attempt to capture that strange polarity, that binary logic of the American cheerleader: pretty on the outside, gladiator underneath.

Ke$ha, "Tic Tok" and "Take It Off"
Kanye West, "Stronger" and "Gold Digger"
Missy Elliot, "Shake Your Pom Pom"
These songs speak to the kind of bad-ass rallying cry music that ac-

companies cheer routines, competitions, and girls together wreaking havoc. Suburban girl fantasies of "thug life." Bratty swagger. Pop with glittery barbs.

MIA, "Bad Girls"
"Live fast, die young, / Bad girls do it well." This one stands in for all the great songs made for girls driving in cars ("My chain hits my chest / When I'm banging on the dashboard"), high on their own power, half knowing that power is, at best, a game, at worst, a desperate illusion. Realizing too late, the dark parenthesis of the song: "My life, I broke it."

St. Vincent, "Cheerleader"
Darkest cheerleading song ever. And it's not even really about cheerleaders. But it also kind of is.

Pixies, "Winterlong"
Cults, "Abducted"
For the romance and mystery and longing and heartbreak that all feel softest and sharpest during adolescence.

Gorillaz, "To Binge"
Elusive, dreamy, dark. The perfect love song for the love story in the book—all three of them.

Hole, "Miss World"
No band ever conveyed it better: How hard it is being a girl.

This post first appeared on the website *Largehearted Boy* and is reprinted with permission.

QUESTIONS AND TOPICS FOR DISCUSSION

1. *Dare Me* explores the world of high school cheerleading, which has become more competitive and dangerous in recent years. What is the appeal for Addy and the other girls?

2. Addy and Beth are, or were, very close friends. What do you think their connection is? How does their personal history impact what happens in the novel?

3. We see very little of Addy and Beth's parents. Do you think their parents' role in their lives affects their behavior?

4. While Addy notes that Coach's life seems perfect—a loving husband, beautiful young daughter, lovely home all her own—Coach seems unhappy. What is missing for her?

5. Coach is an important mentor in Addy's life, but she also has questionable boundaries. What do you think of Coach's behavior toward Addy?

6. Beth accuses Coach of many things, ranging from being a bad coach to a bad influence to a criminal. To what degree are her charges founded or unfounded?

7. The male characters in *Dare Me*—Will, Matt, the other Guardsmen—appear on the fringes of the story yet exert a huge impact on what happens. What is the place of men and

boys in the world of *Dare Me*? Does that place make us more or less sympathetic to them?

8. Beth may be seen as a quintessential "mean girl," but she can also be seen as loyal, fiercely protective of Addy, and sometimes an effective leader. How do you view her? What do you think drives her behavior throughout the book?

9. There are repeated references to Beth and Addy's experience at cheer camp the previous summer, when Addy became friends with another girl, Casey. Why does the experience keep reemerging? To what extent did it impact their friendship?

10. In many ways, Addy is caught between two powerful "leaders"—Beth and Coach. Where does she land in the end? And is it a good place?

11. In some ways, *Dare Me* is a book about power, how to get it and how to hold it. But is it also about female power, or does power operate among males in the same way?

12. Did you play a sport in high school, or were you a cheerleader? If so, do you identify with the way cheerleading consumes the characters?

13. Is there something specific about adolescence that creates friendships as intense as Beth and Addy's? Did you have friendships like that, or witness them, in high school?